Shadows & Reflections

A Roger Zelazny Tribute Anthology

For Carl Yoke

©2017 Positronic Publishing
Individual stories copyrighted by their authors

Cover Design by Jay O'Connell

ISBN 13: 978-1-5154-1740-8

Shadows & Reflections

A Roger Zelazny Tribute Anthology

Edited by
Trent Zelazny
and Warren Lapine

Table of Contents

The Two Rogers

by George R. R. Martin

I was twice as fortunate as most. I knew two Roger Zelaznys. One was the writer. The other was my friend.

I met the writer first. It was 1967, and I was a college student, back home for the summer between my freshman and sophomore years at Northwestern. Though I had been reading science fiction voraciously for several years, the genre magazines seldom made it to the candy stores and spinner racks of Bayonne, New Jersey, where I bought my comics and Ace Doubles (Two Complete Novels for 35 cents, couldn't beat that), so I had missed all of the early short stories that launched Roger's career. The only hardcover books I could afford were those offered by the Science Fiction Book Club.

And then one day the club newsletter *Things To Come* turned up in my mailbox, and one of the offerings was a novel called *Lord of Light* by a writer whom I'd not heard of previously, though it claimed that he had already won both the Hugo and the Nebula. It was there in *Things To Come* that I first read those fateful words, "His followers called him Mahasamatman and said he was a god. He preferred to drop the Maha- and the -atman, however, and called himself Sam. He never claimed to be a god. But then, he never claimed not to be a god."

I bought the book, of course. I wanted to hear more about this fellow Sam and check out this new (to me, at least) writer.

I had read Heinlein, Asimov, Vance, Bester, de Camp, Van Vogt, Andre Norton, Eric Frank Russell, Fritz Leiber, H. P. Lovecraft, Jack Williamson, Pohl & Kornbluth, all the classics. I fancied that I knew my science fiction, had even begun to write some of my own. . .but nothing that I had read previously prepared me for *Lord of Light*.

This was not like anything that had gone before. The poetry of the language. The way the author played with myth. The colorful background, the inventive world building, the non-linear structure. And of course the characters. Sam especially, who never claimed to be a god. By the time I closed the final page, Roger Zelazny had become one of my favorite writers. Not one of my favorite science fiction writers. One of my favorite *writers*.

Lord of Light was an awakening. For me and for the field. It won the Hugo Award and was nominated for the Nebula Award for the year of its publication, and if it were up to me, it would have won the Pulitzer as well. *Lord of Light* is one of those books that you need to reread every few years. Each time you do, you will discover something new. It has been almost half a century since I first encountered it, but age has not withered its power nor custom staled its countless charms. Now, as then, I would rank it as one of the five best science fiction novels ever written. If you have never read it, do not call yourself a science fiction fan.

In the years that followed *Lord of Light*, I sought out everything by Zelazny that I could get my hands on. *This Immortal, Creatures of Light and Darkness, Isle of the Dead, Jack of Shadows, Roadmarks, Doorways in the Sand, The Dream Master* ("He Who Shapes"), and the rest. Each of them is unique, and each of them is wonderful in its own unique way. (Yes, even *Damnation Alley*.) Zelazny never repeated himself, and he never disappointed.

And then there came *Nine Princes of Amber* and the rest of Corwin's saga; not sequels, truly, but rather a continuation of one long, epic story. With Corwin of Amber and his troublesome siblings, Zelazny gave us all a cast of characters as fascinating, complex, and charismatic as any the genre had seen since. . .well, since Francis Sandow, Render, and Sam. Amber and Chaos and their infinite shadow worlds were something we had not seen before, either, a unique fantasy setting worthy of being ranked with Tolkien's Middle Earth, Howard's Hyborian Age, and Vance's Dying Earth. The tale itself, with its cliffhangers, reversals, twists, and maddeningly complex spiderweb of plots and counterplots and layered revelations, was truly virtuoso. And of course the writing itself was pure Zelazny, full of poetry and wit and action, a song in prose with moments that will linger long in the memory of anyone fortunate enough to encounter them.

Zelazny's short fiction was just as extraordinary. Early in his career, he wrote "A Rose for Ecclesiastes," the last of the great "old Mars" stories, written just as NASA's probes were about to prove that the real Mars was something very different and far less interesting. An instant classic, it was soon enshrined by the Science Fiction Writers of America in their *Science Fiction Hall of Fame*. Then, as a bookend, he went out and wrote the last "old Venus" story too, and called that one, "The Doors of His Face, the Lamps of His Mouth."

In those days, the typical career pattern for a new writer was to make a name writing short fiction for the magazines, win a few awards, and then switch to novels, where the money was. . .but Zelazny never abandoned the short story. His shorter work only grew stronger over the decades, with brilliant tales such as "The Keys to December," "The Last Defender of Camelot," "Home Is the Hangman," "Permafrost," "24 Views of Mt. Fuji, by Hokusai," and so very many more.

The author of all those stories, the first Roger Zelazny that I came to know, was a writer of surpassing brilliance, one of the true giants of our genre. . .but like Heinlein and Vance and F. Scott Fitzgerald and many other authors I admired, he was someone I knew only through his work. I had no inkling then that Roger would one day become a dear, close friend.

As best I can recall, the first time I ever met Roger Zelazny in person was at Discon, the World Science Fiction Convention in Washington, D.C., in 1974, where Roger was the Guest of Honor. He was only 37 at the time, very young to be a Worldcon GoH, an accolade that is usually bestowed on distinguished gray-bearded gentlemen (and gentlewomen, though their beards tend to be shorter) toward the end of their long careers. . .but so profound had been Roger's impact on the field that only the most hidebound old phans ever questioned the propriety of honoring this *wunderkind* at such a tender age.

Our first meeting was hardly the stuff of legend. I had sold a few stories myself by that point and was up for my very first Hugo at that very convention (I lost), but I was still in awe of Roger, so when I found myself in his presence, the best that I could do was shuffle my feet, stare at his shoes, and mutter something about how I really really *really* liked his stuff. He was appropriately gracious and thanked me between puffs of his pipe, and that was pretty much the end of it.

In the years to come I encountered him at other conventions, but it was not until the spring of 1976 that I spent any extended period of time with him. That year Roger had been hired to teach a workshop for aspiring writers in Bloomington, Indiana. By that time I had published quite a few more stories and even won a Hugo of my own, so the good folks running the workshop had offered me the gig as Roger's assistant. I accepted with alacrity, as much for the chance to learn at the master's feet as for the modest stipend.

There in Bloomington we spent the better part of a couple of weeks together, reading and critiquing stories, working with the students, talking books and sharing meals. The Indiana workshop did not follow the famous Clarion model, where all the students read and critique one another's stories. Instead the workshoppers heard a series of lectures by Roger and received their critiques from him and me. Truth be told, I think I learned as much from Roger's talks as any of the students.

"Where do you get your ideas?" is the eternal question that every writer dreads, generally because we have no answer for it. Some will say "the muse," some may say "Schenectady," some just say "That's a stupid question," but the truth is most of us have no idea where we get our ideas. Roger did, though. "From the Yellow Pages," he would say. I saw him demonstrate the process at that Bloomington workshop. He had the students open the Yellow Pages at random, close their eyes, point. . .and write a story about whatever listing their fingers came to rest on. That was where "The Doors of His Face, the Lamps of His Mouth" had come from, he told them. He opened a phone book at random, closed his eyes, pointed. . .and hit "Bait Shops." (Or so he said. But then again, he was also known to say that he wrote *Lord of Light* entirely for the pun, perhaps the greatest groaner in all of literature. Not everything he said could be trusted. There was a playful side to Roger that strangers seldom saw, a twinkle in his eye that meant mischief.)

As for the critiques, the two of us slipped naturally into good cop/bad cop roles. I was the bad cop who tore apart the stories and left them bleeding on the ground. Roger was the good cop who put them back together. He was as good a teacher as he was a writer; gentle, soft-spoken, and supportive, capable of finding something good in even the most wretched manuscript, always ready with constructive suggestions and improvements. His story sense was as sharp as his prose.

Those weeks in Bloomington deepened my admiration of Roger the writer, but they also gave me my first glimpses of the person behind the prose. Those who knew him in his youth have often told me how shy he was as a boy and a young man, and some of that shyness still remained even in 1976 and could make him seem reserved and cool. Once you got to know him, though, Roger was one of the warmest people I have ever met, a wonderful conversationalist with a rare, dry wit. He was truly a Renaissance man; an aikido master (and later teacher), a collector of Persian carpets, Navajo rugs, rare first editions, and rarer comic books (he owned a near-mint copy of *Marvel Comics #1*, the comic that introduced the original Golden Age versions of Submariner and the Human Torch), a lover of good food, good drink, and aromatic tobaccos, who could discuss classic literature one moment and recite Green Lantern's oath the next.

In the years that followed, Roger and I continued to bump into one another on the con circuit, but after Bloomington our relationship was closer, and we often found time to have a meal together. Then, in December of 1979, I left a home and job in Iowa and moved to Santa Fe, New Mexico, to take a stab at being a full-time writer. I also left behind my troubled four-year-old marriage, which finally collapsed during the move itself, leaving me to move to New Mexico by myself. Though I had some friends down in Albuquerque, an hour away, I knew no one at all in Santa Fe itself. . .except for Roger Zelazny. My first year in New Mexico was a lonely one, a year I spent largely by myself, bent over my typewriter in the back room of my little house on Declovina Street, working on the book that would ultimately become my novel *Fevre Dream* and hoping I could finish it before my dwindling funds gave out. It might have been a truly unbearable year if not for Roger. Though our previous acquaintance had been relatively slight and entirely professional, Roger and his wife Judy took me under their wings, asking me to their home for dinners, drinks, and conversations, introducing me to their friends and to many of the local writers, inviting me to parties, wine tastings, book signings, literary luncheons.

Meals with Roger became a regular and important part of my life in Santa Fe. Breakfast burritos and blue corn pancakes at the Tecolote Café, where Roger's favorite was the Sheepherder's Breakfast, a blend of potatoes, onions, chile, cheese, and jalapeño peppers with a poached egg on top, the hottest thing on the menu. Lunches at the Shed, where Roger always made certain to order the lemon souffle as soon as we sat down, since it had a lamentable tendency to sell out early (still does). A memorable dinner at Chez Renée Captain's Table (long since vanished, though its empty building still stands decaying on Cerillos Road), where we celebrated the sale of my novel *Fevre Dream*. Countless dinners at the Palace (another landmark Santa Fe restaurant, now gone), a former brothel, where the dessert cart was a wonder to behold. Roger loved desserts and would often eat two or three of them, confusing waiters to no end. "I'll take the apple pie," he would say. "Very good, sir," the waiter would say. "Yes, and that German chocolate cake looks good." The waiter would frown. "In place of the apple pie, sir?" he would say. "No, I'll have both of them. Oh, and the zabaglione as well. What flavors of ice cream do you have?" (And yet he never gained an ounce and remained rail thin all his life.)

One day we were driving down to Albuquerque to attend the monthly First Friday writers' luncheon and talking shop along the way, as we often did. Our mutual friend, Fed Saberhagen, had just sold an anthology of science fiction and fantasy stories about chess (eventually published as *Pawn to Infinity*) and had asked both of us for stories. My own pals Gardner Dozois and Jack Dann were putting together a theme anthology as well, about unicorns (eventually published as *Unicorns!*), and George Scithers and Darrell Schweitzer had written Roger to sound him out about contributing to their anthology of stories set in bars and taverns, *Tales from the Spaceport Bar*.

"The thing to do," I said, "is write a story about a guy who plays chess with a unicorn in a bar, and sell it to all three anthologies." Roger chortled at my joke. . .

. . .and then he went home and did it. The guy who plays chess with the unicorn in the bar he named "Martin." He did indeed sell the story to all three anthologies, and to *Asimov's* as well. "Unicorn Variation" went on to win the Hugo Award, beating one of my own novelettes in the process.

That was the sort of literary challenge Roger loved. He was a writer who took his art seriously, but he never lost his sense of play. The huge, page-long sentence in *Creatures of Light and Darkness*, that infamous pun in *Lord of Light*, the inventive structure of *Doorways in the Sand*, those were all glimpses of his playful side. So too his contributions to Wild Cards, the series of shared world superhero anthologies that I edited, starting around 1984. Knowing Roger's love of comic books, I knew he would give us something wonderful, and so he did. The character that he created—Croyd Crenson, the Sleeper—became in many ways the essence of Wild Cards, both hero and villain, always the same and always changing, a character who could be adjusted to fit almost any role a writer needed him for. Roger designed him that way quite deliberately, and he always got a kick out of seeing what other writers did with Croyd. The Wild Cards series is still going today, twenty years and twenty-one volumes after it began, and the Sleeper is still a part of it. . .and will continue to be for as long as the series continues. In Croyd, we like to think, a little bit of Roger still lives on.

13

As I write this, I realize that it has been fourteen years since Roger died, since that dark night that I drove him to St. Vincent's Hospital for what would prove to be his final stay. It doesn't seem possible. His face and voice still linger in my memory, so vividly that one would think it had only been a week since I last saw him.

I knew two Rogers, and I miss both of them. I miss the writer that I first encountered in 1967 and the tales he would have told us if he only lingered here among us longer. And I miss the friend I made in 1976 at that workshop in Indiana.

He left us too soon, and we shall not see his like again.

—George R. R. Martin
Santa Fe, New Mexico
August, 2009

Playing God

by Steven Brust

Heads-up poker—one on one—has never been my best game. Once, back in the twenty-first century, I went up against a kid named Stu Unger, and he cleaned my clock so badly I've been afraid of the game ever since. Seriously. Oh, "cleaned my clock" is an expression from when telling time involved—no, skip it. Point is, I'm more comfortable at a full table.

Well, but sometimes you're forced out of your comfort zone; and when one of the richest sons-of-bitches in the galaxy wants to play heads-up cards with you, you go for it. Especially in a world where a good poker game has been getting harder and harder to find. These last years, Ren has been mostly supporting us (a good UI specialist is never lacking work), and I'm enough of a fossil to be just a little bit uncomfortable with that.

I had kissed her good-bye, apologized again for missing Thanksgiving with the kids (it's an old, old holiday invented during a war right here on old Earth—go graze it; our family still celebrates it when we can), and boarded the liner. I'd have liked Ren to come along. She'd have liked to come along. But the invitation was for me, so that was that.

Out of habit ingrained from the days when travel was dangerous, I looked around for seat restraints, and felt vaguely uncomfortable that there weren't any; then the inevitable announcement started, in the middle of which was just the slight shift, jar, bounce—and we were in space.

In space, where communication was still tricky and where, more importantly, I was cut off from the Garden. No matter how much space travel I did, that was one thing I couldn't get used to, and didn't like at all, at all—especially this time, because the invitation had been now or never, with a hoversine at my door, barely time to pack, and no time to learn anything about my host beyond what everyone knew. I'd have liked to get to the Garden to graze for him. I knew I was only cut off for a few days subjective time and almost none in real time, but it made me more nervous than the idea of heads-up poker with one of the wealthiest men who'd ever lived. I tried to put it out of my mind and enjoy the trip.

The me of just a few hundred years ago would have been excited as hell to be traveling through space, much less through artificially created wormholes and mathematical abstractions that ought not to exist. The me of a few thousand years ago would have been trembling, curled up on the floor, and making his clothes damp with sweat and possibly other fluids. The me of now relaxed, let the seat roll back and adjust itself to his form, and closed his eyes as we made our way to Homefree.

Just under a week later subjective time, the *Lady Gaga*—a huge, elegantly misshapen transport owned by Sandow Travelcorp and full of travellers and with all the comforts of etc.—made a stop just to let me out. That made me squirm a bit. At the bottom of the jump-tube, there was a professional greeter who professionally greeted me, and if there was a hair out of place on her head I couldn't find it. It was only later that I realized that her dress, hair-style, language, accent, and manners were all right out of the twenty-first century (or maybe the twentieth; it was after the internal combustion engine but before interstellar travel, all right?).

She told me her name was Sylvia and that my suitcase would be taken to my room, and asked if I needed some time to refresh myself. If she had said "wanted" I would have said yes, but I took the hint and shook my head. The weather was perfect. This was Homefree, also called Sandow's World, and he was not only absurdly rich, but a worldscaper; between the two, the weather would always be what he wanted it to be. Here, where the *Lady Gaga* had docked, we stood on a beach of pink sand that ran for what looked like a mile or more before meeting a blue, blue, oh my god blue ocean full of the sort of waves that made me wonder why no one was surfing. But almost no one surfed anymore, anywhere, and almost no one came to Homefree.

Sandow's world was whatever he wanted it to be, here and everywhere. While I'd never want him for an enemy, here, where the very dirt could be seen as an extension of his nervous system, I most certainly wouldn't want him for an enemy. Opponent, of course, was different.

There was a hoversine nearby, the twin of the one that had brought me to the ship. I got in, and Sylvia sat across from me and pointed out the sights. The trip, which couldn't have lasted more than five minutes, brought us from the beach, past a mountain, and eventually into the middle of a forest. Nice trick, that.

We got out, and she led me along a path in the woods until we reached a glade surrounded by deciduous trees in which a poker table with three chairs sat looking absurd. Next to it was a sandy-haired alien dressed all in white, standing almost as if at attention. He had a couple of extra arms, and if I kept up on things, I could tell you what species he was.

"This is Tony, the dealer," she said. "I'll leave you in his care. Mr. Sandow will be along presently."

"Thank you," I said. "It's been a pleasure getting to know you."

She pretended not to catch the irony. She climbed back into the vehicle, which silently rose, turned, and headed off.

I shook hands with Tony; his smile was automatic and professional; a lot like hers. He used his upper right hand to shake, and that may or may not have meant something. Next to each chair was a small table laden with fruits and chocolates, an ash tray, and a place for a beverage. I'd have bet money that, somewhere just out of sight, was a full bar; and that there were concealed microphones so that a bartender—human, no doubt—would be able to hear and fulfill any orders in seconds.

"Feel free to sit," he said in English with no trace of an accent.

Position doesn't matter heads-up, of course, so I took the closest chair, stood next to it, and waited. He appeared in less than a minute.

Francis Sandow, one of the hundred wealthiest people in the Galaxy, looked a lot like a college student. He wore sneakers, jeans, and a Beatles tee-shirt from the Sergeant Pepper era. His hair was light brown and well-kept, his eyes were blue, he was clean-shaven. He walked up to me with his hand out, and I took it. His hand-shake was firm.

"Phil," he said.

17

"Mr. Sandow."

"Call me Frank," he said. "I have no choice but to call you Phil, as there isn't a last name recorded anywhere."

"Phil is fine," I said.

He sat down, and so did I. "Or rather," he said, "many last names are recorded, but none of them go with Phil."

I kept my face neutral. "As I said, Phil is fine."

He nodded without taking his eyes off my face.

"Drink?"

"I'd take a ginger ale."

He nodded, and seconds later an extremely attractive young woman wearing very little appeared from between two trees. She was holding a tray with two glasses on it. I looked at her, then at Sandow.

"Based on the costumes worn by cocktail waitresses at Mandaly Bay, approximately 1990," he said.

"Based on, or an exact replica?"

He shrugged and smiled a little.

The waitress gave us our drinks—he had something in a brandy snifter—and went away. I manfully resisted the urge to watch her leave.

He turned to Tony and gave a slight nod. The dealer reached under the table and pulled out a familiar-looking lacquered wooden box. Sandow opened it. "Cigar?" he said.

"No, thank you."

"Mind if I have one?"

"Not at all."

He withdrew one and lit it with an archaic cigarette lighter. A light breeze came up, blowing the smoke directly back behind him; I didn't think that was an accident.

He removed a roll of bills—actual, physical bills—from a pocket and handed them to Tony in exchange for chips. I handed Tony my card and eyeprinted the receipt, surrendering almost twenty percent of my bankroll. And if you think that wasn't scary, you've never played poker professionally. Tony pushed some chips to me across the authentic, antique speedcloth.

"How was the trip?"

"Comfortable," I said. "Restful. Luxurious."

"The food was all right?"

"Better than all right."

"Good to hear. But you've lived in luxury at some point, haven't you, Phil?"

"Not often, or for very long. We live pretty simply now."

"We?"

"My wife and I."

"Oh," he said. "You're married? You should have brought her along."

"I would have," I said, "but you didn't want me to."

His eyebrows rose a little. "Now, what makes you say that?"

"Sylvia said my suitcase would be taken to my room."

"And?"

"She said suitcase, not suitcases. You can't be following me closely enough to know I only brought one suitcase and not know about Ren. Not to mention your remarks about my name. If you didn't invite her, it was deliberate."

He smiled a little and nodded to Tony. "Let's cut for the button," he said.

I wasn't at all surprised that we were using real, actual, hold-each-one-in-your-hand playing cards. They brought back memories. The poker variant was Third Box. I opened the first hand to three blinds without looking at my cards, just to see what he'd do; he studied his hand for a while, then threw it away. The next hand I looked at, raised again; he let me have that one, too. Since he seemed willing to be pushed around, I did so, and in five hands, I knew I was a much better card player than he was. Whatever he'd been doing for the last thousand years, he hadn't been living and breathing poker.

"You're very aggressive," he said.

19

No, you're just passive, I didn't say. I smiled and waited for the next hand.

People say you can learn a lot about someone by the way he plays poker, and that's true, but it isn't as simple as some would have you believe. Devious or straightforward, passive or aggressive, loose or tight: those were key elements of someone's game, but they don't directly translate to what the person is like outside the game. My point is, if I picked up on elements of Sandow's personality, that was fine; but right now I was just concentrating on how he played cards. And if you think that because he was on the passive side as a player he was passive as a person, you're being an idiot.

He opened a hand, and I was sufficiently confident I was beat to throw mine away. I stole a couple more, then he opened again, I came over the top, and he thought for a long time, studying me, then mucked.

"You were in a big hurry to get me here," I said.

"That's the thing about wealth," he said. "You can indulge yourself without waiting. If I get in the mood to play poker with one of the best, I can find out who that is and get him here in less than a day."

A little later, we both had hands; he undercharged me for a draw, I hit, and got a decent payoff.

"You like being rich?"

"That's an odd question," he said. "Did you?"

I resisted the urge to squirm. That remark, the name business—was he probing at me? Trying to learn things he'd been unable to learn otherwise? And why did he care? Then again, I might just be over-reacting. I kept the thoughts out of my voice, face, body.

"Haven't done it much," I said. "I like not being scared about running out of money. That part is good. Raise."

He mucked. "Yeah, beyond that it's indulgence. For me, it just sort of happened. I did what I wanted, and it ended up producing—he gestured around himself—"all of this."

"So you indulge yourself?"

"Are you judging me, Phil?"

20

I thought about it. "No," I said. "I don't know what I'd do if I were in your position."

I threw away a good hand when he opened big, because it wasn't quite good enough.

"No, you don't. Wealth was never a goal of mine. Still isn't, really."

"What is?"

"Building. Making. Creating. Leaving something worthwhile behind. I'll call the blind."

"Laudable," I said. "Raise."

"Maybe. Call. Don't you feel the same way?"

"I don't think of it as creating something new as much as improving what already exists."

He nodded thoughtfully and checked. I bet and he called again. I'd take the chance that he was trapping me; he struck me as a more straightforward player than that.

"Still worthwhile," he said.

"I think so."

He looked at his hand, hesitated, then said, "I'm all-in."

"Call."

He laid his hand down. "I caught my second pair."

"Yeah, I got a set."

"Ouch. Well played. Do you give lessons?" he asked.

"I just did."

He chuckled.

I said, "All right, Frank. So, it's obvious you didn't bring me here for poker. What have I just been paid for?"

"Are you hungry?"

I nodded.

"Good. We'll talk about it over dinner. You may as well cash in. Want bills, or shall we send credits?"

"Sending credits is fine."

Tony refused a tip, saying it was already included in his wages. It's kind of fun when, after being alive as long as I have, you can have a new experience.

Dinner was served outdoors on a grassy patch next to a brook, with enough candles to make me think of a Buddhist monastery. I could see the guy's house from there, and if I had a house like that, I'd hang out in it once in a while. A fellow of the same species as Tony served deviled eggs, asparagus with truffles in seasoned butter, roast chicken ala L'Ami Louis, and crepe Suzette. I had two glasses of a burgundy that must have cost more than I'd just won; he had a chocolate milk shake.

When the server or the chef or whoever he was left us alone, Sandow lit another cigar; I declined again. We both had a golden colored desert wine, and he said, "So, Phil. I have a question."

"Yes, Frank?"

"What was Jesus actually like?"

I feel pretty sure my face gave nothing away, but my heart hammered at me, and I immediately began going through the Fibonacci sequence in my head.

"Hey," he said, clapping his hands in my direction. "Over here. I need you here, Phil."

He wasn't going to let me engage my fore-brain. Unless he thought I was trying to graze. Either way, it meant he knew things about me he couldn't know. His earlier remarks seemed more sinister now. I was scared.

"How much do you know?" I asked him.

He reached into his pants pocket, extracted what looked like an antique $1 bill, and put it into his other pocket. "I just lost a bet with myself," he said. "I was guessing that would be question two, after you asked who else knew, with question three being how I know."

"You were right about question three," I said.

"I know about the exobrain you were just trying to reach," he said, "and some of what you people have done through history. And you are old enough to have known Jesus."

He knew about the Garden; yes, he'd thought I was going to graze, and he'd been interrupting me so I couldn't. Well, all right. I was in his world—literally and figuratively—and my heart was still pounding. Time. Time and knowledge. All right.

I said, "Did you actually want to know about him, or more precisely, them? Or was it just supposed to be a shocker?"

"I wouldn't mind knowing more, but it was mostly just to cue you in that I knew about the Incrementalists, and your exobrain, and your talent."

Yeah, he did. A hell of a way to let me know, too. I'd done that myself: the shocking statement out of nowhere. It was a pretty common technique, for example, when recruiting: you meet someone who thinks you're a stranger, then you reveal that you know that he's not a stranger at all. Sometimes I'd do it to gauge the recruit's reaction, other times to communicate as much possible as quickly as possible. Was I being recruited? Or evaluated? If so, for what?

"Who else does know?" I asked him.

"No one. And I'll keep it that way, as long you don't do what you do to me. What do you call it again?"

"Meddling. Meddlework."

He chuckled and drew on his cigar, his face momentarily vanishing in a cloud of blue smoke. "Good term for it," he said.

"I won't meddle with you," I told him.

"Then I'll make sure no one besides me learns about you. Besides," he gestured with the cigar, "it isn't as if I don't like what you do, what you've done. I do. This lousy, screwed up universe would be even lousier and more screwed up without you guys."

"We like to think so," I said. "How did you find out about me? Us?"

"You told me. Eleven hundred years ago, you told everyone. Remember?"

I used a bad word.

"I have access to a lot of information," he said. "Not as much as you have, but a lot. I was digging around, looking for something else, and you showed up, and then I dug some more, and found out where you'd left the information out in plain view."

"It was supposed to be taken as a metaphor. We didn't think anyone would believe it," I said. "I mean, not in the literal sense."

"Back then, no one did. But this isn't back then, and I'm not anyone."

"What do you want?"

"Your help."

"With?"

"I want to rebuild the Earth as it was three thousand, one hundred years ago."

"You're a worldscaper," I said.

"Oh, sorry, I assumed you knew."

"I did. It's just that I didn't put it together. I mean, you can actually do that."

"Yeah. And I intend to."

"What happens to the present Earth?"

"Such as it is?"

"Yeah, such as it is."

"Nothing. I don't plan to touch it. I'm going off into a different part of the galaxy, but there's a lovely G3 star there. I've already started forming the planet. I'll send out word. There are plenty of re-creationists around who'd love to colonize a place like that."

"Why three thousand one hundred years?"

"Because that's as far back as your memory goes," he said.

"Oh."

"Will you help me?"

"You want access to the Garden. You want me to help you learn things you couldn't otherwise, to get as close as possible to the old Earth. Is that it?"

"Exactly."

"Why?" I asked.

He caught my eye and held it, cigar forgotten in his hand. "To see if we can do it right this time," he said.

I nodded. "I'll help you," I told him.

*

We entered his "house" eventually, and I was shown to a room about the size of the house Ren and I lived in. He left me there, saying he'd see me tomorrow. I unpacked and relaxed. I wondered if the room were bugged. From what I knew of Sandow, it wouldn't be, but it didn't matter that much anyway. I sat down and stretched my legs out. This was a pretty new Second for me, and was considerably shorter than my previous had been, so my feet seemed too close. A strange feeling, but one I'd had before.

For the first time, I had the chance to get to the Garden. I didn't right away, however. I checked the time-translator and found I still had almost two standard hours before the rendezvous, so I set an alarm for an hour and forty-five minutes and caught a nap.

I nap when I can; it's one of my great pleasures.

I woke up, but didn't enter my own Garden. I closed my eyes, and heard the distinctive, never to be forgotten sound of ocean waves breaking against rocks; and the tartness of good apple cider tantalized my tongue, and there I was: not my Garden, but our Garden. It was a place the like of which had never existed before Ren and I created it, and the like of which no one else had ever created, and there's a whole story in that, too. But for now we'll just say that Ren and I could meet in our shared Garden.

The product of our joined subconscious minds had turned out to be a library, in the same sense that the Taj Majal was a cottage. If you want full details on the place, and how we built it, I keep that seed as a blue pitcher next to my sink; go ahead and graze it if you want. It was mildly frustrating we couldn't actually take down and read any of the books, but it was a comfort to be surrounded by them. We met each morning in our little corner, and wandered the stacks of our minds as we talked. She appeared to me as she had in her first Second; apparently I appeared to her as I did when we met. This implies many things that you're welcome to speculate on or research as you please.

25

I was there for less than two minutes before she appeared; she'd always been punctual. I squeezed her—an odd experience, as the sensations were sharper and the emotional impact weaker—and she squeezed me back.

"How is everything at home?" I said.

"Would you like to know what your dog did?"

"Uh oh. What did your dog do now?"

"Remember that nice teak end-table we used to have?"

"Oh. Harsh. You know, it was right in the book that they chew furniture at this age. You knew that when you got him."

"When you got him," she said. "I've never had a dog."

"Uh huh."

"How's the poker?"

"Good. I won."

"Yay! Does that mean you'll be coming home?"

"Turned out he wasn't really trying. Let me tell you what he wants."

She listened the way she always did—with total focus. When I'd finished, she said, "Strange."

"Yeah."

"You're going to help him?"

"Unless I can think of a reason not to."

She chewed her lower lip. "I wish you were here."

"Yeah. I'd like to curl up on the couch with you. BWIMF."

She smiled and rested her head on my shoulder. "How is the schedule?"

"Local time here it's evening; I'm guessing I'll usually be with Sandow then."

"Should we switch to morning your time? Say, fourteen hours from now? That'd work for me."

"Yeah, let's do that."

"So I'll see you in fourteen hours."

"Love you. Pet your dog for me."

"Your dog," she said, and vanished before I could reply.

I relaxed a bit, drank some water, then sat down again. I closed my eyes and imagined the scent of cherry blossoms and the taste of chive, and I was back in the Garden, this time my own Garden. It appeared to me as a somewhat modified Roman Villa, because three thousand years ago my subconscious had determined it should be. Three thousand years ago, I'd never imagined that there was such a thing as a subconscious, but it seems to have worked without my knowing. Three thousand years ago, there were many, many things about the Garden we didn't know. A few hundred years ago, Ren, along with a couple of others, had figured out the process by which death sent an Incrementalist's stub into the Garden, which is how some of us manage continuity of existence; that left everything else. After long, long argument, we leaked that knowledge, which had led to Earthgov's system of recall tapes, and the ability to restore someone to life if deemed necessary. I have mixed feelings about the whole thing, but over-all I think it's good. My point, however, is that, for the most part, we have no more idea of how the Garden works than we did three thousand years ago; or forty thousand. But it works, and I used it, walking through the interior landscape of my mind, exerting conscious control over things I could, discovering things I didn't know, holding objects that didn't exist. I took questions with me, and brought knowledge back.

I went down imaginary stairs to a place below my villa and walked aimlessly. Upstairs and outside, direction mattered, because I had locked those "places" into my head, planted seeds of memory there. Down here, there were no seeds, no places, nothing. Anything that has ever been communicated in symbol from one person to another in all of human existence could potentially be found here; so full, so packed, so dense, that it was empty; because it is as hard to hear when there is too much sound as it is when there is too little. I walked through the familiar emptiness.

Francis Sandow.

I pictured him, and let the little I knew of him roll around in my head. Presently I saw a bicycle—the sort with the oversized front wheel. For reasons I couldn't remember, it was linked in my mind to a strange 19th Century television show about which I could recall very little. But I climbed onto the bike anyway, and a picture formed in my mind of a

Strantrian temple. There were statues there of many of the gods in their Egyptian-like pantheon, but my attention was focused on the one who looked like a man, his hand raised, a quiver of thunderbolts at this side, his skin bizarrely lime-colored.

Interesting.

I collapsed the bike into a small stone and put it into a tote-bag that appeared over my shoulder because I wished it there. I moved on, looking through knowledge, sifting it, touching it, feeling it; playing with ideas as if they were tangible things. A little later a stream cut across my path, and I took the cold water into my hand and drank, and I understood more of what it meant to be a worldscaper: to bend nature to your will on a staggering scale. The stream became another stone, and that, too, went into my pouch for later contemplation.

Further on, a child's kalidoscope showed that Sandow was psychic. I wasn't certain I believed it, but that was the claim. Into the bag.

I listened to an old Irish tune played on the penny whistle, and I learned a little about the god I'd seen: Shimbo of Darktree, who inhabited Sandow's psyche in a way that I hoped had a lot to do with abnormal psychology, because the possibility that it didn't was too scary to contemplate. It clicked against the other stones in the bag, and I walked on.

And on.

When the bag was starting to feel heavy with facts and theories and knowledge, I climbed back up the stairs. I turned the bag into an ancient instrument called a Fender Stratocaster, which I'd never learned how to play very well, and set it on the stone table in my atrium.

I opened my eyes then, returning from the Garden long enough to get some food and relax a bit, before returning to do what Sandow had asked of me. This time, instead of walking through the unknown of random knowledge, I walked through the known of the carefully organized—bits of my own life, recorded, as it were, for eternity, or at least a reasonable facsimile there-of. They were all there, because once you've put something in the Garden, it never leaves. And your own seeds are the easiest to find.

I limited myself to an hour or so, because if I wasn't in a hurry to learn about him, he'd better not be in a hurry to learn about me. We would take our time, both of us.

Then I napped again, because spending that much time in the Garden takes a lot out of you. Still later, Sandow and I ate a late dinner—a less formal meal this time—and we talked about what I learned. Not about him or Shimbo; I kept that research to myself. But I told him about the Earth three thousand years ago, memories that had faded, but were now, again, sharp and clear.

That set the pattern for the next few weeks: In the morning, I'd go into the Garden and spend some time with Ren, then I'd go into my own Garden and learn what I could about Sandow, which I'd keep to myself; and I'd bring back seeds of my old life, with their clues about ancient Earth, which I'd share with him over dinner. Sometimes, in the evening, we played more poker.

Sandow learned a lot in that time: he learned how to make a Roman shoe, which market in Judea had the best fruit, where to find salt, which blacksmith made the cheapest needles. And more. So much more. Things I had forgotten that I had forgotten; things it would never have occurred to me to wonder about. Sandow drank it all up.

I learned things, too.

I could have learned Sandow's switches—those bits of sense memory we all have, that generate emotions that generate brain chemicals that make it possible for an Incrementalist to meddle with someone—but I had told him I wouldn't meddle with him, and I meant it, so I didn't look for his switches. But I did look for him. I wanted to know something about this man, this Earthman whose body was more than a thousand years old.

I wished the Garden had had more about Strantri; I learned enough to be intrigued, but not enough to actually understand it. It was like Tibetan Buddhism in the way the supernatural elements seemed to slip through your fingers when you tried to grasp them, leaving nothing but practical advice in your hand; it was like Judaism in the way hard lines separated the mystical from the mundane so that it took years of study to learn how the one led to the other; it was like Catholicism in the way its priests functioned as mediators to and from the gods, accepted as normal and natural by its followers. I didn't run into indications of anything I'd call fanaticism, though there were hints that long, long ago that, too, had happened.

Sandow, it seemed was a priest—or maybe a high priest, the translations were inconsistent. But it meant that there was some sort of symbiotic relationship between him and the god Shimbo, which relationship was one of the things that permitted him to do the work he did. There were more sources that insisted he could read minds, and, I admit, the evidence started to sound convincing. I remained skeptical. There was some discussion of the magnetic fields generated by planets, and how these generated places called "power pulls" that a Strantrian priest would use to draw the god into himself. All of this stuff walked the line between practical and detailed enough to be believable, and nonsensical enough to be dismissed. For example, according to tradition, the god would chose the man rather than the reverse, but I didn't find that entirely credible. For one thing, it would imply that the god had an actual, independent existence which, if you have memories going back forty thousand years during which time there's been no evidence of the existence of gods, takes a bit of believing. And Sandow himself, it turned out, wasn't entirely convinced.

But, I figured, I could be wrong. It's happened before.

Sometimes, in the evening, Sandow and I would sit in some glade somewhere, or in his rooftop garden, or in one of the seemingly numberless sitting rooms and just talk. It was strange how relaxing it was to me to be able to open up to someone who wasn't an Incrementalist. For his part, he seemed delighted to speak to someone who had memories that reached back as far as his.

We drank wonderful booze and ate spectacular food and spoke of his long-lost family, and my long-lost friends. I told him about the first time I died, of something that I'm pretty sure was tuberculosis; and he told me about finding a reason to live, just when he thought there could no longer

30

be one. I explained that, to me, memory was place; he explained that, to him, money was fuel.

We spoke of loneliness, and we understood.

And every day I went to the Garden, filled him in on old Earth, and learned about the new Galaxy.

Even now, after all that's happened, those seem to me to be good days. I miss them. They continued until one day when I happened to graze some of Sandow's recent history. It freaked the hell out of me, and changed everything.

*

I had been keeping Ren informed of what I was doing, and what I'd discovered; not in any deliberate way, but just as we talked. She told me about what the kids and the grandchildren and the great-grandchildren were up to, and the latest adventures of Wolf, our Altaran Bijihound, and her current meddlework, and I told her about Sandow, and we often argued about whether Shimbo might really exist. Ren thought it was possible, I remained skeptical.

That day, she took one look at my face and said, "What is it?"

"Something I just learned. A hedge I found. I still don't understand it, and I'm not sure if I really believe it." I stopped talking. Frowning. Thinking. She waited. I finally said, "If you want to graze it, it's the marigolds in the pot just outside my front door."

"Do you want me to graze it, Phil? Or would you rather tell me about it?"

"It's something that happened—that may or may not have happened—a few years ago. Um, to make a very long story drastically oversimplified, it looked like another of the Pe'ian gods may have moved from one host to another."

"What do you mean?"

"I can't say it any more clearly. As near as I can tell, one of the Pe'ian gods took it upon himself to change hosts."

"But that means—"

"They're real. Yeah."

31

"And that means—"

"I know."

"Two people, then? The god and the man? Each one existing independently, but sharing a body?"

"That's pretty much it," I said. "If true. And it seems true."

"Then which one—"

"I don't know."

She frowned. "I have to admit, the bit about recreating the Earth from three thousand years ago seemed dubious. I should have said something."

"I should have seen it."

"What do you think he's after?"

"Sandow?"

"No, the god."

"Oh. Well, what have I got?"

"Oh," she said. "That's, I don't know, horrid. On several levels."

"Yeah. One them being, I don't know what to do about it."

"Can you leave? I mean, if you asked him to let you just go home, would he?"

"He would," I said. "But if we're right—"

"Oh. Yes. The god wouldn't."

"Yeah." I sighed. "I miss Jimmy."

She took my hand. It wasn't the same as in real life, but it felt good anyway. "Me too," she said. She kissed my cheek and I opened my eyes to a place unfathomable light-years away from her.

*

After that, as far as I could tell nothing obvious changed in my conversations with Sandow, but I was more wary, and I was listening to him in a different way. If he noticed anything, he didn't let on. And I spent even more of my time in the Garden trying to learn what I could about Shimbo of Darktree, Shrugger of Thunders.

Shimbo: real or not? Sandow: psychic or not? Me: totally screwed or not? If the first was true, the others sort of followed naturally, and it seemed pretty clear the first was true.

Information on Shimbo was scarce and sometimes contradictory; The Garden doesn't seem to gather much information from alien species, which is an important clue about its nature, and someday someone will use that clue to figure something out. I'm sure of it.

But, both in the Garden and in the real world, I was able to gets bits and pieces. For one thing, Sandow didn't mind talking about him; or else considered it a fair trade for what I was giving him. I learned of the worlds he'd built, and I looked at them, hanging in space like lanterns of life. I learned of the chants he used, and was able to record one into my i-card. And I found more things in the Garden, considered them, saved them.

And I learned about a flowering plant called *glitten*.

It originally came from the Pe'ian homeworld, and the root is sacred to various Strantrieen rituals. The petals are broad and white, with streaks of pale yellow; the eye is blue or indigo, depending on the time of year. It gives off a scent like oranges mixed with a hint of peppermint. By tradition, the Stranti priests keep the flowers floating in pools as long as they can find flowers in bloom. And, if you choose to believe it, they only grow near a power pull.

I don't know.

I could probably have asked him if he had any of them, and where they were; but the Garden contained the information that he'd dictated instructions about them to his gardener, so I could just go find out, and I did. It was a walk of a couple of miles through woods and fields and past beaches; changes in landscape that shouldn't exist that close together. Eventually I reached them in a patch of Eastern exposure where they'd be shaded most of the day; a place where it was warm and the humidity was higher than in the surrounding area—I guess a worldscaper can do things like that. I knelt next to them, inhaled, enjoyed. Then I picked a handful of flowers.

"Something I can do for you?"

I turned around. "Hey, Frank. Possibly."

"Do you know what you have there?"

"Yeah, I do."

His eyes were narrowed, and he seemed tense. It occurred to me that, for all I knew, I could be surrounded by weapons, held by people or machines or both, all pointing at me. I should probably assume I was.

"I don't think those will work as a, what do you call it?"

"Switch."

"Yeah. They won't work as a switch on me."

"No, they won't. And I said I wouldn't meddle with you. Can't you read minds? You should know that."

"I can't read yours."

Well, that was a relief. "Interesting," I said. "I wonder why."

"The ability doesn't come with a guarantee. Why do you have the flowers?"

"Why did you bring me to Homefree?"

He studied me. He had track shoes on, I was wearing loafers. I suppose you could say this gave him an edge if it came to fighting, but that would be silly—in this Second, I was shorter than him by seven inches and lighter by fifty pounds, and he knew how to handle himself in a fight and I didn't; he was very possibly armed and I wasn't. The shoes were beside the point, but for some reason that's what popped into my head just then. It was late afternoon, and the shadow of an oak tree stretched out behind him. Among the meadows and brooks and woods were some gentle hills that gradually sloped up into mountains, snow-capped and purple majesty and all like that. We stood in a kind of basin, like a scooped out field of wild grass, uncut, with some trees scattered about to provide shade. I had the feeling that if I spent enough time on it, I'd find a pattern in those trees, like, maybe a question mark or something—something that would make Sandow chuckle to himself when he thought about it. He was that kind of guy. I turned to study the sunset.

"You seem nervous," he said.

"I am."

"Why?"

"So far as I know, you've never had anyone killed unless it pretty god damned necessary."

"That's why you're nervous?"

"No, I'm nervous because there's always a first time."

"This won't be it."

"I'm glad to hear you say so."

"And I hope it won't be necessary."

"Me too."

"Although death isn't as scary for you as it is for the rest of us."

"Death is pretty scary for us. Figure there's a fifty-fifty chance you'll be the one who comes back out of stub. That means there's a fifty-fifty chance you won't."

"Better than a hundred percent chance."

"Yes," I said.

"In your case, it has to be better than fifty-fifty, or we'll need to rewrite the laws of probability. That would be how many coin-flips in a row?"

"I like talking to someone who knows why it's called a coin-flip."

"Yeah, me too," he said.

"Remember what you told me about the universe being a little less screwed up because of us?"

"Yeah."

"You too."

"What's your point?"

"We're sort of alike, Frank. When the opportunity comes up, we use the resources we have to fix things a little, here and there, don't we? And sometimes it means we have to throw our weight around, just a bit."

"I'm still waiting for your point."

"And we hate it when someone does that to us. You use money, I use oxytocin, but we still push when we need to, and we hate being pushed."

"How about if you just say what's on your mind?"

"Why did you bring me here, Frank?"

"I told you. I want to recreate the Earth of three thousand years ago."

"Yeah, only I don't believe you."

"I haven't lied to you, Phil."

"I don't think you're lying. I think you believe what you told me."

35

"I think I'd know."

"That's sort of the issue. What made you want to rebuild the Earth?"

He frowned. "What do you mean?"

"When we meddle with someone, if we do it right, the Focus never knows he's been meddled with. We just change his actions—subtly—and push him a bit. He feels like a free agent. And he is a free agent—it's just that he's a free agent who's a little more inclined to do the right thing."

"Keep talking."

"So, when did you get the idea to do this?"

"Are you saying one of you did this to me? Meddled with me?"

"No, not one of us. When did you get the idea?"

He stood there and looked at me for what seemed like a long time, and I was scared. "You said you wouldn't—"

"I meant it. I'm not. I won't." Now I was well and truly into the scared zone. I said, "Now, when did you get the idea to recreate the Earth?"

He nodded slowly, with the look of a man ready to accept an unpleasant truth—or maybe of someone who'd had to accept unpleasant truths before. "All right," he said. "Let me think."

The sun was going down, splashing red on the rocks behind him, making the sky orange in the west; the scent of pine-needles came with a breeze that should have been chilly but wasn't.

"It was a few years ago," he said at last. "I was looking at pictures from old Earth, and I thought about how we'd screwed the place up before we managed to get off it, and how I'd love to see what it would have been like if we hadn't."

"And it suddenly came to you to try it out, to learn more."

"Yes."

"And to enlist me to help."

"Yes."

"So you already knew about me, about us."

He frowned. "I guess I. . . I don't. . . I must have."

"Yeah."

"I don't understand—"

"We aren't the only ones who can meddle, Frank."

"I'm not sure what you're saying," although the look on his face suggested that, maybe, he was starting to figure it out, and that he didn't like it any more than I did.

"Not sure, or don't want to believe it?"

"Both."

"We're standing at a power pull, Frank. You know what you can do here."

"What is this about, Phil?"

"Ask the god, he set the whole thing up."

"He can't do that. He can't do anything unless I—"

It's just like making a scary play in poker: once you're committed, you're too busy to be scared. I ploughed on. "Remember Mike Shandon and Belion, Frank?"

"I'm not likely to forget."

"The god jumped from the Pei'an to the man, and did it without the Pei'an even being consulted."

"Special circumstances."

"Maybe."

"What do you imagine Shimbo wants?"

"Immortality. The Garden. Me."

"I don't believe—"

"You don't want to believe, Frank. You've never been sure how much is you and how much is the god. He's made you angry, proud, frightened; but you've always wondered if he was real. Well, he's real, Frank, and he has his own agenda. He wants to leave you, Frank. He wants me, for my access to the Garden, for my lifetimes of past and future."

He was quiet for a long time after that. Then he said, "You know, Phil, even if you're right, I'm not sure I'd mind so much."

"Maybe, but I can't let that happen."

"That's why you picked the flowers?"

"Yeah, to tell him that."

"You think he'll listen to you? I haven't had much luck getting him to listen to me."

"No, I don't figure he's going to listen. But I'm not just going to wait around. One day you'll ask me to take a walk, and we'll pass near a power-pull, and Shimbo will manifest, and then he'll be gone from you and he'll be with me. I'm not going to wait for that to happen."

He shook his head, standing next to me. We both watched the sunset. "Did it occur to you to just tell me you wanted to go?"

"I understand that every time you try to leave the world, the world doesn't want to let you. I have an idea that, mysteriously, it wouldn't want to let me, either."

"You may be right. But if what you say is true, you're an idiot to piss him off."

"Maybe."

"You have a plan," he stated.

"Maybe."

He shook his head. "You aren't the type to just let things happen to you. Any more than I am."

"Exactly," I said. "Any more than you are."

I turned away from the sunset, and faced him fully. "It isn't going to work, Shimbo. I don't want you."

Sandow looked different, though at that moment, I don't think I could have explained how. More focused, maybe? Something deeper behind his eyes?

"I know what you want, Shrugger of Thunders: you want the Garden; you want forty thousand years of accumulated knowledge and to know that if your host dies you'll go on. But you can't have it; I'm sorry.

"If you inhabit me against my will, I swear by all the good I've ever done, I'll never go near a power pull. You will never manifest, and when this body dies, the others will keep me in stub for a hundred years if they have to, to make sure I'm gone. To make sure you're gone. I promise this, Shimbo. We don't want you."

I was concentrating so fully on Sandow's face, I barely noticed the storm-clouds gathering over our heads.

Sandow tried to speak—tried, but then he was gone, and there was another in his place. Whatever my opinion of psychic ability, one thing I know for sure is that I don't have any. So what I saw in Sandow I saw with my eyes. He filled his body more; he took in more air, and spread out, from his feet, into the ground below us. I'm sure that if I'd been able to measure him just then, he'd have been the same height he was five minutes before; but he was taller; man-sized and yet somehow bigger. His arm was raised, and I knew—knew that when it came down, I would be dead. I hoped I'd only be stubbed, back in the Garden, waiting to start over; but the man before me was a god, whatever that might mean, so who knew what he could do?

The rain came down, the thunder roared, the ground shook; it was hard to stay upright. There was nowhere to run, nowhere to hide.

Was Sandow in there at all, any more? Was there enough of him left to give me the ten or fifteen seconds I needed?

There was a crack of thunder, and the rain came down in torrents. Sandow's—or, rather, Shimbo's—eyes fell upon me, and I understood that I was about as significant as a gnat that was annoying him.

If I managed to live through this, it was going to produce one of the most interesting seeds in the Garden.

And he hesitated; and that was Sandow, inside the god. Was it force, or pleading? Control, or reason? I had no way of knowing. But now I had my few seconds. Just me and Shimbo.

I pulled the infocard from my pocket, flicked it to life, and held it out, letting it show him what in my head I still called a slide show—3D pictures of world after world, hanging in space. World after world that he would know.

"You aren't simply a beast, you know," I told him. And flicked the infopod again; the soft, low rumble of chanting in Pe'ian occurred, just barely audible.

I made myself hold his eyes—ancient, powerful, terrifying eyes. I wanted to sink into the ground. Of course, with the way everything around me was shaking, that was a possibility in a more literal sense than I cared for.

"You create as well as destroy. I know of your wrath, and I know the worlds you have helped to build. You can be either. The man who holds you is human, and he, too, creates as well as destroys. So do I. Is it so much to ask that he, and I, be permitted to live out our lives? Shimbo of Darktree Tower, do you need to control so much that you spread unhappiness? Is that who you wish to be, how you wish to be remembered by all who come after? I am asking you to consider, to think about it."

And still, he hesitated. He hadn't yet destroyed me, and that was something. But his hand was still raised; all he needed to do was lower it, and I'd be no more. So I looked up at the most powerful being I had ever heard of, much less encountered, and said, "One other thing, before you toast me." And, just like a hippie from a millennium ago, I stuck a handful of flowers in his face.

Take that, I thought.

"You are more than a servant," I said. "Can you be less than a master?"

He stood there, arm upraised, inhaling the scent of a flower sacred to him, seeing his worlds, hearing his chant; and I waited.

And something changed, and it was Francis Sandow who stood before me once again. The rain slowed, slowed, and stopped; and above me the clouds broke up. Sandow looked at me. Before he could speak, I said, "I promised not to meddle with you; I didn't say anything about him."

"You'd have made a good lawyer," he told me.

"Ouch," I explained.

We stood in the darkening dark, there, in the hand-crafted world, and I breathed sweet air, glad that I was still able to, and that it was still me doing it. He was quiet, either because he sensed that I needed some time, or else because he needed some, too.

Night came to Sandow's World.

40

"Let's go back to the house," he said at last. "Want to walk? I can send for a craft."

"Walking is fine."

"I'll have the *David Bowie* come for you tomorrow."

"All right. You saved me, you know."

"After putting you in a position to be killed. Or worse."

I shrugged. "Are you still going to build that world?"

"Yeah, I am. At this point, I kind of need to."

I chuckled. "Redemption?"

He shook his head. "Not funny."

"No, I suppose not."

"Phil, I'm sorry—"

"Forget it."

"Maybe I will. But you won't. Ever. I don't envy you that."

"Then have your chef cook me something I won't want to forget."

"I'll do that," he said.

And he did.

Keeper of the Keys

by Kelly McCullough

I felt the dragon coming before I saw him, a whirling and curling in the clouds at the very limits of my perceptions. Moonbird, greatest of Rondoval's dragons, and astride his scaly neck, the castle's long absent master. My master, Pol Detson.

He had his guitar in his hands and a song to speed the journey on his lips, though his voice sounded cracked and tired rather than sweet as it usually did. It had been nearly three years since I'd seen him last—my much missed accursed master. Far longer than he'd expected to take unlocking the secrets of the Keys.

I would have sought him out before now, but he had commanded me to remain behind, and defend Rondoval castle against a possible assault by the greatest of the madwands, Henry Spier. He had also charged me to do what I could to continue the renovations he'd begun after his return from the technological mirror world where he'd grown up.

I disapproved of that—the banishment, not his return. The place for the master of Rondoval was here, where the castle's curse could keep a proper eye on him. But the family politics of my accursed master's line were. . .complex, full of strife. It was Pol's grandfather, Mor, who had sent him into exile as a baby, only to bring him back again as a young man. The banishment had followed a sorcerous duel in which Mor killed Det, who was Pol's father and Mor's own son.

Then, it had been too dangerous to allow the young Pol to live in the world of Rondoval. Later, it had been too dangerous to have him anywhere else. At least, that's how I understand things to have happened. I was physically present at the duel, but not yet in any shape to pay attention to the thing, having only just been summoned into the world myself. Summoned? Perhaps it were better to say created, or even cast, for I am as much a spell as anything, the—

"Belphanior, come to me. I need you."

The words were little more than a whisper, but coming from Pol's lips I would have heard them half a world away, for I was the curse of Rondoval and I had been created expressly to serve or avenge her masters as they needed me. I spun myself up into a tower of crystalline light and raced to meet him, finally freed from my long confinement at the castle.

"What is your wish, oh accursed master?" I asked as I manifested myself in the air before him.

"You've been consorting with demons again, haven't you?" asked Pol.

I had cause then to be glad that I couldn't blush, for he was right. I liked demons, being one myself, though very new to the game.

"I can always tell when you've been chatting with the one you met at the gathering at Belken by the way your diction goes all grandiose," he continued. "But that's neither here nor there. I need you to take Mouseglove ahead to the castle for me, and see that you hold the enchantments in place, he's badly hurt and I haven't the strength to keep them there much longer."

It was only as he mentioned the little thief that I registered Mouseglove's presence, so focused had I been on the return of Rondoval's master. Pol's eyes glowed for a moment and a thick rope of amber light detached itself from the dragon-shaped birthmark on his forearm, drifting over to attach itself to me. The other end was connected to a network of multicolored strands that wrapped cocoon-like around Mouseglove, and I felt a heavy drain on my resources as I took over the maintenance of the spell and lifted the thief from Moonbird's back.

"I'll be along as soon as I've seen to things in the caves, but only briefly," Pol continued. "I need to act on what I've learned and, quickly. If it weren't for Mouseglove I'd have gone straight on to Avinconet, but I can't trust him to Merson's care, or my brother's. So I have to attempt things out of order."

As I carried Mouseglove down to the castle, I studied the spell that bound him. It was a beautifully crafted bit of magic, worthy of Det himself, or maybe even old Mor—far beyond what Pol could have managed the last time I'd seen him. That was shortly after the confrontation with Henry Spier at Avinconet. It pleased me that Pol was continuing to grow so rapidly in his spellcrafting, though it did not surprise me.

He was a madwand, from a long line of madwands, natural sorcerers all, save only his older brother. Laric had been ruined by Ryle Merson, Det's onetime partner and later nemesis. And now an uneasy ally of my master—more of those complex family politics. The formal training Merson had inflicted on Laric had cut him off from the dragon blood that Mor's great great grandfather had brought into the line along with the dragon-form birthmark that graced the right arm of every child of the house.

Though Det had made me, I couldn't conscience what he had done to his older son by giving him to Merson as a hostage. Laric's loss of his madwand's soul was a goodly part of why I chose to recognize Pol as the true heir to Rondoval and my master over his older brother's claim.

*

Pol sagged in the saddle as he watched Belphanior bear the wounded thief away, only too glad of the battle straps that held him in place.

Moonbird canted his head to one side, looking back at Pol worriedly. *Are you all right back there?*

I'm fine, old friend, just very tired. Pol cased his guitar and slid it into the pocket dimension where he kept his most precious possessions. *Very, very tired.*

Pol wanted nothing more than to land at Rondoval and fall into his chambers for a week's sleep. But as he had backtracked his father's steps across the eastern continent, he had felt the presence of Spier more than once as both sought to discover the secrets of the Keys. It was a deadly race with knowledge and power as the prize.

Pol had won the course, but only barely and at great cost to his friend Mouseglove. Pol wanted to unmake the statuettes, Spier wanted to make more. If what Pol had learned was true, both of them were doomed to failure, but there was much that each could do with the secrets they now possessed.

The statuettes were Keys to another world, older, wilder, filled with ancient and powerful magic. Pol's father had created them to open a door between the two. He wanted the other world to flood into this one, remaking it into a place where magic conquered all, and sorcerers stood astride the world with the madwands among them the next thing to gods.

Each of the little figurines held the soul. . .no, *was* the soul of a powerful sorcerer that Det had defeated in sorcerous combat, madwands all. Somehow, Pol's father had been able to capture them in the moment of death and condense them down into the shapes they now wore. As part of the process, each was bound to the purpose of increasing the power of magic in the world by opening that Gate or by any other means possible.

It had taken Pol three long years to trace the path Det had taken in learning how to transform a soul, and the knowledge that had come with the years had both stained and strengthened his own. He glanced at the mark on his arm, and wondered if the red dragon there was looking back at him with as much of wonder and worry as he felt. For the secret of chaining a soul lay in his dragon blood and his madwand's art.

But then Moonbird was landing him in the courtyard, and Pol could no longer focus on anything more than staggering into his bedroom and the long dark that lay in wait for him there.

*

My master called to me as he fell into his bed and ordered that I wake him in a scant six hours. He was asleep before I could respond, so I returned my attention to the injured thief. Mouseglove had deep claw marks scoring his back and right shoulder. A fraction of an inch deeper or farther left and his spine would have been severed—not an insurmountable problem with the right spells, but a much greater challenge than simply maintaining his body and speeding normal healing.

Pol's spell was a cleverly crafted thing, but I thought I could see ways to increase the pace of healing, so I set about strengthening this strand of magic and sliding that one over a touch. Nothing that would rise to the level of noticeable interference, just the tiniest sorts of tweaks that only a creature of magic like myself might think of.

I was just finishing when I heard the angry buzzing of a frustrated dream-sending trying to find its way through the defenses of Rondoval. Something from Spier most likely, though it might also have come from our "ally" Merson. Both had played that trick on Pol in the past, which was why I had added a tightening of the etheric structure of the castle to my program of restoration.

As the sending slid along the outer edges of the wards looking for entrance, I opened a tiny hole for it congruent to the window in the room where I had placed Mouseglove. The sending slipped inside a moment later. I reached out with what will I could spare from my assigned task and crushed it, releasing a bitter, bright nugget of power that tasted of Spier. Quite delicious, and I amused myself afterward with a meditation on how best to prepare and present the sorcerer himself should I have the opportunity of indulging my taste for my master's greatest enemy.

*

Despite the destruction of his sending, the shadow of Henry Spier continued to haunt Pol's dreams. The older madwand was always close to the edge of Pol's consciousness these days, waking or sleeping—a grim presence that never quite went away. Not even in dreams of his old home in the other world.

Pol woke tired, leaving behind a smoky bar and the even smokier voiced Betty Lewis. As he opened his eyes the details of the dream left him one by one, starting with the song the two of them had performed in duet and ending with Henry Spier carrying away the basket that held all their tips and the only remaining copies of the album they'd recorded together. The latter left him with a sense of loss all out of proportion to the theft.

For a few long beats Pol considered simply going back to sleep, but the Spier of his nightmare quickly shifted into the one that worried at his waking mind and started to gnaw away. With a muttered word and a twisting gesture of his right hand where it lay on the coverlet, Pol spun a rippling orange strand of magic into existence. It reached across the room and lifted the water out the basin on his washstand, forming it into a rough sphere.

Another twist of his hand pulled the ball of water across the room to hover a few inches above his face. With a reluctant sigh, Pol lifted his head and plunged his face into the floating water which moved of its own accord now to scrub away both dirt and sleep. It was brutally cold—another effect of his spell—and he couldn't bear it for long, but when he finally exhaled and dropped back onto his pillow, he felt much the better for a clean face and a clear head.

Sighing, he raised his hands from the coverlet and sank them into the water as well before sending it back to the basin. Sliding a hand across his cheek, Pol reinforced the magic that kept the hair of his beard from growing—ironically, a variant of the sleeping spell that Spier had used to bind Merson's daughter once upon a time.

Moonbird, sent Pol, *meet me in the courtyard. Avinconet awaits.*

I come.

"Belphanior."

A curl of green fire shaped itself into a face a few yards from Pol, sliding along ahead of him as he walked. "Master?"

"How fares Mouseglove?"

"He will recover, though not quickly. His hurts are deep and serious."

"Guard him well. He took those wounds saving my life. . .again." He frowned and shook his head. "Silly of him, really. I see that Rondoval has largely been returned to its former glory. You have done well. I'm especially pleased that you've restored the northwest tower. I've need of something in its foundations and I wasn't looking forward to having to move several tons of masonry. Thank you."

The face in fire blinked bemusedly and then nodded. "You are welcome, master."

Pol snapped his fingers and the smoke dispersed. A few minutes later, he was descending a flight of spiral stairs that ended at a small crypt. He touched his dragonmarked forearm to an apparently unmarked spot on the right hand door pillar. In response, the heavy stone slab that sealed the tomb puffed into a thick cloud of purple smoke and rolled out of the way, revealing a small chamber centered by a black marble sarcophagus. Applying the mark to the stone caused the lid to slide silently aside.

A man's body lay within. Tall, well built, its long white hair centered by a single black streak in a sort of inverted mirror of Pol's own. He was wearing loose pants of rough silk and a sleeveless shirt that exposed the dragonmark on his right arm, and if Pol hadn't known better he would have guessed the man only hours dead.

"Dragon blood," Pol whispered.

"What was that, my master?" a voice whispered in dark.

"I should have known you'd keep an ear out, Belphanior. I said, 'dragon blood.' That's what's preserved my umpteen times great grandfather so well. Arn is the first of my family to have the blood of the dragon flowing in his veins from birth and the second of the great madwands."

"I've never quite understood how that works," replied the curse. "Arn's father didn't marry a dragon, did he?"

Pol laughed. "No, at least not literally, though Maris was an exceedingly tough old sorceress in her own right. If what I learned in the east is right, Vul exchanged a part of his soul with the dragonlord Firewind, for this mark—" Pol touched his arm "—and the blood that comes with it, 'unthinning for him and his heirs unto eternity.'"

"Interesting. . ."

"Terrifying is more like it," Pol mumbled to himself.

But Belphanior didn't answer and Pol went back to examining the body in the sarcophagus. A dense net of dark threads like the web of some eldritch spider clung to the dragonmark on the dead man's arm—spellstuff, though not active. Pol stepped around to the far side of the plinth and then leaned down and placed his own dragonmark against his ancestor's.

Wings in the wind. . .towers of red air like slow burning heat lightning. . .the taste of brimstone and charring meat. . .red eyes in the darkness. . .claws gripping, tails twining, falling together toward the sea and sexual release. . .scales sliding along worn stone at the ancient hatching grounds. . .the shattering of an egg from within!

Pol flicked his wings aside and opened his outer eyelids—no, stretched his shoulders and opened his eyes to meet the concerned gaze of the face in the green fire.

Belphanior blinked at him. "Are you all right, master?"

Pol thought about it for a moment and then nodded. He blinked a couple of times and the world beyond Belphanior's green fires shifted into focus. He was lying on his back on the flags beside the sarcophagus. It felt strangely comfortable, which he put down to his dragon-tinged perceptions along with a desire to spit fire on Henry Spier and then devour him whole.

"What happened?"

"I activated a very old spell, and I was not entirely ready for the consequences. Given my druthers, I'd have constructed a ritual and done it with one of the Keys ready to hand, but I don't have the time to waste going to Avinconet and coming back here again, so I had to manage it the hard way." He flicked his tail angrily, pushing himself to—no he didn't have a tail and hadn't moved.

With a sigh Pol grabbed the lip of the sarcophagus and pulled himself upright. "And now, on to Avinconet."

*

I didn't like the way something seemed to have jumped from the corpse to my master when they made contact, not one little bit. Nor the way that when he first blinked himself awake his eyes had looked like dragon's eyes, complete with slit pupils, if only for a second.

And I especially didn't like that it had all happened mere minutes before his departure from Rondoval and my watchful care. But accursed

50

masters will do as they will and there's nothing a poor bound demon can do to stop them. All I could do was watch him out of sight and then return to tending Mouseglove.

*

Will you not play for me? Moonbird asked, breaking Pol's reverie.

Absentmindedly, he reached into otherspace and pulled out his guitar, tuning it briefly before starting into one of the pieces he'd written for Betty Lewis. While his hands played the familiar melody his mind wandered forward to his next task, the retrieval of one of the seven Keys. Merson was going to be a problem. He didn't. . .had never trusted Pol, not even after they had fought together.

Thank you, I haven't heard that in a very long time. Moonbird's unvoiced words drew Pol's attention back to the present.

Seemingly of their own accord, his hands had started a new tune, a gliding, sliding, wild sort of music unlike anything Pol had ever heard before. As soon as he noticed, his fingers lost their way, and the guitar thrummed discordantly as he fumbled to a halt.

What was I just playing? He asked Moonbird.

The great dragon coughed and growled low in his throat. *Or, in your tongue, it might be rendered as—*

The Flaming Spire, Pol responded, realizing that he had understood Moonbird's original, dragonish answer without the translation.

Yes, that's it. The great dragon turned his long neck, looking back and down at Pol. *Few of your people understand our tongue. Fewer still learn it late in life and all in one moment. Your father was one such, and. . .*

What? asked Pol.

I'm not entirely sure it was a good thing for him. There were other changes in Det at the time. He became crueler and colder, less like one of your people and more like one of mine.

You almost make it sound like you don't approve of dragons.

Not at all. We are what we are. But we are not human, and Det was, or ought to have been. Which is not to say that he didn't already possess cruelty and coldness in abundance, just that they became more accentuated at that time.

Moonbird tilted his head from side to side in a manner that Pol recognized as a shrug. *On the other claw, there are any number of draconic tendencies which he didn't exhibit either before or after that moment. Perhaps whatever he did simply intensified those bits of his personality that he shared with us.*

That's. . .you've given me much to think about, old friend. Now I just need to find the leisure for it.

Pol sighed. He certainly didn't have it now. With time so short, he'd told Moonbird to take them via the shortcut—a sort of hole in the fabric of the world that would quarter the flight distance at the cost of temporarily turning them inside out. At least, that was how it felt, and it would render Pol mostly useless for a good hour afterward.

That meant that if he was going to contact his brother Laric before his arrival he had to do it now. He turned the idea over once again. Laric really didn't like him much more than Merson, but their shared blood might count for more in this case, given what Pol had learned in the east. Beside, he couldn't think of a better plan. So. . .

Pol exchanged his guitar for the shell of a darkwater island clam that he'd fitted with a golden hinge to replace the one nature had originally placed there. Opening it exposed an irregular mirror on one side and a trio of small tools attached to the other, making it look quite like the lady's compact he'd stolen the idea from.

Using the fine-pointed stylus made from the fang of a manticore, he quickly sketched a series of sigils just above the surface of the mirror, rearranging the tight coil of spell strands that lay within into something much more geometric. Then he very lightly stroked the mirror with the tiny sphinx whisker brush.

The silvery surface fogged for perhaps a ten count then cleared again, though it no longer reflected Pol's face. Instead it gave a bird's eye view on a window in the western tower of Avinconet. Pol took the third tool from his clamshell, a thin tube of bone from the wing of a harpy, and raised it to his lips. Taking careful aim, he pointed it through the mirror and blew sharply. A tiny ball of onyx like a black pea shot out to lightly strike the window.

A moment later the window opened and Pol's point of view zoomed in, passing through the window and finding another mirror waiting on his brother's desk where Laric now sat, waiting. He looked very like his brother, complete with a white streak running front to back through his thick dark hair.

"What do *you* want?" he asked Pol, his voice gruff and distant.

"I need to collect one of the Keys."

"That's impossible. Merson would never consent to any of them being removed from the matrix that holds them trapped now, especially not by you. I agree with him, madwand. We can't trust you or any of your kind."

"Yeah, I kind of figured that would be your initial answer."

"It's my final one too, Pol. Just because you're my brother doesn't mean I have to like you." He reached for the mirror.

"Hold on, I'm not terribly fond of you either, but you're going to want to hear this. I think that I know how to re-key the Keys if you will, and I'm probably the only one who can do it."

"Probably?"

"Probably. It's possible you might be able to do it too, and if I die trying you'll get your chance, but there's nobody else alive who's got any hope of managing it. And if one of us doesn't do it, this whole world is going to be devoured when the Gate finally opens."

Laric blinked several times. "But we've got the Keys contained."

"For now, perhaps. But they cannot be destroyed, only remade, and even if Spier doesn't break them free, someone else will eventually, or they will do it themselves."

"And only you or I can remake them?"

"Yes."

"Is that because we are Det's sons and he made them in the first place?"

"Sort of, it's got much more to do with how they were made and that we both descend from a very clever madwand named Vul Iverson." Pol raised his forearm to the mirror. "He's where we got this."

"I'm listening."

"Good, let me tell you a story about dragons. . ."

When Pol finished Laric shook his head. "I just don't know. You're sure the Keys can't be destroyed?"

"Positive. The dragon scrolls were very clear, souls can never be destroyed, only transformed. Even a soul devoured by one of the great demons isn't truly unmade, it is simply subsumed into the substance of the demon until such time as the demon itself dies or is devoured. That's why Det made the Keys the way that he did, to take advantage of that principle. They're essentially crystallized souls tempered in the fires of magic."

There was a long silence until, finally, Laric's shoulders sagged. "Merson will fight to prevent you removing any of the statues from the ward matrix, and you can't afford what that will cost you, not even if you win. Let me talk to Taisa. Between the two of us we should be able to keep him distracted long enough for you to slip in and steal one. I think I can convince her of the necessity. Wait till one hour after the sun goes down and then go in through the catacombs."

Before Pol could thank him, Laric waved a hand across the mirror and severed the link between them. A few minutes later, Moonbird found his hole in the sky, and after that Pol was too busy losing his breakfast to worry about his brother any more.

*

Pol brushed dust off of his shoulder as he closed the tomb's door behind. "Damned mummies. I don't know why anyone wants to keep the things around."

Merson's would not be bothering anyone again soon, not till they'd gotten themselves untangled at least. Somehow, Pol didn't think they'd be very good at untying knots. Another hundred yards and two turns put him in the room where the Keys stood in the midst of a gigantic interlaced pattern of ward spells.

Pol sighed when he saw it. His memory of the structure hadn't failed, alas. Having read his father's notes, and the dragon scrolls on which the spells had been built, Pol knew which figure he most wanted to start his gambit with, but that wasn't going to be possible. The etheric structure of the spell was built in an interdependent spiral working outward from the innermost ward and figure to the outermost.

That meant he had to start at the end and work inward. There was no safe way to pull any figurine out of the structure but the last that had been placed—a robed and hooded woman with a distinctly serpentine cast to her features. He knew her name now, Issalia, and she presented a particularly difficult challenge. But, there was no helping it, so Pol began the careful work of freeing her from the warding structure.

As soon as he broke the outer ring, her voice spoke into his mind and a small hovering flame appeared in the air in front of him.

You have returned at last, Detson. Does freeing us mean you are finally ready to continue your father's holy work and open the Gate?

Pol answered aloud, "Let us say that I am ready to discuss it again, and leave it there for now. Nor do I have time to free all of you. In fact," Pol broke another line and then reached down to snatch up the figurine despite the still partially intact state of the ward—it cost him a nasty shock and he gasped in pain, "I don't have time to do more than collect you and flee."

In seeming punctuation of that statement, a horrible bellow echoed down from somewhere high in the castle above. Pol opened a pouch at his hip and started to move the figurine toward it.

Hold, said the flame, and Pol felt himself slowing down as though he were a bug trying to move through hardening pine sap. *There are warding runes on that bag that will impede my abilities. If you are going to put me in there rather than free my fellows or help us to open the Gate, I must move to oppose you.*

Ever so slowly and painfully, Pol opened the hand that held the figurine and began to turn it over. "It's your choice, but if you do so, I will be forced to flee without you. That will leave you here to be reimprisoned by Ryle Merson. Come with me willingly and you may get the chance to complete your purpose."

The figurine began to slide out of his hand. *Wait. I will comply for now.*

Pol closed his fist around the little statue again, then shoved it into his pouch. As soon as it was closed he ran for the room's only window.

Merson's voice cried out from behind him, "Dammit, Madwand!"

Pol jumped onto a little table below the window and dove straight through the glass filling the narrow gap. As he fell away from the opening, a burst of flame went roaring through the space above him. He had dropped perhaps ten feet when a great handlike claw caught him out of the air—Moonbird!

*

Hours later, Pol found himself reinforcing the wards on the bag by playing yet another song of soothing. The thing within had just made its dozenth attempt at breaking free, and despite Pol's exhaustion, they still had many miles to go before they would reach their intended destination.

You're going to put me to sleep if you keep that up, Moonbird said into his mind.

Pol sighed. *Yeah, me too.* Then, with more resolution, *This isn't going to work. You'd better take us down before this thing breaks loose and I end up having to deal with it a-dragonback.*

Anywhere specific?

Good question. Pol scanned the area below them, hoping to spy a stone circle, or sacred grove, or some other such site, but couldn't see anything appropriate along the coastline they'd been following. *There's a stony little island or something out there at the edge of what I can see. It's not what I'd choose, but it's got some magical potential and it's better than anything I see ashore. If nothing else it will isolate the aftermath if I lose.*

As they got closer, Pol's assessment of the island—a red stone sea stack perhaps a hundred feet tall and fifty across the roughly flat top—didn't improve. The barren little island did have a few threads of magic clinging to it indicating some past history with the art, but nothing half so useful as the deeply set wards and even deeper history of the ancient magical dueling grounds that had been his first choice.

Is this wise? asked Moonbird.

Almost certainly not. From what I've learned of the creation of the Keys I should be doing this in the place where Issalia was originally bound into this form. Or, failing that, at Rondoval or some other place where I have deep magical roots. But the bindings on the bag are already fraying and I've simply run out of time.

Is there anything I can do?

Return to the air after we land. Watch. If I am killed, fly back to Rondoval and have Belphanior alert my brother and Merson as to what has happened and where I fell. Perhaps they can retrieve the statue and the situation, or at least my body.

Pol tucked the guitar back into the pocket dimension and retrieved a metallic rod and a large stick of green chalk inscribed with symbols Pol had found in the east. The chalk was one of seven such, each tightly bound in a cocoon of braided spell strands all in bright blues and golds. The scepter had belonged to his father, and now he tucked it into the back of his boot.

As soon as Moonbird touched down, Pol slid off the dragon's neck and slapped him on the shoulder. A moment later Moonbird jumped over the edge, dropping nearly to the water's surface before catching an updraft and soaring back into the blue skies above.

The young sorcerer was barely aware of his scaly companion's departure, having started to inscribe a series of complex designs on the rock as soon as he landed. Initially he worked with one hand holding the chalk, and the other clutching the bag that he'd removed from his hip while occasionally mumbling a word of binding. But, as soon as he'd gotten a series of three small concentric circles in place and connected them with a half dozen carefully drawn glyphs, he dropped the bag into the innermost circle.

Within seconds the red velvet of the bag had begun to smoke and char, quickly turning black as the thing within worked to free itself. Seeing that, Pol swore and redoubled his efforts at completing the figures. As each line was drawn, a corresponding thread of magic slid free of the dense braid on the chalk and melded with the diagram.

The stick itself was a very sophisticated piece of magic, and the end result of a formalized magical ritual of the sort that Pol could never have managed even a year previously. He kept glancing at the smoldering velvet as he worked and mentally measuring the unnaturally rapid diminution of the chalk against the ongoing destruction of the warded bag. Finally, he closed an arc that looked like it didn't quite belong in this world and completed one last glyph. The process finished off the last tiny lump of chalk and finished unbraiding the spell he'd built into the matrix of the stick.

It was only just in time, as the bag suddenly puffed into ash, exposing the little statue within. It lay on its side in the center of the circle for several seconds, then shook and rocked until it finally righted itself.

A flame appeared in the air between Pol and the figurine and spoke into his mind, *What is this?* For the only time since he'd first encountered them, one of the Keys seemed unsure. *I don't recognize these figures. . .but they still seem familiar somehow.*

"That's because the last time you encountered something like them, you were more or less dead."

What are you planning, Detson?

"This." Pol reached forward with both hands, catching the first upwelling of magical threads rising from the final glyph.

He pulled and twisted, activating the spell and sending magical sparks fountaining along the lines that connected him to the figurine. The Key raised a shield of light that flared momentarily when the sparks reached it, then contracted to form a sort of second skin around the figurine. For perhaps ten heartbeats it looked like nothing more was going to happen, then the figurine began to grow and twist.

I don't understand! it cried. *What are you* "doing to me?" The last half of the question was spoken aloud as the tiny figurine finished its transformation into a tall pale woman with a snake's eyes and shimmering robes. "I. . ." She trailed off and looked down at herself, her mouth widening into an astonished gape. "That's not possible."

"Not for long, no. I'm sorry, Issalia, truly. If I could restore you fully, I would, but that's beyond my powers."

She moved her hands through the beginning of a spell of transportation, but froze in mid-gesture before she could complete it, her face twisting painfully. "I'm me. . .but not. My will is still bound. . ."

"To the purpose my father made you for, yes. You are still one of the Keys to the lands beyond the Gate and wholly subjugated to his goals and vision. There is only one way to change that, and even if I succeed, you won't be restored to your humanity."

Issalia looked thoughtful for a moment before nodding. "You propose to defeat me in a duel as your father did before you and then, should you succeed, you will be able to alter my purpose and enslave me to your own will. Clever, and cruel beyond measure to restore me so, only to re-imprison me to serve your purposes. You truly are the son of Devil Det."

"That's not exactly how I see it," replied Pol. And then, because he felt he owed the sorceress some duty for what he was about to do to her, "though I can't argue that it might look that way from where you're sitting. Shall we commence? The spell that lets you temporarily return to your original form won't last for long."

"Wait." She held up a long delicate hand—it was shaking visibly. "The purpose that drives me forces me to this duel, but I can hold it back for a time and I would breathe the clean air of the world a bit longer. Also, I have a question. What happens if I defeat you?"

"I die."

"I'm not sure it's that simple," said Issalia, whose eyes had been darting back and forth across the diagram that connected the two of them. "If I read this right, there's a chance that you will become what I am now, another Key for the gate."

Pol blanched and looked more closely at the structure of his spell. "That. . .hadn't occurred to me, but yes, I think there is a possibility of that."

"More than a possibility," said Issalia. "In order to transform my soul into your tool, you must risk your own. In fact, if I'm reading this spell aright, I may even be able to shift this curse your father inflicted on me to the son he left behind. . ."

"Wouldn't that violate your purpose as a Key?" Pol asked nervously. Things were rapidly going from bad to worse.

"Not at all. The compulsion is quite specific. I must advance the cause of magic in this world at every opportunity. As Det's son you are very likely as powerful a sorcerer as I, and since I would like to see the Gate opened of my own account, a world where you were a Key and I was free to wield you is a world that is several steps farther along the path your father set out, than it is right now. Yes, I think that might work very well indeed."

Without any warning at all, Issalia clapped her hands together, sending a small arc of silver light flying at Pol's chest like a thrown blade or metallic bird of prey. She followed it with another and another as she continued to clap.

Pol flicked the first out of the air with the tip of a green spell strand snapped like a whip, but his tool was too unwieldy to catch the second and he had to drop to his knees and twist aside to avoid the next couple. As that was happening, the world shifted around him, the threads and strands that were the way he usually saw magic vanishing to be replaced by simple geometrical shapes like the wire-frame polygons of early video games.

Grabbing a passing cone, Pol pointed the broad end at Issalia and quickly caught a half dozen of her silver arcs out of the air. Then, guided by one of the madwand impulses that raised his magical skills to an art, he lifted the point to his lips and blew the silver spell shards back at their originator.

Issalia clapped faster, knocking five of the six out of the air. But the last one drew a sharp line of blood across her hipbone. She stomped her left foot then, and snapped the fingers on both hands. In response a line of destruction shot from her foot through the rock of the island toward Pol, like the trail of some demonic mole, while twin lances of blue light scissored in toward either side of his neck.

60

Pol's vision shifted again, replacing the wireframe polygons with loose sheets of light like tumbling towels in a dryer. Without thinking about it, he caught one and snapped it down and across like a toreador wielding his cape. It broke the twinned lances and cut off the ridge of burning stone. One of the blue lances clipped his shoulder with bruising force as it spun away, leaving a charred mark on his shirt and blistering the skin beneath as he climbed back to his feet.

Before Pol could recover, Issalia snapped her fingers again and stomped one foot and then the other, moving into a rhythm not unlike a flamenco dancer as she sent one attack after another at him. He now had a second sheet in his other hand, and was able to continue to fend off Issalia's ongoing assault, but only barely and at the cost of his ability to counter and several more painful burns. She was stronger than he was and much more experienced.

He desperately needed to change the terms of the duel, or he would be destroyed. He shifted his magical perception again, this time consciously, forcing the shape of Issalia's attacks and his own defense to conform to the strands he was most comfortable with. Here, the snapping fingers and stomping feet produced unrolling strings of energy like the fiery tongue of some demonic frog, and Pol's own sheets of defensive energy transformed into fringed nets that flipped and flicked like large fans.

Before Issalia could shift the field of battle again, Pol slammed his two nets together into one and then flung his arms apart to expand them outward like a huge spider's web hanging in the space between them, then let it go. She was shredding the web, but it gave him the time he needed to draw his father's scepter from where he'd tucked it into his boot earlier. Touching the scepter to the web, he sent fresh power to the strands, restoring and strengthening them.

For a moment he felt that he had the upper hand, and he started to push the net forward toward Issalia. But his triumph didn't last, as Issalia upped the tempo of her dancing attack, adding hand claps between the snapping of her fingers. Razor edged loops of silver spun forth then, slicing away the juncture of his web faster than he could repair it. Once again, Pol was losing and badly.

Pol didn't realize Moonbird had joined the battle until Issalia suddenly leaped backward to avoid a falling spatter of chemical fire. But he didn't have the chance to take advantage of the shift as she shouted something into the air that sent the great dragon tumbling away toward the waves beyond the island.

Pol was going to die. Or worse, become one of the Keys that would open the Gate between the worlds and drown this world in the baroque magics of another.

The bottom segment! It was Moonbird's voice speaking into his mind, weak and weary yet urgent. *It's the*—But Issalia let out another shout and the dragon's voice suddenly broke off.

By then Pol had been driven once more to his knees by the more powerful sorceress's ongoing assault. He was about to join the world of the soul-bound unless. . .the bottom segment? Wasn't that the one that Moonbird had used at Anvil Mountain? It was; the dragon's segment. . .fire magic.

Pol glanced at the dragonmark on his arm. The blood of a dragonlord. . .he pressed the mark to the base of the scepter where carved demons cavorted amidst stylized flames.

Contact!

Words growled out of his mouth, harsh, ancient, sibilant and snarling—the tongue of the dragons. Fire erupted across the whole top of the island, brightly burning and furious. Pol's own clothes burned away, though the flames left his skin untouched. Issalia's clothes burned too, and the flesh beneath them. She screamed and fell, burning and bound once again, collapsing in on herself like a building devoured by an inferno. Gold and black, burned and burnished, a jeweled figurine once more.

The flames subsided around Pol, though he could still feel them burning within. He crossed the short distance to the place where Issalia had fallen. As he lifted the statuette, the woman's screams seemed to ring in his ears once again and he could feel her pain in the depths of his own soul, feel exactly what her imprisonment meant to her, feel the absolute despair that bound her as firmly as any spell.

More than anything, he wanted to fling the statuette into the sea, to let it go unchanged, and never have anything to do with the binding of souls again. But if he did, he might as well just concede the world to Henry Spier then and there. As long as the Keys existed as Keys the risk to this world, his world, would stand. If Spier was allowed to break the seal between the worlds, a hundred million souls would drown in the corruption of the elder gods.

Pol spoke the words of binding, reshaping the Key to hell into a Ward against the falling dark. They were the hardest words he'd ever said, knowing as he did the price for saving all those souls from the darkness was the darkening of his own.

*

I watched suspiciously as my accursed master set the jeweled figurine on the table beside Mouseglove's couch. I'd had contact with the little monstrosities before and hadn't liked it in the least. Worse, the thing was clearly responsible for the weight that seemed to have settled on Pol's shoulders.

"You say that this is on your side now?" Mouseglove tilted his head to the side dubiously.

"Not exactly. It's on the side of. . .call it stasis. The other six exist to increase the power of magic in this world, and the most effective way to do that is to throw wide the gates of Prodromolu, the opener of the way, and let the magic of the old ones enter and drown ours. Now, Issalia has been retasked to maintain things as they are. As long as that remains my goal, she will serve me."

"Those things are dangerous tools, Pol, and liable to turn in your hand. You'd do better to leave them all bound at Avinconet."

"I wish I could, I really do. But this is the only way I can see to defeat Spier and prevent the gate from opening. I took a big step in that direction with Issalia here. A very big step indeed, though there are more to come."

Mouseglove frowned. "I hope you know what you're doing, Pol."

"So do I, old friend. So do I."

I left them then, to fetch another bottle of wine—theirs would soon be empty—and to ponder on the ways of men. My master seemed harder and colder than before, but when I looked into the fires of his heart I still saw the same Pol Detson I had always served. There was a lesson there, if I could only figure it out.

And Fountains Flow

by Mark Rich

"The Graveyard Heart". . . later in time. New character (Tina Adiatso) and old ones (Wayne Unger, Mary Maude Mullen, etc.). Tina is a nod to "The Furies," too.

"How interesting—that of all the Sleepers, you should ask about two who stopped Sleeping," he said. "They debarked and waved goodbye to the great *Somnolence* forever. And that—how long ago?"

Her eyes darkened like opening doors. Auburn hair. Black and crimson streaked her gray garb.

And he, moving toward those doors. . .although no longer the round-bellied snowy-owl poetry-shouter of olden times, by no means did he cut the dashing figure of a bard starving beside Time's Avon.

Rumble-voiced, Unger remained—and reeking of dry rot and freezer burn.

"I suppose," Tina said, "that in the Party Set you no longer talk about those two."

"We move on. We forget."

"Ever see them again?"

"Once. A few weeks later. Years—for them. And Al and Leota. . .they looked the same in so many ways, if older. But *different*—as if in the Set I knew them as fragments. Patterns. Like flat images that became whole, out here."

Alvin Moore. Leota Mathilde Mason. Brightest of the Set, sleeping through the years and making exception only for the waking dreams of the Perpetual Lifes of the Parties. Wayne Unger remembered seeing them embrace on the sands beside that last island's pavilion gardens: tall, tanned and tensed before taking the leap—the leap off, while the Set moved on and left them behind. Sun-scorched sand-smell. Wreaths of cirrus above. . .*and how jealous I felt, and feel. . .*

"All lives are shipwrecks."

I spoke. And I was thinking something else.

"Shipwrecks?" said Tina.

"What a philosopher once said. But I do remember thinking that it must feel like jumping into disaster—to leave the Set, to re-enter the world of mundane cause and effect. Waking, sleeping. Your *real* sleep, not our cold one. And then you must fall slave to weeks that run through their seven days in order, rather than leaping as we do from a Friday in March to a Tuesday in June. Sun up, sun down, *blinkity-blinkity-blink* in a mad rush for the end. Am I ridiculous?"

She answered with a contained smile.

A katydid whirred to the table. *I am here*, Unger thought on its behalf. It whirred off, secure in its sense of being, thanks to having no sense of being. The table, artfully made to appear aged and crumbling cement, with flecks milky-green as of lichen: *I am not wholly here.* Much of the world outside the Set said that.

Tina Adiatso had suggested this park near Blue Bay Pavilion, where the Set had arrived for a therapeutic, not Party, stop. Lovely, really. Gravelly expanses and eucalyptus trees like artful arboreal nudes here and there. A few hedges, rusty-green; rock walls, dry fountains, mosaic walks. Unger would have lost himself in his thoughts in the quiet here, once upon a time, letting his fancy conjure whatever it would, first in the air and then on the page; and on later days he would revise and dream again. . .letting words spin away. . .but not in these days: for now his year-spanning Sleep chopped short his days at the ends like pieces of rolled dough. Assembly-line biscuits.

Whence such thoughts? Was it the salt-touched air, in this place?

"So," she said. "Tell me what you are working on these days."

"As Set member?"

"As poet."

"I speak the truth, when I can. *That* is all that is left of the poet in me."

"But you—and your poems—are so popular! You *must* be writing."

"Vogues are nice. They come and go. On and off like switches. Or. . .forgive me. Do you know light switches?"

"From footnotes. But the interest in you is *real*. The launch of the Party Set is seen as marking the start of a new cultural age. And your poems are part of that moment. They define it and make it real for those of us looking back."

*

Seeing Tina Adiatso's agitation he felt stirrings in a soul-chamber he thought emptied of all but the afterimages of old, half-sated passions. Nothing familiar. . .yet this felt like a relaxing into notion and dream—such as had happened in his youth when muses still strode through his days, making stones whisper complaints and treetops rattle with skyborn secrets.

The minor irritant of being reminded of Al and Leota faded. He leaned forward—for he was opening to Tina. It disconcerted him to experience this upwelling, to hear his own words begin slowly in steady tones from his dry lips and then move faster, more loudly rumbling as though now he sipped something he had not tasted, not from those Grecian springs, for a dozen decades or more. He spoke of matters that long ago had ceased mattering—as if that ceasing itself now ceased. He spoke of the natural movements that sounds will pursue and follow—of visual music—of poetry as vegetative growth—of the way a verse might bend gently near like a low bough of spruce, prickly and in reach; or how it might jut out, robust and thick—an oak limb, inaccessible but always there to the eye. Immortality of a different sort: he had concerned himself with that, once. Immortality by means of the transient and ephemeral. Sparse words, soon over.

Her one fingertip, no more, rested on his hand. He imagined, irrationally, the finger curling and the red polish on its nail leaving a streak between his knuckles.

When she leaned away his skin yearned for more. *I should leap from the Set and stay here.* In all likelihood she stood where he did—in actual years lived. Why not such a feeling of connection? He had insulated himself too well, within the Set and its Parties. He needed to emerge more—to see strangers face to face. To engage in conversations and not idle chatter. Mary Maude Mullen, damn her leathery hands, would laugh dryly in triumph: for she had insisted on these non-Party days for all in the Set. And along with most others he had fussed about it.

"You know what I think?" she, Enigma, said.

He kept still, his lips sealed against more release. Had his overflow contained any cavorting brilliance? Had any shrunken sprite of old Unger the White Lion played in those floods?

"You have stopped sharing," she said.

"I share all the nothing I have."

"The inward face. . .the talons taut around the wind-race."

"'The Choking Beast.' Is quoting me against myself playing fair?" He tugged a clump of his white hair and laughed, although his lightning-quick thought about leaving the Set had in truth made his throat tighten.

"The un-Set never play fair, with the Set."

"You seem most fair, in admitting this."

"I keep things on the table."

"Of face, I mean."

She smiled, unembarrassed.

"In any case I am not throttling myself. But by the way—are you attending tonight?"

It would be a non-Party gathering of Set and un-Set: group functions, bull sessions, *blow the winds blah-dee-blathery high and low, blow!. . .*Mary Maude's Therapy Day, to keep the Set grounded and sane, or at very least sanitized.

"I—can't."

She did look tired.

At her lightest touch in farewell his thoughts again eased themselves out quickly and agreeably, phrases forming before he knew they had reached his tongue. And what had he said? More nothings that were his to share. He had promised nothing, certainly.

O wind-torn leaf in the creek, swept around rocks. I last felt thus. . .when?

Unger, across mosaic squares—tesserae creatures from other shores and waters below his heavy feet—moved slowly. Even though a far Dart-journey away from the nearest House of Sleep, his each step pointed toward his cold bunker.

Cries of gulls, the snoring complaint of a lion of the sea, muted conversational murmurs. . .and buoyed up by such musical concordance memory resurfaced.

How could it have slipped so quickly? Then slipped back? He had, too, promised. . .to meet her again when the Set next emerged from the ice. Thousands of miles and months away by her reckoning: she would be there. And he. . .he would come bearing poetry.

His pulse quickened. Due to her thinking his talent only slumbered? *Like the rest of me.* Breeze brushed his fallen-snow hair like stirring hope—hope that he might again feel muse-breath on his cheek, and might go forth with coals newly aglow in the cold hearth he carried within.

Then why not step off? And why not now—here?

. . .because what might catch up. . .if I stopped. . .

. . .like a white wolf loping behind me, its waving mane of all those winters flying in the wind. . .

*

Al Moore had urged his stepping off, too, during their last encounter—decades, a century ago?

After Unger and Leota exchanged a few words—she expressed surprise at his slightly leaner look and healthier glow—he stood chatting with Al while Leota chased children who ran away across windblown sands.

"Pleasant, here?"

"Enough," said Moore. "There?"

"The question is never asked."

"No."

"And what do you do—now that you have all this time—"

"When we were in the Set, Wayne, *we* were the ones who thought we had all of Time."

"But now you have all these days—continuously. And none of those wasted hours freezing down and boosting back up to consciousness."

Al let out an easy laugh. "We have kids to make up for our not wasting enough hours. And we have occupations—other than wining, dining, dancing. Although we do toast the Party Set even yet."

"Occupations—"

"The dust settled. . .and I had offers."

"Ah. The engineer."

"No. The anachronistic tinker. I am curator in a museum of outmoded machinery."

"How strange."

"For all I know, my own century-old trust funds created the position. Do I care? I enjoy my tasks, overseeing arrays of antiques, oiling them, keeping them fit. And when the whim strikes me, I fire up my own old water-purifier, the one that made my fortune, and make water from wine."

"Leota?"

"You remember—an architectural student before joining the Set. She resumed after leaving."

"And now she is practicing."

"Yes."

"Successfully?"

"We may find out in a few years. You—in a week or two."

Bitterness, in Moore's set of face? Or amusement?

"Why have you stayed on?" said Moore. "Life is possible here among the un-Set. This is still a culture of quick change, however many years have passed—and Leota and I are oases of discontinuous memory—memory not contiguous with the moment Now. Once the avoidance ended. . .for the un-Set did avoid us, at first: we looked *wrong*, in their eyes! Me—I was Orpheus except that I *did* emerge from hell with my wife. That upset the way the applecart is supposed to tip over. But after we had adjusted to the simple life, people started consulting us. We offer a corrective view.

History has become the electronic preservation of infinite detail, with the criterion for significance being the frequency of a detail's iteration.

"Any insignificant matter, such as you keeling over drunk at the bar—if repeated a million times it becomes more important than a poem repeated only now and then."

"You have kept up on me."

"We keep behind on you."

Amusement in his eyes—not bitterness, clearly.

Something relaxed in Unger. Maybe he did wish (*decades, a century ago?*) his poems would find oblivion. He could accept being Silenus with the cup, then, and forget his worries about being no longer Great Pan with the pipe. He could embrace being Wayne, waned.

"Glad you enjoy it out here."

"*In* here," said Moore. "That is how it feels. We are *in* our lives "

Me—out. In the cold—I who fear. . .

Both your way, and mine.

*

He knew other Parties, other years, had touched here in the Southwestern-state solitudes, but saw nothing familiar when he went strolling away from Red Mesa Pavilion—not even desert views. New construction had accreted like coral around the dining and dance floors. He walked up stairs and through halls and doors to find a garden acres in extent yet covered over with opaque, blue-white panels: he had chanced upon tomorrow's meeting place. He kept walking.

In his old cache of personal possessions Unger had found what he wanted, just before that last dip into those stilled waters where Hans Brinker skates for eternity. He pocketed them on awakening to keep handy: the mechanical pencil, the pad. Antiquated technics? So be it. If Moore could revive them, so could he—while still flipping idly through the calendar leaves.

He gazed out a window at a series of ruddy towers rising in ranks and growing smaller into the distance: jagged prehistoric teeth in an immense jaw. They would catch a fish yet. University towers, he suspected.

A Party Set pavilion by a university, though? No such thing. To his recollection, anyway.

When he came across an isolated alcove he heeded the call of his antiquated technics. He wrote random thoughts, phrases, words. He thought of books he wished handy, to open at random. Antiquated desire? How was he to know, in these days celebrating pre-Set culture?

Returning later to the pavilion he found himself wondering if Set schedule would allow him enough time—time to rethink, to weigh each word. How many lines had he written? A few. A phrase, maybe two worth keeping—but if worth keeping his words might lead to other phrases, other lines.

Then he laughed at himself for worrying about having time, in the Set. If not Now, then Then.

A shadow among Party Set shadows, he passed through clouds of hovering lanterns shaped like darting aircraft. Dome-shaped miniature skies hung dimly above each one, etched with moving strobes. A creature like a miniature pig drifted by on a tasseled pillow, blowing lightly over panpipes. Poppy petals—blood and snow, and scented with sleep—fell to his shoulders.

Hugh Jameson waved him over to a table where an immense smoked fish lay in partial ruin surrounded by admiring smiles of lemons and limes.

"You look happy," said the cherub-haired man, his eyes felinely jealous.

"Happy? No," said Unger. "Or maybe so—at a day properly misspent."

"Out collecting royalties for reprints, then. "

"A nice thought. But I was spying on the enemy's spies. We are attached tonight to a university. Maybe it will be gone tomorrow, though. Who knows but that universities now fly around the four corners and settle wherever the windy topic of the day rests."

"We are the topic of the age, not the day."

"Then it must be coincidence, that we and the university both landed in the same spot."

Juniper aroma wafting from Jameson's glass made Unger think of the desert sands he had failed to find outside Red Mesa. He turned toward the bar—surprisingly not a barmat. Human tenders stood there with no buttons nearby to push, adeptly pouring from bottles into jiggers and looking almost natural in so doing. Students, he guessed, earning historical-practicum points.

When heading away with a drink he found Jameson alongside him still. A glowing jet-fighter, mid-Twentieth, strafed the air above his left ear. Dancers arm-in-arm drifted by. How we are all infatuated with each other, Unger thought.

"I hate the thought," cherub-hair said. "Scholars hovering around, tabulating our drinks."

How many winged martinis can dance on a pinhead? "They have done so all along."

"The bastards! Yes, I imagine so. At least until a certain hour."

Yes—and then when the barmatics shoved out the earnest young students, the Set would let down its guard the slightest bit. In this day and age, whatever day and age it might be, did it matter, any more, what privacy the Set might desire? The watchers might turn away for the moment's discretion. By morning, however, this Party would be history and thus worthy of scrutiny. The rich and famous will always be put through their motions—for their motions so quickly become redolent of old ways and old thoughts. . .and so educational.

"Did you see classes?" said Jameson.

"Classes of classes. I saw students attending a lecture, while other students watched through windows, taking notes on the lectured."

Jameson laughed.

Unger turned toward his rooms and saw, stirred up in the darkness by Jameson's words, the students as before but now gazing carnivorously his way. His sip of scotch burned, having started down the wrong pipe.

After an hour alone facing words that refused to take wing off the page, he took his empty glass back to where jet fighters strafed the crowded, festive night.

*

When in the morning Mary Maude Mullen, Doyenne of the Set, called his name he was following a beckoning satyr toward the woodland where the wilds of the world rose in coy, contained facsimile below skyblue glass.

Even so he paused. He saw a shadow, likely the legal man, behind her in the office.

"I suppose that was a stab at being funny," she said, her tone half statement, half question.

"Stab?"

"Your inquiry into leaving. Of anyone here you, Unger, will always be the last to think of leaving the Set."

"A whim," he said. "I had forgotten protocol and thought I would sleep better knowing it."

"I will send it. Your sleep is my concern. Off to see your young poet?"

You knew? Instead, "My poet?"

"She is a poet of some sort. Not that I fear a poet to be an enemy. But she makes herself out to be employee of an entertainment juggernaut, too, so I suspect she is not a poet, really. What poet allows herself to be hired by a juggernaut?"

"A poet speaks against juggernauts, rather. She must be just a company woman who dons the midnight cape, dark and poetical," said Unger, drawn in somewhat against his desire.

But what is my desire?—even as hands at a table rose to mind.

"I am never one to give advice," said the Doyenne, whose frail-boned fingers played life-strings. The Set jerked to animation at one twitch, then flopped clattering to stage floor—*exeunt*—at the next. That she, too, had strings stretching into the catwalk darknesses overhead made her ease her clutch not a whit.

"Never," said Unger, walking on.

So the Doyenne had voiced caution. He supposed he had earned her stepmotherly concern, given his standing as first major violator of the docile civility of the Set. If she feared another act of angst-crazed Poetic Mind on his part, though, so be it. His ravings would appear in a zero-circulation rag, set there by the company woman.

When he stepped to the top of the red sandstone stairs leading down into the covered gardens, his *Arctic Review* caped romantic waved from a table set far in, at a spot surrounded by circles of polychrome pavers, shading walls, and bends in a slow-moving stream. She again wore decorous gray—simple of lines, but no starving artist's garb. Other poets before her had clung to soul-damping jobs, for the filthy lucre. Stevens, Eliot, Larkin and others had lived comfortably enough. Not to mention Unger.

When their conversation came around to her hope—"You brought a new poem"—he pursed his lips and shook his head.

"You have written something, though."

He felt around his hesitancy. Speaking about what he was writing: not the same as about things written and published. Bygones. *That was in another country, and besides the poet is dead.*

"A few lines," he said. "By the way, I reacquainted myself with your world in that towering library you have here, and discovered I still have a publisher. It seems people still read books."

"And some look like this." Her hand-motion produced a rectangle in the air, faintly aglow and whispery. He had seen and heard similar at the library.

"A page of a book. . .by Diane Dean? A poet?" he said, seeing the name by the page number.

She twisted her hand and pulled back the page. "Another who wishes she were," she said, not unsmiling. "Shall we?"

As before he found his hesitancies and qualms beating a quick retreat. His tongue and lips then surprised him by decanting liberally of old wine he long ago had forgotten he had cellared. Conversation moved again toward Leota—who had set his heart afire for perhaps its last time. Muse-hungry—had only he admitted that to himself!—and the self-appointed and self-defeated Bard of the Set: Unger had blundered, buffoonlike, in her pursuit. Then Moore, unmoored from time-bound earth, arrived to win her, to lose her, then to. . .

Unger felt new, sharp discomfort: for in speaking to Tina his thoughts circled nearer pivotal points in the untold tale. How to unveil them? If at all? Leota's pregnancy, her decision to leave the Set. . .and that catastrophic Party that unfolded beneath a brittle-crystal black-as-blood Christmas Eve sky. . .

Tina no longer touched but clutched his hand.

Her eyes: tunnels into which he plunged.

. . .and that image that for so many skipped-over hopscotch-square years had refused to return with the finality of certainty, as anything more than bric-a-brac dusty-shelf surely-not-fact: now it arose like a doomed white owl, shrieking and settling its cold claws into his tongue, poising itself there to fly out his opening, numbing lips: *for I see through my vodka-steam breath the ghosts of my hands—there before me in the frosted sleep-chamber—not my own bunker—and why am I here?—in the House of Sleep, the House of the Set: I see my hands clutching white stake and black mallet, the sharpened point downturned to that frozen, frozen. . .*

No! he cried within—just as outside a piercing trilling pulled him back outwards, away from himself.

A thumb-sized wren had landed on Tina's shoulder, instantly bursting into song, note-running throatily in a tonal cascade without cease. She raised a hand to shoo it.

Wings blurred suddenly silent.

"You are—"

He lacked the word.

He thought she nodded, then saw her head sagged with fatigue.

"Forgive me," she said. "This—faintness. Happens to me. No—no help. Please. I will be—right back—"

She hurried stiffly away.

Unger waited, absorbed in the revelations of his own verbal torrent.

Toward what falling-off cliff had his words pushed?

He had arrived wanting to see her again. And her eyes—of promise, of threat. She created. . .a link. Unger of old turned in his sleep and nearly cracked open an eyelid in her presence. Yet were that inner, old Unger to emerge—would not the world see the wrecked, ruined corpse on the shoals of ice and stone? The walls around the Set—walls of time-flitting sleep, walls of lifeless cold—saved him from exposure. He could hide, unrevealed, in his cold-bunker traveling between far-spread calendar days.

At least he had not torn from his pocket his few penciled lines:

Not for us winds blow, earth rests,
skies turn and fountains flow. . .

Winds were just winds—or winds of chance; earth, the world of the un-Set; skies, the heavens seen in their turnings by the un-Set—

So skies were the Set.

And fountains?

Fountains stopped him. Were he to believe his own words and his sense of their meanings, then he had erred from the beginning in climbing aboard the Somnolence.

Fountains—into which poets dip their daemonic, Orphic toes—flow in a non-place apart from winds, earth or skies.

Yet they flow, all the same—

For the un-Set.

He knew this, having been of them, once.

The Set moved differently through time—granting him a different View. From the beginning he had hoped to emerge from his journey carrying the Lyre whose strings only he, Unger of the Set, could pluck.

But skies turn—and he, with the skies. . .

And fountains flow. . .just not for us. . .

His emptied glass, the night before, had refilled with memories—one of them fortuitous. How nearly had he cribbed! Centuries before dry-lipped Unger, George Herbert had penned:

For us, the winds do blow,
The earth doth rest, heaven move, and fountains flow;
Nothing we see, but means our good. . .

And nothing *we* see, with our View from the Parties, means *our* good.

Unger started from revery. He moved to pocket his lines, then realized he sat alone even yet.

And children run away across the sands.

A wren, perhaps the same, uttered its song now and then nearby, while birch leaves shook beneath the blowers.

Later he received a note of apology with a request for one more meeting. The two of them, she said, had just reached a point. . .

*

He had just reached a point. His mind ajar. . .frozen shut, for so long, and now melting around its hinges and reopening: for in Olden Times. . .in that chamber where his muse, lost to him forever, lay after being drawn bloodless and sucked breathless—freezing down to her lone arctic zone between Parties. . .

There—he, Wayne Unger, went first in departing from Party Set supercilious decorum. He threw aside his grace-under-lyre poise with such force the mere rumors unsettled both Set and un-Set: for he murdered the Lotus Queen of the Parties, Leota Mathilde Mason. Or rather he murdered Leota Mathilde Mason Moore: for she had just married Alvin Moore and taken his name. . .good incitement to brute violence. . .for there, in her chamber, he found himself standing with stake and mallet in hand. Al Moore, distraught, then murdered Unger in a frenzy, with that mallet. Al himself then died, in punishment for his crime—and did so, in fact, before Unger, already dead, could die in punishment for *his*. The poet needed to be revived before justice—"symbolic death"—could be meted out. Then meted back in. So Leota died, then Wayne died, then Al died—and then Wayne died. They met later to laugh over it. Even so, symbolic death had felt distinctly unpoetic. Ending score: Wayne Unger, one. Al Moore, one. Society, two.

On which side of the Moebius strip of Set-life sat irony? The House of Sleep was infected with it, the proverbial louse of arch Modernity. . .and whatever happened to lice, anyway? Consigned to their own freezer-lockers, saving their genetic codes: for the world might need itching, scabs and disease once again. *Just walk away from it all. . .*(and where had *that* notion winged in from, yet again?). . .*into the arms of the foe, o thou louse.* How tumbling-over-each-other came his thoughts! Another for the glass, o faithful barmatics! To embrace what the "I" is, the Self must embrace the multitude of thoughts within its unkempt mansion. Jumbled learning and stumbling pratfall, sordid Sordido. . .just think of Al's "Maud" (*The red-ribb'd ledges drip with silent horror of blood*: Al Tennyson, not Moore) and Mary Maude the impaler. . .and the blanketing solace that words provide—or once did. Might they again? The woman, damn her face—sprouting serpent hair and dripping red at the eyes like a shrieking Erinye on Unger's Oresteian trail. *But I never killed her, my mother-muse. Or did I—?*

Leota on her bier, her bed-casket freezer, her catafalque now a barge. . .launched down the tunnel of give-up-all-hope.

And the spike in her heart—driven in by whose hand?

Of the four deaths one fell with finality: that second death, when Moore had murdered most unsymbolically. When Unger handed his penny to the boatman, the boatman smiled, knowingly—and kept smiling after the bribe, too, was paid and dead Unger was rowed back to the warmer of two shores. Unger's head and body parts, hammer-bruised and shattered and pulped, came back together in the rotund wooly shape of Unger of old, to all outside discerning eyes. Yet Unger, *new* Unger, knew.

Mary Maude Mullen and her lawyer-minion greeted him when he awakened—she, clucking like a wizened hen at having to quash the furor Unger had raised: all those rumors of mayhem and murder. . .or attempted murder as it might be considered, historically, since the Set would manage to mend and revive dead Leota. Once a Lotus Queen, always.

Blind dead bled drunk I remember nothing nothing nothing at all: Unger pled at the inquest—after which he was sentenced—he, a poet, *sentenced* to death—and sent, tensed, to be gassed in the chamber with red-ribb'd ledges, that the boatman might take his coin (a second time) and his bribe (ditto).

Yet Unger knew. He who was no more. He blacked out no longer beside the barmat. He no longer stole, drunkenly sleep-walking, into pleasure craft to gain entrance to other festivals of love than his own—festivals of drunken delight, festivals of exclusion. What was the Set but exclusion? Each member raised walls and dug moats to keep out others. For all that the Parties knit them together they froze into solitary silences—to survive, somehow, and not end up subsumed completely into the dancing amoeba made up of identically softly swaying components.

He had set up his barriers. . .for without them everyone would see, surely, how he had gone away, perhaps never to return. Wayne Unger, the frozen man: killed, revived, executed, revived. . .now cold-bunkered, now thawing, now freezing, now waking. . .a man alive; a Poet, dead. . .

In the Set. . .and out. . .and in. . .and out. . .

*

"Have you heard of the Epirrani," she said with her tone of flat-finality questioning.

"Not that I recall."

"Not surprising. Keeping up on news is hard, on ice. Paranorms are rare, anyway. And their talent is costly to have."

"Costly?"

"Its deployment comes with a price."

"I see. I think." Unger found himself recalling Tina shakily rising from the table.

"I went on doing your research for you and found it was not completely a lie that Tina Adiatso is a poet, since she does seem to share your leanings—which makes sense, given her extreme sensitivity."

"Extreme sensitivity. That is the talent you are talking about? You say Tina is like this—Epirrani?"

"Sensitivity is not it. Not exactly. The talent is to stimulate something like that in someone else. To set feelings in motion. Memories, too. To open others. Whom she touches."

Cold spread inward from his hand.

"I see you begin to see," said Mary Maude Mullen. "Her name is not real—of course. We traced this Diane Dean all the same and found her real employer is one with an old grudge against the Set. Ever since that affair involving you and Leota and Moore they have been trying to get the real story—looking for something sensational, something to cast us in a worse light than the dim one in which we already appear. Because they would bring us down to their own tawdry level this anti-Set group has sent Diane Dean to you. She felt flattered to be hired, I imagine. She has written about you before, in magazines. For that she was hired—not just because she is Epiranni.

"And so, Unger. What have you said to her?"

"I have small idea, really. Words. . .they just came out. Before I was thinking them, it seemed."

"As I feared, from what I have read of these Epiranni. What gives us a chance is that the charade may not begin until Dean has recovered and can fully share her information. And even then they may wait until you are in cold sleep again before using your sensational words in their campaign."

"Until she has recovered?"

"As I said, the Epiranni pay a price. Diane Dean is already in an induced coma. It may last weeks. Her body and mind require it after overextending. She was in coma for a week after your first meeting—and that was brief, was it not?"

He absorbed this. "But about waiting until *I* am in cold sleep—"

Rarely having seen Mary Maude's smile, Unger greeted its arrival warily.

"You are writing again," she said. "Well. Should *you* write the book *they* want, before they have the chance, and draw it all from your memories. . .do you see? Your star is ascendent again among the un-Set. You will be heard. And the topic itself will draw readers—for the Leota affair remains one of the great fascinations, one of the great mysteries of the Set."

You owe us, she was saying without saying.

It startled him that he could express his horrified comprehension with a simple nod.

I cannot stay in this world where my only choices are to wake or to dream. If I do not depart from here, if I do not leave by Sleeping, this moment Now will seize me—and the ice-muse with that stake in her heart will catch up to my clay-footed soul. . .and then all the world will know I am finished. I am dead. I am gone.

He opened his lips to say this. Instead: "Tina, I mean Diane, requested another interview—"

"Good," said Mary Maude Mullen. "So you have not told all. That gives you even more time. The other matter—as to whether you are leaving the Set for good, or just for now: we can leave that for later.

"And I am so glad, Unger, that we can agree so well."

*

Days fled like. . .

No: *flew* at him, buffeting and grasping, taking him up in gray talons and holding him aloft from the slippery earth over which he had glided all this time—holding, then releasing him like a leaf. Attenuated and insubstantial after all his time in the Set, he floated earthward. *Not wholly here.* Nor there. He worked, dozed, slept, ate, stared at empty pages, scribbled nonsense, shivered, lost weight, read the works of great ancients and gained despair: *Yea, o Emerson: I am the dwarf of myself. . .*when at last before his eyes appeared, late in a night, not his ice-white staked-heart dead Nemesis but one whose forehead rippled as her scalp gave birth to the snouts of rising auburn serpents and from whose eyes dripped blood-tears. She reached to touch his hand as he struggled to awaken from dream. . .

Whatever else thou art, thou art muse.

For now as the Fates caught up, night by night, with the fallen former Eternal, Unger found at last that his pencil, antique, and paper, antiquated, and writing hand—kept on ice against the ages—trembled together. The fractured hearth within him, set ablaze again, at last could spread its winter-flake ashes to cover all.

The Headless Flute Player
by Jane Lindskold

The rapping was loud and decisive. I opened the front door of my small house to discover a headless torso, clad in water-stained garments, standing on my doorstep. Its right hand was raised, as if about to grasp the Shang bronze serpent that served as a knocker and rap a second time. However, when I pulled the door fully open, the hand fell limply to the torso's side and the entire gave me its expectant attention.

How my visitor knew that I'd opened the door was beyond me, for the head was well and truly gone, not tucked under an arm or carried in a basket or some such. Without a head, the torso could neither see nor hear. I suppose it might have felt a change in the air currents.

Dismissing this minor mystery—for minor it was compared to having a headless body come calling—I wondered what I should do. The torso solved the problem for me. Fumbling in its bedraggled left sleeve, it pulled out a scrap of fabric and presented it to me with due solemnity.

Inscribed upon the fabric in reddish-brown ink was, "I wish to enlist your aid in retrieving my head."

The message was clear enough. Nonetheless, I read it through several times before grasping my unusual visitor on one shoulder. I let my talons prick through the fabric of his robe, wordless warning as to the consequences of abusing my hospitality. Then I towed him inside. He—I assumed my caller was a "he," although inspection of his motley attire left gender open to question—permitted himself to be led.

I settled my guest on one side of a low table, then I poured myself a cup of tea, a relatively new indulgence from the world of humans that was taking the demon realm by storm. I considered pouring my visitor a cup, shuddered as I contemplated just how he might drink it, and, instead, placed a writing tablet in front of him and a freshly-inked brush into his right hand. Then I guided his left hand so he could feel the paper.

He immediately began to write. He must have had a good sense of touch because, as soon as the brush began to scrape for lack of ink, he made a dipping gesture. I obliged by putting an inkstone within his reach, tapping it against the tabletop so he could feel the vibrations and by these know where it rested.

I took advantage of his absorption to study him more closely. By reading his aura, I confirmed my first impression that he was indeed human, not a demon shapeshifted into that form. There were several peculiarities within his aura, but I put them aside for later study.

Next, I inspected the area where his head should have rested. The neck had been cut cleanly through, slightly above the folds of his robe. The stump of the neck had sealed over so neatly that had my caller not already inquired after his head, I might have hazarded that this was his natural condition.

Based on his attire, my caller appeared to be a street beggar of very eccentric habits. Although the temperature was midsummer warm, his robes were bulked out as if he was wearing heavy winter undergarments. His outer garments mingled those of a man and a woman, so, by the end of my inspection, my confusion as to his gender was increased, rather than otherwise. He also looked as if he had recently been for a swim with all his clothing on, although, when I had grasped his shoulder, the fabric had been completely dry. However, this immersion probably explained the lack of bloodstains on his clothing.

My caller carried very little in the way of possessions, although his bulky robes might conceal just about anything. A flute was thrust through the sash at his waist. This was a lovely instrument, glossed with the patina of frequent use. On the other side of the belt hung a pair of finger cymbals. From these, I conjectured that my caller might make his living as a street performer. At that thought, a memory quivered for attention but, before I could quest after it, my caller finished writing and thrust the tablet across to me.

"You may call me 'Lan,'" the text began. "I am a wandering musician, earning enough to keep body and soul together, with a bit left over to share with those less fortunate. Yesterday, I was approached by a man who asked if I was interested in earning shelter, hot meals, and some coin. When I learned that all I would need to do was entertain some unexpected guests at his home, I was very willing.

"I followed my patron in the direction of a pleasant district where the richer sort lived. We were passing down a deserted side street when, without warning, a large, heavily-muscled warrior with a great, bristling beard stepped out of an alley. He held a sword in one hand and an enormous sack in the other.

"My patron cried out in shock and alarm, at the same time pushing me away. I took the hint and started running

"For all his size, the bearded warrior moved with a tiger's swift grace. He leapt after me, catching up before I had gone ten paces and dropped the sack over my head. I kicked him in the knee. He knocked me to the ground. I heard my patron shouting.

"Then. . . My head was in one place, my body in another. Without any conscious prompting, my body resumed running. My head tried screaming, but my mouth got full of bag. I got dust in one eye and couldn't rub it out. I—by this, now, I mean my torso—ran blindly. Literally. I couldn't see nor hear nor smell, but I could definitely run.

"I'm a bit uncertain as to how far I ran since, between one step and the next, my footing vanished. Suddenly, I was over my neck in cold, racing water. The current grabbed me. My sodden clothing dragged me under. Breathing didn't seem to be an issue one way or another. Since underwater I could better escape capture, I let myself drop. I swam until I touched bottom, then grasped about until I found a heavy stone. I picked this up in case my soaked robes weren't enough to keep me under. Then I started walking.

"I felt much safer. I remembered in which direction the river flowed. This gave me some small orientation. I recalled that when my patron had approached me, the day had been well past noon, getting on for the Hour of the Ram. I resolved not to emerge from the river until after dark, so found myself a quiet pool outside of the main rush of the current and settled to sit on the bottom. Other than the occasional small fish who came to nibble upon me and decide I wasn't edible, I was left alone.

"I won't pretend this wasn't a peculiar situation. If I tried, I could more or less sense my head. I no longer shared its sensations, but I knew where it was. Enwrapped in darkness, I became nothing but thought and touch. I wished desperately for help. As I did so, I felt my string of coins tug from where I had tied them inside my garments. I inspected more closely, discovering that one coin in particular was the source of the disturbance.

"I recognized it as part of my haul from the day before. Since it had appeared to be solid gold, I had given it a closer inspection, noticing that although superficially it was a normal coin—round, with a square hole in the middle—it bore strange markings. I had resolved to keep this coin until I could dispose of it safely, for I dreaded either being suspected of counterfeiting or of having knowledge of some ancient hoard.

"In my earlier inspection, I had not detected anything else unusual about the gold coin but now, perhaps because my sense of touch was intensified by the lack of the other four senses, or perhaps because of my peculiar isolation underwater, I realized that the coin emanated a peculiar energy. Moreover, just as I could sense my detached head, so I could sense that this coin seemed to be guiding me somewhere. Directionless as I was, it seemed wise to follow this prompt.

"After nightfall, I emerged from underwater. I had no idea if anyone could see me or if the appearance of a headless torso was causing alarm. My lack of awareness was both frightening and strangely restful. After I wrung out my garments, I tore a scrap from my underclothing and, using my blood for ink, wrote this message."

Memory stirred. I felt I couldn't be blamed for not recognizing my caller—one did tend to focus on the absence of the head to the exclusion of all other details. Now I realized that I had indeed seen this man before. I had crossed to the human world to purchase supplies, including the tea I was currently drinking. Passing along one of the busy streets, I had been attracted by a lovely tenor voice. I had diverted from my course and found Lan—for now I realized who it had been—singing a playful song, the lyrics of which concealed—if one had any knowledge of current scandals—a scathing indictment of a local official. Lan had accompanied himself on the very flute that now rested in his belt.

As I passed by, I had tossed a coin into the cap that rested on the pavement. Only after I had returned to my own plane had I realized that I had thrown a gold shen coin rather than the copper I had intended. I had shrugged. The gold in the coin was good and, if the street musician held onto the coin, the *chi* stored within it might benefit him.

For a fleeting moment, I wondered if the shen coin explained the torso's remarkable post-decapitation mobility, but I dismissed this as unlikely. There simply wasn't enough *chi* stored in that single coin. What Lan's possession of the coin did explain was how his torso had made this unlikely journey, safe and apparently unremarked upon. He had wished for aid. To one who might grant that aid, the coin had brought him.

Now that Lan was here, what was I to do? That it never occurred to me to reject his request for aid should not be taken for any indication of great nobility in my character. At this point in my life, I was but a brash young demon, possessed of a good deal of raw power, eager to prove myself. Therefore, it would be by my deeds that I would make my reputation. Here was a quest of great promise.

First, I must find a way around Lan's current physical impediment. His note said he could sense the location of his head, so he could be my guide. However, a guide I must lead by the hand and protect against every small misstep of the way held little appeal. I sought out a string of gourds I had hung to dry in one corner of the room. Gourds are inherently suited for storing magical energy. I had grown these in soil imbued with powdered ginger, ginseng, and cinnabar. There was in me the desire to be more than a warrior, to be a creator. As of yet, I had found neither art nor craft to suit me.

Inspecting the gourds with senses other than those five I shared with humanity, I selected the one that would best serve my purposes. In shape it was rounded, with a fat neck that I carefully sawed through until it was a match for Lan's own. Leaving the dry seeds inside, where they would provide a reservoir of *chi* that my workings could draw upon, I poured into the open neck of the gourd any number of powders and liquids, shaking until the interior was well-coated. When I could feel the powerful hum of dormant magics awaiting activation, I crossed to my guest.

Lan had remained seated, the embodiment of patience. He flinched slightly when I pressed the gourd over the severed stump of his neck. Laying a reassuring hand on his shoulder, I bound the gourd into place, adapting for the purpose a routine mending spell. Then I stepped back, confident in my casting.

I had expected Lan to gasp, which he did, to raise his hand to feel this ersatz head, which he also did. What I had not expected was for him to turn his smooth gourd face to "look" at me, then scream in terror.

"Who. . .? What are you?" he asked, his voice sounding precisely as did his natural one, for I had willed it so when designing the spells.

I was a little hurt. Hadn't I been his benefactor? Then I recalled that Lan had never seen me in my natural form. If he remembered the person who had tossed him the gold coin, he remembered a young human male of his own race—which meant straight black hair, dark brown eyes, and skin the golden brown of ripening wheat.

What he saw standing before him was humanlike, but not in the least human, not unless humans had rich blue skin (shading slightly into purple), purplish-black hair, and eyes of such a dark black that no pupil was visible. The skin surrounding those eyes was ornamented with angular patches of ebon-black that made my eyes seem to glow. My hands were human-like in that they possessed five digits, but not at all human in that my fingers—and my toes as well—ended in very sharp talons.

When I considered this, I could understand why Lan had screamed. Briefly, I considered shifting to my human guise, then decided that the transformation would be at least as upsetting. Besides, Lan deserved to know what sort of being he had associated himself with.

I reached for the teapot and filled my cup, hoping that such a domestic act would calm my guest. As I did so, I said, "The enchantment I have worked upon you creates the guise of normal sensing, as well as granting the ability to speak. You still retain the advantages you mentioned in your note. You do not need to breathe. Nor do you appear to need any sustenance."

"I don't, do I?" Lan said. Only hearing as excellent as my own would have heard the small quaver of fear. "How very odd. Then again, I am accustomed to going without meals. The life of a street performer does not provide such on a regular schedule. May I know what to call you?"

"Kai Wren," I replied, offering a courtly inclination of my head.

"Kai Wren," Lan repeated. "Are you a *hsien?*"

The word he used pertains to many sorts of spirit beings. I shrugged. "So we have been called. We have also been called demons, because our aspect is terrifying and, as such, assumed to be inimical. However, there is a greater difference between my people and the *hsien. Hsien* are denizens of your world, belonging to it as do humans or dogs or trees. My people dwell in a plane that touches upon your own, but is not of it. Long ago, we learned to travel between planes, and frequently visit yours."

"Ah." Long pause then, "Which plane am I on now?"

"My own. I would hazard that when you followed the tug of the *shen* coin, it drew you here."

That Lan accepted what I told him without protest did not surprise me, for the tales of his people are full of remarkable supernatural events. He next said, "Will you help me find my head? Nice as this facsimile is, I do miss my own head. For one, without breath I cannot play my flute."

"I understand. Yes. I will aid you. To be honest, I'm interested in the puzzle. Perhaps if we find your head, we will also learn how you manage to survive without it. It's a neat trick, one I wouldn't mind adding to my own repertoire."

"If we find out," Lan said generously, "you're welcome to borrow it, as long as the borrowing doesn't hazard my own continuing existence. It would do me little good to regain my head if in doing so I bartered away my life."

"Well spoken," I agreed. "We have a deal. In your note you said that you could sense your head. Is that still true?"

Lan did not shut his eyes in concentration, for he did not have eyes to shut. Nonetheless, I had the impression that he was doing something along those lines.

"Yes, I can. It feels a long way away, though."

I smiled, remembered what a fearsome sight that could be, and tamped down on the broadness of my grin. "No matter. I can provide transportation. Can you ride a horse?"

"Not really," Lan said. "Horses are for the fine folks. I'm just a wandering musician."

I had my doubts about that last, but this wasn't the time to argue the point. Nor was it the time to teach him how to ride. I considered my options. Since I didn't know whether Lan's head was in the demon realm or the human realm, summoning a dragon—I had a few bound to me—wasn't a good idea. The lesser dragons, such as I commanded, were elemental spirits. I couldn't risk taking them out of their element, not to mention that I didn't want to invest the *chi* necessary to keep such a showy mount unnoticed.

"Got it!" I said. Moving to the shelves on one side of the room, I removed wooden figure of an ox pulling a cart. A few years back, I had studied wood carving. This figure had been the best of my efforts. The ox was typical of those used by peasants, with a broad brow and spreading horns, its solid strength and stolid temperament visible in every line. The cart was simple and practical, of the sort used for hauling.

My lessons had not merely been in carving. I had also learned how one worked with the grain of the wood so that the latent *chi* was intensified, somewhat after the manner of *feng shui*, by the lines and curves of the carver's knife. Although my teacher had said I had talent, I had let my lessons lapse, feeling this wasn't the art I could feel calling to me.

Head bent, I cradled my head above the carving, allowing my *chi* to mingle with that inherent in the piece. A breath, two, three. A surge of power and it was done.

When I set the figure down in the road outside my front door, it grew to a life-sized replica. "It will carry us both easily," I explained to Lan, who, despite having a head conjured from a gourd, was still capable of marveling at miracles, "through this plane, your own, or the sideways spaces. The cart may look slow, but that's deceptive. Both ox and cart travel slightly above the ground. Unhampered by friction, they are capable of moving as swiftly as the fastest running horse. Spells of misdirection cause it to be overlooked. Any who notice it will simply think that this cart can't possibly be the same as the one they passed earlier, for everyone knows that ox carts are slow and plodding. Now, up on the seat. In what direction do you sense your head?"

After taking his place, Lan bent his head and concentrated. "There, in the direction of the ox-tiger. The signal is faint but true."

"Northeast," I said, giving the ox his head, and thus we set off in search of Lan's.

Initially, our journey took us through the demon realms, where neither our conveyance nor my companion as much as raised an eyebrow. Eventually, though, Lan's directions sent us through the sideways spaces, to emerge in the human realm a great distance from the town in which Lan had suffered his loss. There I changed my shape to that of a farm lad, strongly-built and handsome in a rough way. We concealed Lan's gourd with a hooded cloak that also served to cover his motley attire.

"My head feels closer," Lan said in response to my query, "but not close. Drive toward those mountains."

We did, continuing after dark, for neither of us needed rest as humans did. I naturally saw in the dark, and I'd made certain that Lan's gourd head could unnaturally do so. Night travel also meant that our ox cart could trundle over fields and rivers—rather than going around them—without raising comment. Or, if we did raise comment, it was to add to the ample fund of Chinese ghost stories.

91

Other than orientation, Lan wasn't getting much from his head. It had been transferred from the sack to a box and was suffering all the discomfort Lan was missing, having a dry mouth, sore eyes, and too much to think about. Lan admitted that if he had to be imprisoned, he was rather glad that he was cut off from his head.

I'm not sure what I expected to find at the end of our journey. Lan's description of his assailant made him sound like a classic bandit. I was completely surprised when Lan's "turn right," "go straight," "take us up that hill" led us to where we could overlook a minimally fortified, multi-building complex.

"That's it!" Lan said. "My head is somewhere down there."

"I believe," I said, after studying the compound, "it's a potter's establishment. "There's a clay pit, ample water, and, see that glow to the back? I think that's a kiln. I'm guessing those longer buildings are workshops. They probably double as dormitories. The master and his family probably live in the other wing."

"It's awfully quiet," Lan commented. "I know it's the middle of the night but, given the number of people who are living there—see how large the gardens are?—there should be someone awake and about."

A flare of reddish-orange light caught my attention. "Someone's up tending the kiln's fire, at least."

"It's still too quiet," Lan persisted.

I didn't argue. Lan was human, after all. Although I went into the human world to shop, I certainly wasn't an expert on human habits.

"Do we go in now or would you prefer to wait until morning? It's your head on the line."

Lan considered. "Now. We might as well take advantage of the darkness. Maybe we'll be able to grab the box with my head in it and get out before we're noticed."

"Fine. We'll leave the wagon here and I'll glide us in." I checked to make sure I could get to my sword, which I carried concealed in a bit of portable sideways space. I had a few other tricks tucked up my sleeves, which were much roomier than they looked.

Grasping Lan under my left arm, so as to be able to reach my sword with my right, I caused my *chi* to spread forth, catching the night air beneath invisible wings. When we landed lightly inside the compound's central courtyard, Lan pointed directly toward the kiln. Drawing my sword, I spread shadows and silence about us, and we gusted forward. Even as I took these precautions, I wondered if they were necessary. Lan was right. This place was virtually deserted. I sensed only three or four life forces. All were gathered near the kiln.

We ghosted closer. Two men were were visible by the kiln, intent upon what they were doing. I didn't need Lan's hand tightening around my forearm to let me know that the armored man with the bristling beard was the same who had cut off Lan's head. The second man was completely hairless, of middle years, possessed of powerful shoulders and arms, although otherwise hardly a prime physical specimen. His expression was sour and unpleasant.

Lan gasped when he saw what held the two men's attention. On the table lay a girl child of about eight. She was very beautiful, with dark, silky hair swept into loops over her ears, and expensive silk clothing embroidered with butterflies and peonies covering her innocent form. Her slippered feet faced the closed door of the kiln, which was as large as the door of a house. It was impossible to escape the impression that the two men intended to shove her inside.

Seeking to read her *chi*, to learn whether she slept or woke, I realized that the girl was no girl at all, but rather a statue made from the purest white clay, her features cunningly painted on, her hair some clever artifice.

As Lan and I closed to just outside the circle of light cast by the kiln, we heard the bandit say in a rough, guttural voice. " Hsin, when will the fire be ready?"

The bald man bent to study the color of the light. "Patience, Wang. What you desire demands a hot fire."

"Will the head be enough? Won't feeding it in cool the fire?"

"I have taken the head into my calculations. You came to me for my expertise. Now you second-guess me?"

Bandit Wang's shoulders slumped and, momentarily, he looked pitiful. "No, but enough has gone wrong. I don't want to take any chances." He glowered at the potter. "Nothing had better go wrong, understand?"

Hsin's expression was bitter. "I understand. I warned you, you're asking for miracles."

"You'd better give me one," Wang growled, "else. . ." He made a slashing gesture that managed to convey that the potter wasn't the only one at risk.

Potter Hsin's gaze flickered over the empty buildings of his compound, then rested upon the bandit with something like hatred. I understood but, before I could consult Lan, he strode into the light.

"I know the story," Lan said without pause, "of how the gods challenged Pu to make pottery with all the characteristics of living flesh, and how Pu realized that only a fire fed by his own life would work the charm. What nonsense is this?"

Doubtless, being addressed by a torso with a gourd for a head stopped the bandit's ready blade. Not trusting him to remain astonished for long, I slid forth and pinned his arms, then removed his sword and threw it to clatter across the courtyard.

"Nonsense?" Bandit Wang growled. "I'd heard Hsin here boast that he was the equal to Pu, his very son. I'm only demanding he make good on his boast." Then his voice broke. "My little Mei died of a fever three days ago. When I prayed for her life to be given back, I received a vision of this place and so came to enlist Hsin's help."

Potter Hsin sour features twisted with indignation. "Enlist? Is that what you call kidnapping my household and promising to kill each and every person if I don't bring your daughter back to life? Tell them the rest of your vision, madman!"

Wang hung his head. "I was told a willing sacrifice was needed. I thought to offer myself, but my dreams made clear I was unworthy. I must find one possessed of great virtue."

He looked at Lan. "I'd crossed your path more than a few times. I had seen your generosity of spirit, how although in rags you gave away most of your coin, how although without power, you did not hesitate to challenge ministers and kings. I thought that if I showed you Mei's body, explained. . . I thought. . . But it all went wrong."

Lan stared at him in wonder. "Why didn't you ask me to accompany you? Why the sword, the sack?"

"I was afraid you would refuse." Wang shook, though whether from sorrow or in an attempt to break my hold, I couldn't tell. "I only understand force. I knew your sacrifice must be willing. I thought that if I showed you how many lives rested on your choice. . . I thought. . ."

"Thought!" snorted Hsin.

"If I help you," Lan asked, "will you free the potter's household?"

Nod.

"And give Hsin treasure to compensate for his anguish?"

"I planned to in any case," came the muttered response. "I didn't want to say so because he'd think me soft. I'd give all my gold to have Mei, my greatest treasure, laughing and alive again."

"Give me my head," Lan said. "I will gladly go into the fire."

"Lan! You can't mean this," I cried, appalled.

Lan shrugged. "One life for many and a daughter back into her father's arms? How could I not? My only regret is that Wang did not think to ask."

I was shocked to the core. Demons are capable of self-sacrifice, but for strangers? This was purest insanity. Moreover, Lan had no assurance his death would restore this child's life. Gods are tricky sorts.

"This is all wrong!" I protested. "There must be another way." Remembering Pu's legend, I thought I saw a way. "Master Potter, as I recall, the gods where shocked when they realized the sacrifice Pu had made to fill their request."

"Yes," Hsin replied. "The gods had only wished to learn if Pu's power was from heaven or hell. When they learned what he had done, as an apology, they made him the patron god of potters."

"Very well," I said, "let us assume the gods do not wish Lan to die so that another will live. That would be an unprofitable exchange. One for one. Lan has made the offer. I am in his employ. I insist on taking his place."

Lan shook his gourd so wildly that I thought it would fly off. "Kai Wren, no!"

I smiled and dropped Wang to the ground, certain he was no longer a threat. "I offered to aid you to find your head. I'm not going to let you burn it to ash as soon as we do. You know something of me. Let me undergo this trial in your place."

Lan frowned, but perhaps he remembered what manner of creature I was. Reluctantly, he nodded. I grinned ferociously and lifted a box that rested near the forge. "Reclaim your head, that my first duty will be completed."

Before the astonished gazes of Hsin and the Wang, I removed the gourd from Lan's shoulders and set his head in its place. Retrieving Wang's sword from where I had thrown it, I tapped the severed edges of Lan's neck.

"As this made you two, let it make you one again," and, as simply as that, Lan's head rejoined his neck. I doubted that either Hsin or Wang could see that the tremendous surge of *chi* that sealed the gap came, not from me, but from Lan himself. Wang had been correct—Lan was a creature of great virtue, one of those rare humans who become Immortals, although I do not think even Lan himself suspected this.

"Now, Master Hsin. Is the fire ready?"

The potter checked the color of his flames, added a bit more fuel, and, after pursed lip inspection, nodded.

"I will bear Mei into the fire," I continued. "When I have done so, close the door after me. Keep the fire fed. When the sky shows true dawn, check to see whether you are indeed a true son of Pu."

I gave none time to protest, but gathered the form on the table into my arms. It was heavier than I had expected. I realized that Hsin had shaped his clay over the girl's dead body.

96

"Open the door," I commanded. When Hsin did so, the heat billowed forth like something solid. However, I had bound dragons and knew something of fire. With a nod, I strode over coals into the flames: one step, two. . . At the third, I heard the door of the kiln close behind me.

I had no illusions that I could raise the dead. Mei's living or dying would be up to her father's gods. My task was to supply what *chi* was needed and, incidentally, to keep both her and myself from burning to ash.

I knew something of fire, but that did not mean I was immune to heat or to pain. As I stood in the heart of the kiln, I felt both with an intensity beyond anything I had anticipated. I was tempted to flee—I could do so without even opening the door of the kiln. Wang and Hsin would believe I had burned to death and Mei with me. Lan would make sure that Wang spared Hsin's household. Why then should I suffer for the return of a human's short life? It was laughable.

But more than I craved relief from this suffering, I craved to rise to be among the great. When this tale reached the demons—as it would, whether by Lan's agency or another's—I would have taken a step up in the estimation of my kind, for this was great magic. So I stood in the fire, letting agony burn away my illusion of humanity, centering my concentration on not so much resisting the fire as letting it become part of me. Breathing deeply and evenly, I channeled power into the still form in my arms and waited for the door to open. Then, only then, would I know if I burned alive for naught.

How long passed before that door opened? Objectively, only a handful of hours. Subjectively, I lived more years than had already been mine and—although I was young by the standards of my kind—I was still over a thousand years old. I lived through waves of pain, doubt, fear, regret. . . Time and again, I contemplated retreat. Time and again, held only by pride, I kept my place.

At last the heat of the fire began to ebb. I heard the ping as the porcelain in my arms cooled and settled. Hsin was indeed a master of his craft. Even with this unconventional firing, with the temper of a human corpse at its center, the figure he had formed remained intact, the glazes and paints he had laid upon it fresh and bright as life.

But did I hold a child or only a doll?

When the door opened, I was stiff with stillness of centuries in my bones. I stalked forth, unable to find the *chi* for even a simple illusion disguise. Lan must have told Wang and Hsin something of my nature for, although their eyes widened, they showed no surprise.

Carefully, oh, so carefully, I set the thing I carried upon the table. As we fixed our gaze on this figure shaped like Mei, we knew we looked upon a miracle of the potter's craft. Did we also look upon a miracle of divine mercy?

Stillness. Silence. Sorrow. Then dark lashes fluttered, the child stirred, breathed. Her father rushed to hold her, his tears falling upon flesh that did not hiss as cooling pottery would have done.

"Baba," came a voice as sweet as the music of Lan's flute. "Baba, I dreamed such strange dreams."

Mei's gaze rested upon me without the least trace of fear. I felt glad. It would not do to help bring a child to life to then kill her with fear. I looked over at Lan.

His eyes twinkled. "I believe your promise to aid me is discharged, Kai Wren."

"Thank you." I turned to Potter Hsin. "Truly, Hsin you have proven your boast to be a son of Pu. I would learn your craft from you. Would you take me as a student?"

"Gladly." His face lit in the first smile I had seen, transforming him as fire transforms clay. "I won't even insist upon a fee."

Creatures of Foam and Mist

by Gio Clairval

Set in the universe of Roger Zelazny's Creatures of Light and Darkness:
*On an unnamed planet, the sea stretches above and beneath the atmosphere.
Here, the Prince Who Was a Thousand keeps his wife Nephytha, who was
disembodied and cannot survive on a normal planet. Here also, a large reptile
frolics in the mist.*

Pharaoh, the King of Ter, dreams, and in his dream a waterfall of beer
fills the largest fountain in his garden. The frothy liquid overflows the
stone rim, splashing on his sandaled feet as he bends to replenish his jug.

The court gathers around the suzerain, he who rules over the oldest of
the six human races scattered across the universe. His servants chant:
"Blessed be the divine beverage!"

"Praise Nephytha," the Great Priest intones, "goddess of Death,
darkness shining in the night."

"Praise!"

The King drains his jug and replenishes it.

"Glory to Nephytha," says the Great Priest, "who presents us with the
ever-flowing liquid gold of the divine Pharaoh."

"Glory!"

In his dream, the King's throat and tongue grow tense, and he makes
a sound as if he were choking.

He awakes in a fit of coughing, on sheets flecked with blood, and he
knows he is going to die.

*

Nephytha hovers in mid air, unsubstantial, a breath under the moving
sea that is the ceiling of her world, her playground and her prison. Above,
glowing fish swim at the bottom of the sea, like stars spinning across the

sky. And below, the land sparkles with the reflection of the light on scaly, wiggling bodies. If only she could transport herself away, as her husband does. Nephytha used to be one of the four great gods of the lands north and south of the Mother River, but she renounced her wings when she married the divine Thoth, three times great, wielder of the arts, Thoth the Wise, Thoth the Teacher, self-begotten and self-produced. He who resurrected the dismembered Horus, but could not restore his wife after the Thing That Cries In The Night destroyed her material body.

The birds she created to keep her company sing for her. She must find a way out.

*

The King's servants, seeing their master on the brink of death, call the Superintendent of the Royal Bedroom, who in turn summons the healers. Pharaoh recounts his dream, and the healers pronounce as one that Nephytha should be placated by copious offerings of beer.

A procession forms from the royal apartments to the temple of Nephytha, but, despite the jarfuls of ale sluiced onto the sacrificial altar, the King still chokes, face blue, eyes rolling up into their sockets.

Pharaoh's youngest page, who's been known to discern otherworldly shapes in the clouds, raises his voice to cover the brouhaha of the terrified court. "I saw the goddess Nephytha in a dream."

The healers and the Great Priest snicker, but the lesser priests, upon hearing the holy name, belt out: "Glory!"

"She spoke to me. Let us go down to the Lord of the Fish itself, the Mother River, and pour all of the King's liquid gold we can find into its sacred waters—until the Goddess (Glory!) relents."

Pharaoh nods between two fits of coughing.

While the Nihil River waxes golden with beer, and papyrus boats hurry toward the shores, fowlers refrain from throwing nets, and maybe a smattering of water gods ceases gossiping, the young boy raises his arms and sings:

O luminous Nephytha, darkest angel,
Consciousness glowing in the dead of night,
Flowers of white shall fall in utter darkness,
As the souls—who are cold—disperse in water.
O Goddess bright, mélange of blackened buds.

The King's cough subsides, and he of the holy flail rises from the bloodied sheets to his feet, smiling, for he is healed.

(Glory!)

*

The Prince Who Was a Thousand walks along the beach.

Within the waters hanging above him, there appears the outline of a woman. He takes a step forward then, arms stretched upward as to retain her, but the woman's shape resolves into a school of shiny fish, and his name, which is "Thoth," vibrates in his ears like wind in a shell.

His throat aches as he calls out her name, but no sounds, not the tiniest echo, respond.

Alone, he stands beside the sea and also beneath the sea. He tosses a stone into the waves but, when he opens his hand, expecting the stone to return, nothing comes back. His shoulders droop.

The backwash fills his footprints after he is gone.

*

Nephytha turns to a mastodon-sized saurian she made out of green mist. "Fancy some ale?"

The reptile stares with shining eyes and bows its head.

"Drink the sea, then," she says, "and the beer will come."

Now the saurian arches its long neck to drain the sea that is above and below, and water rushes into its body in never-ending flows—not slimy any more, not any more. The abyss inside the beast has no bottom and a ferocious blizzard roars within.

When the sea has disappeared into the reptile's infinite stomach, the churning beer from the Lord of Fish, the Mother River, gushes into the unnamed world that is the goddess' home, her garden and oubliette. Ale

101

whirls down the saurian's mouth, and neck, and the caverns within. The fishes with translucent bellies are gone; myriad golden bubbles dance on the ceiling of the world; a refreshing surf bathes the shore.

Nephytha plunges into the frothing crests and swims between rushing whirlpools as her soul dissolves into foam. She is free.

*

Sam the barkeep wipes the stainless steel sink. The mirror above the splash-back reflects an old traveler's tired face, obscured by black hand-painted letters spelling the bar's name, *House of Life.*

"So you lost her," Sam says with professional intensity.

The traveler stares at the bottom of the mug. "I wasn't able to save her."

He raises his empty glass. Sam takes a clean mug and drafts a thick creamy stout, but the old man wags his finger. "Not that one. I've been drinking ale."

Sam taps a finger on his lips. "Right. Dunno what I was thinking. Sorry 'bout that."

"You haven't heard a word I said." The traveler holds up a hand to halt the flow of apologies. Something in the old man's movement—a fluidity that belies those round shoulders—catches Sam's attention, makes him perk up.

"I've heard everything," he lies. His hand clamps around the pump.

"I can't see her in dark beer."

"What is it that you see already?" Sam glances at the tag: this patron is at his twentieth pint. Time to shut the tap. But the expression on that lined face is so wistful Sam decides to let the man have one last pint.

"My wife. I see my wife."

"In your beer."

"Ale. It must be clear, pale ale, not too much foam on top."

Sam, who dislikes patrons that criticize his way of drawing beer, lets go of the tap.

"Please." This word is said with no inflection, no emotion, and Sam finds himself filling the mug and knifing the top to stave off the foam, twice.

"And that's why you drain so many pints." He intended to make it sarcastic, but it came out sympathetic.

"Every night, yes. I hope she will forgive me and come back to me. She can do it. I know she can."

"Sure. She must be. . . er. . . waiting for the right moment."

The traveler scratches the grey stub on one cheek, eyebrows knitted together.

Pushing the mug toward the old drunk, Sam glimpses some kind of whirling at the bottom.

He rubs his eyes with two knuckles. Too much smoke. He doesn't approve of the owner's habit of letting the last patrons burn a cigarette before close. Even with the door wide open, it makes your eyes sting.

Despite the tears, he sees. Full lips curled into a smile, and dimples on either side, before the foam erases them like footprints crumpling in wet sand.

"I am sorry," the old man says. "I should have tried harder. Come back."

Doorways In Time

by Edward J. McFadden III

Incidents and fragments continued—

The feeling that I had been here before swamped me like rain on tissue paper. The old Fred Cassidy had done this thing so many times the sun and moon were bored looking down on it. Above, around where the belt that drove the world skipped and looped, a tower with the Earth resting atop its massive frame dominated the horizon.

I gaped at the size and power of Nikola Tesla's creation.

The red brick walls of Tesla's lab still smelled of concrete, and the Wardenclyffe Tower rose into the sky like a metal nightmare, many of the welds on the superstructure still warm. In times of worry he who carries the most burdens will eventually crumble and fall, just as some are crushed by the enormity of a situation, or an object. I was thusly awed. Even Speicus marveled at the towers size, its cross-section of steel and wood a maze of symmetry and strength. Atop the tower a half-circle of wire and metal waited to fill the air with electricity, its core dull and silent.

I can see why Tweedledee and Tweetledum's boss wants this candle lit, said Speicus from his office inside my brain. Tesla lit a series of street lights at a great distance by transmitting electricity through the air like a radio wave. At least that's what I recalled from my ancient history.

The ground around the lab had been cleared, and the patches of green grass and dirt were marred only by a thin road that led to the lab's entrance. I didn't remember walking from the cover of the woods to my current position on the southern side of Tesla's lab. What if I was discovered by security? Would I be shot on site? Tesla had been obsessed with project secrecy, which was born from the fact that some of his ideas had been stolen.

Just because you're paranoid doesn't mean they're not out to get you, Speicus said.

A gentle breeze pushed the grass, and somewhere a piece of metal tapped against wood. I realized it was the flag lead-line banging against the flagpole in front of the lab, which was nothing more than a rectangle of brick.

"Speicus, any idea what we should do? Go knock on the door? And say what? 'Hi, I have no idea how I came to be here but can we have some tea and chat? I need to tell you something.' I'll be shot!"

You know what you need to do. Do you need me to actually rattle your damn noddle? Speicus said.

I walked, and when I came around the corner of the lab there was a man standing before the tower, gazing up at it with a grim expression on his lean face. He wore a grey tailored suite, and a thin dark tie.

"May I help you?" the man asked.

"You are Tesla?" I said.

The man's face twisted like I'd asked him if the Earth was round. "Yes. How did you get in here?"

I didn't know really, but...

"If you cut the fence I'll whip your ass myself! What paper are you with?"

Telsa came at me, and I put my hands up. "I'm just here to talk to you. I'm no reporter." Whether it was my clothes, or the way my voice sounded, or one of the other hundred things that marked me as alien to his time, Tesla's face softened.

"Why do I believe you?" Tesla said. He squinted, and his mouth fell open a crack, as if he didn't trust his own words.

On the periphery of my vision a white cat hid behind a large pipe, its keen eyes studying me. The universe chirped, and everything jumped for an instant. I staggered, and Tesla stepped forward and steadied me.

"You must speak with Westinghouse right away," my mouth blurted. "Tell him of your plan to transmit not only communications via your towers, but electricity as well," I finished, but it was really Speicus. He could take over pretty much whenever he wanted.

Tesla looked hard at me, his eyes tiny black marbles. He was weighing me, trying to hide his surprise. "How did you know that? There is no way you *could* know that," he said, stepping back as I got my legs back under me.

As things swirl I hang on to my sanity as best I can, everything that came before revealed to me in an instant. My time is running short. Where was Dennis Wexroth when you needed him? The persistent little turd.

Oh, I get it. Speicus slapped me mentally.

I said, "That is why I'm here. You must tell Westinghouse. Your future depends on it." The lie flowed so easily from my mouth I shivered. I knew, as did the powers that guided me, that telling Westinghouse would lead to him asking Tesla how he was going to charge people for the electricity running through the air. When Telsa answered he couldn't, Westinghouse would kill the project, thus avoiding the events Speicus and I had seen through the doorway in the woods. The fact that this change would start a spiral that would leave one of mankind's greatest scientists destitute didn't seem to matter. The needs of the many and all that rot.

Knowing there was no possible way anyone could have known his real plan for the tower, Tesla said, "I will."

And he did.

A door closes in the depths of my mind, and I wonder if Speicus has literally slammed the door in my face. Then I'm standing on a beach, the star filled sky rolling before me. The north shore of Long Island has a quiet grace, and The Sound itself defies definition by making very little of it. The gentle lapping of the clear water eases what's left of my mind, and suddenly the beach was full of doorways, and I thought of ladies, tigers, cell phones, TV dinners, purple shoes, ships, sealing wax and other lurkers on the threshold. Soon, soon, soon...

*

Incidents and fragments—

Even though the forest was nothing more than scrub pine, it was still pleasant compared to the buildings and smog of the city. But I think that's what I miss most, the tall buildings, the freedom I felt when swinging high above the fray, like an eagle soaring in the clouds.

Speicus had grounded that bird.

My make-believe wings fluttered, the path before me unclear, and my knees had come unhinged, when the doorway appeared in the trees above. Saintly and majestic it descended through the scrub pine as if held in place by an unseen god or force. The doorway stood before me, like a giant accusing mouth telling me to do my duty or let a more competent team take over.

Through the doorway a circle of blinding light released shards of static electricity that lit the air on fire. The metal fillings in my teeth sizzled. I fought to stay in control, pushing back the constant voice of Speicus. I would decide. Me. Fred, or whatever was left of me.

Lightning scorched the sky, fanning out over the world like spider's legs. The bolts holding together the dimensions came loose and time jolted. Speicus was aware of it. Through the electric haze the doorway showed the cracking of the Earth, a slow butterfly effect that eventually reached the planet's core, and rattled it apart.

I stood on a broken plain, shards of rock protruding from the ground. The piece of earth I stood upon floated amidst other parts of the planet, and then it collided with a bigger piece and was crushed to dust. My heart wavered, and on some level a piece of me died.

A head popped into the open doorway, then a second. Both men wore bowler hats and were dressed in black. One man seemed bald; the other had long grey greasy strands hanging below his hat. "Don't forget about us asshole. Remember me? I'm Rathford, and this is Sunn. And we're about to crush your world, *seeeeee*."

I hear the tinkle of Speicus' laughter.

The doorway is closing.

It's over.

A white cat walks across my path, pausing to look up at me as if to say, "I'm a Whillowhim agent, and I can do all kinds of shit in this dimension."

I blink, and the doorway is gone.

Rays of fading sunlight stream into the forest, and I walk on, carrying those burdens, not missing a step. Crystal clear are the rivers of my thoughts, cold water drenching the innards of long forgotten ethics, and what it meant to be real. I was part of something now. I had a responsibility to Speicus, to the people of Earth who I now protected.

The woods ended abruptly, and dirt and grass filled the open field separating me from a large brick building at the clearings center. I felt maggots crawling across my brain, and for an instant it's as though each little bug is taking a piece, feasting on the white matter that now only serves as a backdrop for what I've become. What Speicus and I have become.

Lost in the bleakness of time, I wonder how long I have to complete my mission. To stop the events I saw through the doorway from happening. Does it really matter? Green faces sprout roots and fill my mind with a tangle of dreams, ideas, and thoughts that make me want to cry. I see children dying, the end of it all. Maybe there would be peace then, when all the humans were gone, our aggressive, virus-like behavior lost amidst the dark matter.

Oh, buck up, said Speicus.

Spinning through time.

Time spinning. I'm lost. Even though I was found, I was lost. I felt so tired, all my life sucked through the tiny hole in my heart, and I remember my old partner Ralph Warp. Crafts? What in all of hell that is holy was I thinking? I hadn't done much thinking back then, with the exception of trying to figure out ways to stay in school and collect my money.

Pain lashes my mind, and everything I see starts to fade. Then the buildings and trees sprout legs and run away.

*

Bits and Pieces—

Nothingness transposed on colorless paper, invisible fish jumping in rhythm with my heart, and a sea of rolling heads knocking and slamming into each other as the ooze of civilization seeps through the pores of a broken world dreamt by a broken mind. Each second is a lifetime and nothing at all. A loss of everything that never was, and never would be, buried beneath inverted black stars looking out on the brightness of the realization that it's over.

Gone.

Kaput.

Then I remember where I am. Cartoon gangster one, Rathford, and cartoon gangster two, Sunn, are holding me captive, but help was on the way. I had seen it lurking in the tall grass beside the path. I laughed, a loud throaty sound that made Sunn reach for his weapon. The tinkling sound of Speicus' laughter haunts me, then I was falling, the pit of my stomach nose-diving through a reality that left me paralyzed.

Charv, the tips of the kangaroo ears on his suite bobbing and swaying, watches Ragma as he runs forward. Neither tweedledee nor tweedledum saw Ragma coming, and in that moment I felt Speicus sitting on the edge of his mental imbalance, pushing me forward into the abyss, where he would leave me for dead and take my body as his own. I shook my head.

You're an asshole, said Speicus.

Ragma, disguised as a dog, leapt through the air, jaws open, sharp teeth exposed, and Rathford didn't have time to respond before Ragma latched onto the wannabe gangster and snuffed out his flame. Rathford's eyes bulged, and he stared at me, as if to say, "We had an understanding." Ragma released him, and the corpse fell to the forest floor with a thud.

Charv strolled through the tall grass into the clearing, and laughed when Ragma turned his attention to Sunn. The large bald man pointed his tiny weapon at Ragma, who paused and snarled. Blood pooled around Rathford, and Ragma was careful to step around it.

"Stay back," said Sunn. He pressed his weapon's activation button.

Ragma disappeared, and then reappeared. He had moved ten feet to the right in a flash of an instant. In the periphery of my vision I caught sight of a white cat as it disappeared into the grass. It looked back at me, its eyes gleaming like opals, and I thought I saw a smile beneath the creature's whiskers.

Sunn reeled back, and lifted his weapon. That moment was all Ragma needed. The black dog coiled its legs and leapt, hitting Sunn's chest with such force the weapon flew from his hand and the breath rushed from his lungs.

When Ragma was done, two bloodied corpses lay before me. "Thanks," I said.

"You just can't stay out of it, can you?" asked Charv, as he released me from my bonds.

I had forgotten how odd it was to talk to someone wearing a giant kangaroo costume. "My job now, you know that." Charv turned to look at Ragma, who still stood over the two dead bodies.

"Let's go. You have the world to save," said Charv, as he turned and walked through the woods.

I followed, my reality becoming clearer, but still nothing more than a giant blotch of color and blood, mixing with an ethereal light that brought neither illumination nor warmth. The stand of scrub pine thickened, and Speicus said, *Long Island was covered in these trees. In our time not one can be found.*

Change. It came whether you wanted it or not.

A breeze blew as the sun continued it's decent to the horizon, and I breathed deep and felt Speicus relish the sensation. I closed my eyes and thought of climbing tall buildings, of dangling atop the city like an overgrown bat. It was there I had been most at home. My head in the clouds. My entire world rushing by in a blur below me. The clouds overhead swirled, and when I turned to find Charv and Ragma, they were gone.

*

Incidents and fragments, bits-and-pieces time.

Like—

"Hands up," said Rathford.

111

I sighed.

Speicus whispered, *Already, Fred? We just got here.*

"I don't think..." I began.

"You feel that?" said the man behind me, who had me by the neck, and was pushing his gun into my ribs.

"Is that a gun or are you just happy to see me?" I asked, and the man brought the gun up, and then brought it down on my head. The last thing I heard before the blackness took me was the tingling of Speicus' laughter.

Candy dreams laced with the horror of reality painted on a dirty canvas crawling with spiders and flies. The scent of roses mixed with shit filled my head, and I thought of my old roommate Hal Sidmore, and how he used to peel the paint from the walls in our bathroom with his high octane craps, only to attempt to mask the stench with rose air freshener. The same kind my crazy mother had used. I'm sinking in mud, dirt filling my eyes.

An epiphany in blood, entrails, and gumdrops.

When I came awake I was tied to a tree, and two large men sat before me. My first thought was that they looked like cartoon characters. All dark black, big, with hats like they used to wear in the old days. That snapped my head around. Speicus and I weren't in Kansas anymore.

"You are?" I asked the men, and one of them chuckled.

"You could say we're friends of Morton and Jamie, though we didn't know them. I'm Rathford and he's Sunn. Not that it matters," said the short man. "But we're asking the questions, here, *seeeeee.*"

If he's trying to do James Cagne he was way off, and a couple of decades to early, muttered Speicus.

"Are you trying to be a gangster?" I asked, the old mocking Fred breaking through.

"What? And you're an expert on 1906 Long Island?" asked the one who called himself Sunn. His voice was high and squeaky, which made me smile.

"That where we are?" I asked.

Yes, answered Speicus.

"Don't play stupid. We know you're here to talk with Tesla," said Rathford. "Boss wants this reality gone—everything and everyone in it. So he said to make you gone."

With wit like that it's hard to see how he ended up a low life.

"Gone," I sputtered. Then I realized the doorway must have brought me here for a reason. I was a U.S. legation of the United Nations, and therefore had a responsibility to do... to do what? Certainly not what these two wanted. "I'm not going anywhere."

The name Telsa sparked something buried deep within my mind. He had been a man of great importance back in the early days of modern science. What was it...

"Really, wise guy. Then I guess I'll need to fill you full of lead," said Rathford. He drew out a small weapon that looked a little like a gun.

Sunn looked at Rathford, and said, "Lead? It's a blaster."

"Oh, shut up!" snapped Rathford.

"You two girls mind telling me what you think I'm up to?" I had learned that trick watching old cartoons and reading police procedural novels.

"You're not going to talk to Tesla. When he lights up his candle at full strength to transmit power, and it works, it will set him on our course. The boss can't let you change that." That wasn't much of an answer, but that's all there was.

Ask him if he knows of a good donut shop around here.

"We don't know exactly what you're gonna say to him that changes things. So, you aint gonna to talk to him at all, *seeeeee*."

Everything faded as he spoke, the world's colors dripping into brown mush. Trees melted, leaving only scarred ground and blackened sticks protruding from dead soil like dark teeth in a lifeless mouth. Bodies of people and animals alike littered the ground, their charred flesh still smoldering. The sun was falling, and butterflies danced with golden parachutes as they floated listlessly through the blood stained clouds, the path leading to the woods obscured from view.

Snap to, dipshit!

The tall grass behind Rathford and Sunn began to shift and sway. Fake ears with white fabric in their centers bounced up and down. It was Charv, clad in his familiar kangaroo suite, and behind him trotted Ragma guised as a black dog. The two alien law officers paused just within the cover of the tall grass and watched Rathford and Sunn as they studied me.

Ragma inched forward, like he was stalking an unseen prey. When he broke into a full out run, I closed my eyes tight.

*

Time.

Fragments, pieces, bits...Time.

Epiphany in Black & Light, Scenario in Green, Gold, Purple & Gray...

Speicus nudged me. I had no other explanation for why I choose the doorway I did. Just Fred being Fred, I guess. But was I Fred? Not really anymore. The worlds that saturate my mind don't have star-stones, or Rhennius machines, but now they have Speicus, who is part of me, and who would record and report. My partner.

Glass beads on stained glass, angels falling, full of sorrow, yet I can see something there. Mists, written over with the blood of those I must deliver to the tall trees at the end of the path, through the doorway where some task, some sleight of hand must be turned down another way, stopping something that blue dogs and fat ladies would frown upon.

Are you there, Fred? asked Speicus.

"Yes. I'm a little twisted through right now. Up not up, and down not down. Shit like that." I heard a tinkle that I thought was Speicus laughing. I hated the sound.

The doorways had a purpose. Even if their creators hadn't anticipated the challenged races that may find them. Wasn't I that race? Hadn't the doorways been provided by my new bosses? Who were they, exactly? The US didn't have that kind of power. How many layers up did it go? Hands upon hands, withering within a cloud of lies, a world lost to simple pleasantries, and wants. A world broken down to its bare essentials, where men feed on men?

Jesus, were you always so grim? asked Speicus.

Another downside to sharing a brain is that you never know when an idea, whether good or bad, was yours, or your partners. I had no doubts about who controlled my brain, but it was nice the way Speicus pretended I had some control. There are spaces between things that are so small I can feel the constant pressure of all the layers of time upon me, pushing my heart into that tiny space where there's no room for anything else. Pain expanded across my body, and there were moments I thought I was done. Either dead, or lost within some netherworld that allowed me to watch myself, as controlled by Speicus, live on into forever, not looking back even once to see the lost life I'd left behind.

If there was anyway it could be different, said Speicus. *You're really better off this way. No?* Speicus, having grown into me, had begun to develop what I thought of as the largest copyright infringement imaginable. Speicus was becoming a bigger wiseass than me. Using my weak material!

"Sure was different before I agreed to give up half the real estate in my head, Speicus." I felt very lost.

Your brain? Half a pea is still just half a pea.

White lines of energy sizzled and popped through the air. One of my metal tooth fillings grew hot. Energy zapped the synapses of my brain, and then I was in the forest at the end of the path... but no, it wasn't that forest...

The sun was falling, but the tower in the distance had legs of lightning shooting in every direction, the eerie light pushed away the fading sunlight and scorched the clods. Everything around me jerked, and I staggered, Speicus screamed something in my mind—right there in the front where it hurt.

Open your eyes!

I stepped over the threshold of the doorway and the world behind was sucked away, and my new world drove the air from my lungs. A kaleidoscope of dark brown, turned to green as I saw a frog sitting on turtle's shell it lurched forward across the forest floor. Scrub pine and ash block my way. The light was fading. The day was fading. What lay before me was unclear.

115

But we must go, said Speicus.

I took one step. Then another. I didn't know what was to come, but at least I had Speicus, and I had gone through the doorway. That usually led to something good. Going through a doorway, leaving one place, and entering a new place.

Coda

by Steve Perry

It was almost closing, Sam had already rung the bell, and only a few die-hards were there, finishing up the last of their beer before stumbling off to greet the dawn. He was wiping the bar when the man in red came in.

Sam's smile was involuntary. It had been what? thirty, forty years? The clothes were of a conservative cut and style, much as he used to dress, even though the man in them wore a different body. The sword on his belt was not much more than a machete, though that was enough weapon to do any job to which he might turn his attention. Sam had never heard of anybody who was as good with a blade, and woe to any fool who tried to prove differently.

The body was young and fit, he probably hadn't had it long, but his essence was unmistakable, if you could see into the spectrum as Sam could.

He found that he was inordinately pleased to see him.

The man walked to the bar, sat on the stool at the end so his back was to the wall and smiled.

"Binder of Demons," he said.

Sam's grin grew larger. "Deathgod."

Yama gave him a tight-lipped grin. "Not in that business for a while."

"You can change what you do, but not what you are," Sam said.

"Sayeth the bartender who slew the demon Taraka like blowing out a candle; who destroyed all but one of the Mothers of the Terrible Glow.

"Dalissa sends her regards, by the way."

Sam nodded.

Yama continued: "Sayeth the man running a pub who fomented revolution using a non-violent religion to defeat the gods themselves."

"Well, yes," Sam said. "With a little help from my friends."

He drew two dark ales, set one of the heavy ceramic steins in front of Yama. He raised the other mug. "Old times," he said.

Yama raised his mug, touched it to Sam's. They drank.

"Pretty good beer."

"My own recipe. Doesn't travel well, but it's not bad for draft. I call it 'Dark Karma Ale.'"

"You'd have plenty of that."

Both took another swallow.

Sam said, "I heard you left Khaipur and. . .had words with the Seven Lords of Komlat?"

Yama shrugged. "Not much of a discussion. We spoke, they disagreed. They came to regret that."

"I bet."

"Smoke? I have some aromatic shag you might like."

Sam nodded. In a world where changing bodies was no more difficult than taking a nap, cancer wasn't a worry. When the Wardens of Transfer took over from the Lords of Karma, the process became even easier. Hobble in old and ill, skip out a new man in almost no time.

Sam pulled out his pipe.

Yama came up with a carved briar with an amber stem, and a pouch of tobacco. Sam scooped some of the tobacco into his own pipe. "Moist."

"Put a little slice of apple in it, keeps it from drying out."

Sam tamped the tobacco down, found a match. He took a puff. "Excellent. Nice aroma."

Yama lit his own bowl, drew smoke, exhaled it. It floated up to enwreath his head. "The Witches still send me a packet every now and then. They really didn't like the Seven."

The rest of the customers drifted out, saying farewells. Sam nodded at them.

When they were alone, Yama said, "How about Great-Souled Sam? Took me a while to find you. I thought you might have gone back into the Cloud."

"I think about it from time to time, but there's no hurry. It's not going anywhere. And there always seems to be more work to be done here."

"You would know about the Cloud."

"Sayeth the man who dragged me back out of it."

Both smiled through the tendrils of blue smoke.

"How fares Lady Parvati?"

Sam said, "Passing well. She had some trouble a few years back, nothing major."

"Not how I heard that story,"

Sam's turn to shrug. "Well, you know how these things get amplified in the telling. Somebody wrote a novel about our adventures, did you hear?"

"I heard. I haven't read it."

"It's not bad. Tends to the hyperbolic, though. We didn't do half what the writer said we did, and it's got a really awful pun in the middle of it. Awful."

The two men smoked and drank without speaking for a time.

"You are wondering why I'm here," Yama finally said.

"Thought had crossed my mind."

"Well. For the last thirty-six years, I've run a little lab in the port of Koona. Become a real city since you and I were there, back in the day."

"A lab. Working with. . .?"

"A little of this, a little of that." He paused. "Mostly human neurology."

"Ah."

Sam waited.

"Took a while to train enough doctors who could find their asses with both hands, but eventually, we managed to do some decent hands-on research."

Sam knew what that would have been, so he asked the next question: "And did you find a cure for it? Transfer-effect brain damage?"

If he was surprised by the question, he didn't let on. "Not as such. Some wounds are beyond the best artificers ability to repair."

"And that part you would know; however, I hear a 'but' in there."

"You were always pretty quick. We didn't find a cure here, but there is a place where such can be effected."

Sam thought about it for a few seconds. "The Golden Cloud."

Yama said, "Yes."

The Bridge of the Gods, it was called, the bronze rainbow that encircled this world, where the red sun turned orange at noon. The place of bliss, as Sam knew, having spent some relative-eons there as self-perpetuating wavelengths when his atman had been projected into the magnetic field by the gods. They had thought it was better that he be there enjoying Nirvana than here, plotting revolution. Killing him outright would have made him a martyr, and they didn't want that, either. Turned out that was just another in a long list of mistakes on their parts. They didn't figure on Yama being able to retrieve him and reinstall him into the flesh again.

Being god and hubris tend to go together.

"You always had the touch when it came to machines."

"It was the song of the universe that did the trick, I just provided the ride there and back."

Yama pulled a gold pocket watch from his jacket and looked at it.

"That a local product?"

He held the watch up for Sam to see. "From Earth. Somebody found it in an attic somewhere. Cost a king's ransom."

"I don't doubt that. You have an appointment, you need to check the time?"

"Yes, an appointment. Tell me, Sam, do you keep up your priest dues?"

Sam laughed. "I am known, among other things, as Lord Kalkin, Maitreya, Mahasamatman, and still considered in some circles as a legitimate avatar of the Buddha, though we both know that was a shuck. Still, nobody asks to see my membership card if I drop by the Purple Grove. Why do you ask?"

Death laughed, a thing Sam still found amazing. He had loosened up considerably since last they'd seen each other.

The door opened, and a fat man ambled in. Just behind him, another man who looked as if he had partied for a week and forgotten to sleep. Both of them grinned at Sam.

As I live and breathe, it's Kubera and Krishna!

Behind Krishna, Ratri, who had partnered with Kubera decades ago. All in different bodies, but all starting to look as they eventually always did, as the bodies shaped themselves to fit the spirits that inhabited them. The essence was eternal, the bodies ephemeral, and flesh would morph to copy the fire.

The Lokapalas, all together again. It had been a while.

But the real jewel was the fourth person who passed through the door into Sam's pub. A beautiful young woman whose essence shined like summer sun through an open window. As had the rest of them, she had worn many bodies and many names. She'd still been Madeleine, when she and Sam had been lovers, centuries ago; Mostly she was known as the Goddess Kali, though for a time, she had also been Brahma; she had been called Murga, and claimed by Yama as his daughter. She was never that. They had been married once, Yama Dharma and Kali, the two deathgods. That hadn't ended so well.

Later, Kali, in her aspect as Brahma, had been mortally wounded at the Battle of Khaipur. Yama had tried to save her, using the body transfer machineries. There had been a problem, and a severe injury to Kali's psyche during the transfer. She had lost who she was.

That was then. But now?

Sam's smile was a large as it got.

"Hello, Sam," the young woman said.

"Kali. Nice to have you back."

"Good to be here. But I wouldn't have minded staying where I spent some time."

Sam nodded. He was one of two people in the room—in the world—who had reason to know that.

Yama said, "So, Sam, got time to perform a wedding?"

"Sure. When?"

"Now is good. It's been a long engagement."

Sam laughed.

Kali moved over to stand by Yama. She took his hand in hers.

A wedding. Two deathgods about to be joined by Buddha. What an interesting thing, life was.

Kubera said something, his voice so soft it was almost inaudible, but Sam caught it:

"The Lokapalas are never defeated."

No, in the long run, they never were. . .

Nights in the Gardens of Blue Harbor

by Gerald Hausman

Roger rarely spoke of literary matters. But we always talked about metaphysics, and quite often, martial arts. Once he told me he had done battle with a daemon. When I asked, "Spiritual?" He said, "No, the kind of daemons I've written about."

Another time he told me he'd moved a manuscript of his, metaphysically, from the bottom of a pile to the top. This was early in his career, he said. Usually his hand-written messages ran like this: "We did not know that the guinea pig—Cassiopeia—we'd acquired was pregnant. We walked out to the kitchen 5 nights ago to find she'd had 3 babies. (They're born with full suits of fur, eyes open, & the ability to whistle & run around—which I guess we already said.) Anyway. . ."

Well, that was Roger. But one day in May 1995, he phoned to say that he'd had a curious dream. It was about a novel I should write. Before I could ask any questions he laid out the story on the phone. There were no specific details as to the events, but he was certain about the place where it had to happen: Jamaica. He then mentioned that James Bond as portrayed by Sean Connery should make several appearances, each of them dream-like. He also asked me to put in some other characters from the oldest Bond films, the ones shot in Jamaica in the 60s.

Roger described the main character: "He should be a writer with a problem, a quest. The quest is finding some kind of treasure." Literary, sculptural, or perhaps a chest of gold? Roger said it could be any of those. He believed there should be a martial arts scene or two, perhaps something from long-ago. When I said, "How about Jamaican stick fighting?" and told him how it came from the time of Robin Hood, he said, "That's good." Then: "Maybe the guy is an older man, maybe a trifle lazy." I hastened to ask if he should like ganja, and he said, "Sure, they have that in plentiful supply, don't they?"

Roger's brief outline was shelved. I guess I was saddened by his death to the point where I didn't want to deal with that last phone conversation. All in all, I think I was waiting for a sign. I had that sign the other day, and so the story comes forward, and next, a bit later, I hope, the whole novel.

Chinkweed

Jed raised himself up from the old four-poster that once belonged to British playwright, Noel Coward.

He smiled, lit a cigarette. In Jamaica, Jed smoked Rothmans, in keeping with the British mood of the place, which was not so run down as it was haunted.

Duppy house, Jamaicans called it. Ghost house.

Jed took a drag, stared at the postcard-perfect coastline. The meeting place, over the years, of Errol Flynn, Ian Fleming, Katherine Hepburn, Mick Jagger, Keith Richards, not to mention just up the road, Bob Marley. Anyone who was someone had stayed at Coward's Blue Harbor.

His cell phone buzzed.

"Hell-oooh," he crooned.

"And there you are!" Jed's agent, Marcia.

Bad news when she called—*lately*. Perhaps because they'd broken up—*recently*. Fortunately, she was still his agent.

"What's up?"

"Well, I don't have *good* news," she began.

"I'll take bad then."

"Well, Doubleday went cold on the book."

"You said they *loved* it."

"Phoebe loved it. But she left. Nadia got it then and was warming to it when I told her there might be a film option, then she lost her job and I had to deal with Maggie someone who doesn't care for your kind of writing, or so she said."

"So the deal's off—what now?"

"Okay, so this may not be *believable*, but it might be *bankable*."

"I'm listening. Better be. I'm broke. You're the one who told me to fly down here and write three more chapters, just three. . ."

Marcia went on. "I have a client who's writing a book about the London art scene circa 1940. This super-rich client is also the owner of Handsel & Bradley Gallery. The long and short is, he owns a sculpture. . . half a body. . . sculpted by Noel Coward. Ever hear of him?"

"*Heard* of him? *I sleep in his bed!*"

Marcia ignored the remark. "You find the missing half of that sculpture and there'll be a fat reward, from which I'll subtract my skinny commission, and you'll get—"

"—The rest. And who'll pay the hotel bill? I'm already in debt down here."

"I just paid your AmEx bill in full. You should be OK."

"An advance. Hmm. But what if I don't find the sculpture?"

"You'll write a story about *trying* to find it. I'll sell *that* to a magazine. In fact, I already have one interested."

*

After Jed got off the phone, he sank back into Mr. Coward's four-poster bed.

The morning breeze had nutmeg in it and he wondered what kind of luck he was falling into. A salvage job wasn't exactly his thing. But being in Jamaica in the middle of a merciless Manhattan winter was. Snooping around the premises for a half-a-sculpture might not be half-bad.

He tugged on his old pair of running shorts, went downstairs. Breakfast was ackee and saltfish, the Jamaican national dish. Ackee, that curious fruit that was also a vegetable. The coffee was fresh-ground Blue Mountain. Not low blue, as they say, but high blue, the flavor register measured by the height of the mountain range above Kingston.

After breakfast, Jed rummaged around the Blue Harbor library. Most of the books were sea-salted, silverfish-eaten hardcover volumes from the 1950s. And then—just like that—Jed saw a small reddish sculpture of a man. It was about twelve inches high and ten inches wide, crudely done but not a bad sort of book end. It appeared to be a man shelling ackees with a knife.

The housekeeper, who was dusting the books, said, "Dat one by Mistah Coward. *O-rig-in-al.*"

Jed turned it over in his hands, looked it up and down. "It's crummy clay, not even fired," he said.

The housekeeper's face lit up. "Dem say if the *masteh* hand touch such work, well, it *must* worth something big!"

Jed thought: *Hell, if I had to, I could make one of these and bust it in half. But if this is an example of his art or craft, Sir Noel was wise to keep his day job.*

The bahama shutters behind the white bookcases were wide open revealing a green wicker garden. Jed poked around a bit more, picked up a science fiction novel and then called Marcia on his cell phone. "Tell me something, Marsh, is it the top or the bottom part of the body I'm looking for?"

"Mmm. Don't know. Call you back. Just keep looking, will you?"

"I'll be here. . . or there," he started to say, but she clicked off. She was as fast on the phone as he was on the computer. And who knows when she'd get back to him.

The day oozed by. He hung around the old, empty hotel dreaming of lunch.

He wasn't disappointed. Lunch was toasted Jamaican hard dough sandwiches, crusts cut-off, and filled with a rusty substance called Solomon Gundy. A kind of delicious, odd peppery mackerel spread. He imagined Elizabethan sailors chomping it down on hardtack. Anything fish he liked. This was no exception. The crustless bread amused him. *Should I call it luncheon from now on?*

After eating he strolled the perimeters of the estate, all nine and a half acres. Sea beach on one side, jungle on the other. The middle part was a grove of disease-resistant Maypan coconut trees mixed in, here and there, with some Jamaica talls, those sinuous, slender beauties that suggest the South Seas. He came at last to a small blue natural spring. He was staring into its depths when a graybeard dreadlock stepped out of a curtain of vines and stuck something under Jed's nose.

"Smell dat, mon!"

Jed took a wary sniff. "What is it?"

"Ganja gum," he said. The whites of his eyes were bloodshot and he smelled of stale smoke.

"Want some?"

"I have enough problems."

"You doesn't know what *problems is*. You want white lady?"

Jed knew what white lady was. Cocaine.

"No thanks, man."

"What you want, mon?" the elder asked.

"I want to make a half into a whole," Jed said with a smile.

"You need a natural mystic fe dat," the man said.

Then he turned swiftly and faded into the bush.

*

Jed decided the science fiction novel could wait and he spent the rest of the day reading Noel Coward's play *Blithe Spirit*. It was a comedy about a ghost, owing a nod to Shakespeare and a bow to Roman comedy. He liked it. It was just about as perky and perhaps as piquant as the Solomon Gundy he had for lunch.

He was fifty pages into the play, sitting upright in a wicker chair, when he drifted off.

*

In the dream, if that's what it was, he saw Sean Connery at the blue spring. First it was the old Rastaman and then he melted away and morphed into Connery. It was the young rakish Connery of *Doctor No*. He looked into Jed's eyes and asked, "Are you a stick fighter then?"

*

Jed woke up, wet with sweat. No, it had rained a little and the sea breeze had borne some droplets in upon him. He looked around and saw an alcove he'd missed before. Jed knew at once that Noel Coward had sculpted there. It was entirely out of the rain, and though the almond trees

127

were dripping, that corner of the veranda was dry. *Blithe Spirit* was wet, he, Jed was wet, the corner was dry. He made a note of it. Then he heard the cook call him to dinner. She banged a bread pan with her palm.

Dinner was even more delectable than lunch. Fried fish and bammy, banana fritters for dessert, more Blue Mountain coffee for a finish. The first tree frogs chimed. The sun set behind the distant John Crow mountains. Jed felt perfectly at peace except for one thing.

Am I the only guest? Does anyone else ever come here? Why do I keep falling asleep? Even now I already feel the desire to crawl into the sleigh bed upstairs and drift off.

The housekeeper appeared. Her name was Pansy. The cook, a large woman named Julie, came out of the kitchen and Jed fussed over her cooking, saying it was the best food he'd ever eaten. He wasn't lying. Pansy, an out of work schoolteacher, told a few little stories about Coward and company. And then, as softly as it had begun, night came on with the exclamations of croaker lizards and tree frogs with their three-beat symphony. They had a regular thing going—sing, hesitate, sing again. The croakers clanked in between. A little farther down the hill the sea gathered shells and spread them around, and then retreated, returned, did it again. *Hypnotic kinesis*, Jed thought. *A circadian rhythm designed to slow you down. Or something else. Maybe to put you in a different place altogether. Whatever it is, I'm helpless to resist it.*

Pansy offered Jed a delicate crystal glass of sorrel wine, saying that Mr. Coward liked it, a little bit. Jed didn't. He liked the Appleton's Reserve rum that was sitting unattended on the sideboard. There was a full rack of Noel Coward recordings. He tried one of them. And sat sipping the five-star rum while listening to Coward's high-toned, humorous carolings.

A painting above the sideboard caught Jed's eye. It was what used to be called "primitif." A portrait in oil of a woman dancing calypso style. Her hair was done in a colorful Jamaican head-wrap. The hotel reeked of bygone times, moldy memories. But the good rum made up for it. Jed thought, *There are no more sculptures in the dining room or the downstairs*

128

veranda. Just that one red clayey hand-me-down. And how the hell am I going to find anything when I just fall asleep all the time?

He was feeling the resonance of the rum warm him head to toe.

A small white owl flew into the almond trees.

Jed blinked, and just like that, he dropped off, sound asleep, glass in hand.

*

Bond again. Or rather, Connery. "Care to have a go, old man?"

Jed stiffened. But there in his right hand was a bamboo pole. Stout and strong, and smooth except for the ridges.

"I do this, now and again, to stay in shape. How about you?"

Against his better judgment, Jed gripped the bamboo. Then he held it before him, horizontally, left hand at one end, right hand at the other. He seemed, in the dream, to know what he was doing, and he smiled at the ease with which he raised the pole straight above his head. He held it there for a moment. Connery did the same.

Then, without a moment's hesitation, Connery swung his pole forward with his right hand. It was an easy, loose and looping arc. Jed brought his pole down to protect his face, but too late. Connery's bamboo caught him on the chin. It was a bone-connecting knock.

"That's one," Connery said, smiling.

*

Jed woke with a start, rubbing his chin.

A teak-faced man wearing a 1930s porkpie hat sat in the wicker sofa in front of him. "I'm Mackie," he said, offering his hand, "manager of Blue Harbor."

"What's to manage?"

Mackie laughed. "Are you enjoying your stay at Blue Harbor?" His voice was deep, soothing.

"I wouldn't quite call it a *stay*. Maybe a *snooze*."

Mackie smiled. He had beautiful teeth. His sailcloth shirt was pressed as were his slacks. Even his penny loafers were shined.

"Keep a likkle one eye open when you sleep," Mackie warned. "So the duppy dem don't dream you away."

Jed was about to ask what he meant by that when Pansy said on the stairs that the bed was turned down, that is, if he wished to sleep lying down rather than sitting up. *Or standing up*, Jed thought.

"Soon come," Mackie said. He got up and was gone.

Jed tossed back the rest of his rum. Pansy was at the foot of the stairs.

"Where are all the guests?" Jed asked.

"Them soon come."

Jed went upstairs and took a cold shower. But the moment he stepped out of it, he felt heavy again. *They should call this place Sleep Harbor.*

Later, reading *Blithe Spirit*, he was gone again.

When he woke, the moon was high in the sky. Pansy had turned off the reading light.

Jed looked about the room. A shadow rippled across the floor. A floorboard squeaked. The shadow froze. The wind rustled the poinciana tree.

The shadow flowed across the floor and stopped at the bed.

"Who is it?" Jed said, the back of his neck all prickly.

The figure started, bolted.

Jed put both feet on the floor, ran to the veranda.

There was a man standing in the moonlight. He was ragged and small with narrow shoulders. There was something lopsided about him. He had a bamboo pole in his hands. He threw it hard at Jed.

It struck him on the point of his left elbow.

Jed ran at him, his left hand dangling, his body off-balance.

He watched as the dark shape leaped into the moonlight.

Like mercury the man spilled into the air off the second-story veranda.

He dropped twenty feet, landed without a sound, disappeared.

Jed felt a painful tingling in his elbow where he'd been bonked.

Then Mackie came up the stairs, as if nothing had happened.

"You see that?" Jed demanded.

"Him get away," Mackie said.

"Get a good look at him?"

"No, mon."

Mackie stared into the moonlit almond leaves, neither curious nor uncurious, possibly amused.

"What was he doing?" Jed asked Mackie.

"What them do all the while."

"What's that?"

"Them duppy. Them do what them want fe do."

Mackie looked at Jed. "Blood fire the Rass. You haff money inna de safe?"

"Safe?"

"Mr. Coward safe. Inna de closet."

Jed said, "I have a few traveler's checks."

"Mek we lock dem," Mackie said. There was no amusement in his face now.

Mackie went through the open double doors of the bedroom, clicked open the louvered door in the hall. "Mr. Coward safe in 'ere," he said.

"Mr. Coward is safe in there?" Jed asked.

"No, mon," Mackie replied. "Me say there *is* a safe in there. Belong to Mr. Coward long time back."

Jed opened the top dresser drawer by the bed and felt around under his socks for the folder of traveler's checks. He found them. He brought it to Mackie who was kneeling under a bare light bulb in the stale-smelling closet.

The safe was ancient. It looked like it had spent all of its life underwater. Mackie fingered the combination, the heavy door groaned, opened.

There was a black flashlight, flaked with rust. The kind of solid cop flashlight made in the 1950s. A bright beam of light poked out of it. Otherwise the safe was empty. There was nothing in it except that ancient flashlight, beam on.

"Did you look in here earlier?" Jed asked.

"No, mon."

131

"Does anyone at Blue Harbor know the combination besides you?"

"No, mon."

"What the—?"

"Yah, mon," Mackie said. "Duppy work dis."

"Old Blue Harbor," Mackie continued as he punched the button on the flashlight. The beam went dead. Mackie turned it on again; it lighted. Shaking his head, he shrugged. "Whole heap a thing happen 'ere. Bob Marley him seh, 'Everyting haffa season, find de reason.' But not here. No reason fe ting an ting at Blue Harbor."

"Why?" Jed asked.

"De duppy dem," Mackie said. He glanced at Jed to make sure he understood. Switching off the closet light, he asked—"You can sleep?"

"Maybe not tonight."

Mackie dug into the top pocket of his shirt. He handed Jed a tightly rolled spliff that smelled of. . . blueberries?

"Special blem," he said, and lit it. He dragged deep, offered it to Jed who did the same. After two good draws, Jed returned the spliff to Mackie, stuck a Rothman in his mouth, but forgot to light it.

"How do they make that herb, Mackie?"

"Dem grow with all kinda berry. A real roots mix."

Jed was marveling at the buzz but, as much as that, the flavor. Blueberry pancakes, a morning in Maine when he was a boy. "What's it go for. . . on the market?"

"No market dis." Mackie laughed. "I know the Chinaman what make it. Him do nuff experiment with fruit and honey and ting. When him sure him have it right, then him sell to big time rapper from a-foreign. Shaggy did smoke dis. Me see him."

"So how much would he pay, if he were paying?"

"For dis one spliff?"

"For, say, a pound. . ."

That made Mackie's eyes roll. He took a sweet suck of the berry-spliff, exhaled slowly through his nose, said: "The cost of a BMW."

"New?"

"Paint still wet."

Jed suddenly felt the need to sit down, as if his legs weren't there, as if sitting was the only way he could talk. The Jamaican undertaker's breeze, as they called it, raked across the island. Jed was soaking with sweat. But he felt like jogging up Firefly Hill, 1700 feet above Blue Harbor.

"You good, mon?" Mackie asked.

"*Real* good," Jed replied.

On the coffee table between the two wicker chairs, there was a crude cedarwood sculpture of a man toting bananas on his head. Jed's elbow still tickled with hurt. Reminding him that he'd been struck hard by a bamboo pole. *Or did I just imagine it?*

"Do duppies throw things?"

Mackie laughed again. "Dem can do what we can do. Only dem do it better, faster. Sometime you don' see dem. Sometime you do, and dem fix you wid dem eye.

Sweet-Sweet, the old man sing Calypso song dem. Him bewitch by duppy. Like dem say, "Him take a drink of 'gone fe good oil'—and him gone."

"What do you mean *gone?*"

"Him turn fool."

"And *stay* fool?"

"Yah, mon."

For a little while there was silence between them while Jed sorted through his thoughts. The herb had put a soft blur on the night, but he was feeling things and seeing things. A croaker lizard was wedged up into the corner of the roof. Jed watched it, as if it might suddenly speak to him.

Hanging upside down was a ratbat. A relative, Jed mused, of the South American vampire bat. *Could be a duppy?*

"Duppies can change into things?"

Mackie smiled. "Change from crab to dog. From dog to cat. From cat to bat and from bat to lizard." Then he laughed, walked to the edge of the veranda, and spat into the night.

Jed glanced at the ceiling. The croaker with the liquid eyes was gone. So was the ass-pointed-to-heaven ratbat. He went to the edge of the veranda and spat the way Mackie did. It took a long, long time for his spit to hit the ground, and when it did it smacked pretty loud.

Mackie took a swing at something.

Jed jumped, involuntarily. "Something there?"

"Nothing to worry you, mon. Just a likkle bat."

"You mean that ratbat that was perched up *there?*"

"No, mon. The bat that was just *here*, between us."

"I didn't see any bat between us."

Mackie's eyes sparkled. He grinned. "We call dem ting you call moth, bat."

Jed laughed. "What do you call frog?"

"Toad."

"What do you call toad?"

"Frog."

Jed shook his head. "I see."

For a while after that the two men sat in silence. Jed enjoyed the cross-island breeze. Cool but not too cool. The night's pulse quickened. It was coming near dawn. The sky was beginning to get red up the coast on the way to Port Antonio.

Jed was drowning in waves of thoughts, one after another.

The facts: someone was here tonight. Someone got into the locked safe and left a flashlight on and closed the door, and got past me, and then struck me with a bamboo pole and leaped off the veranda, some twenty feet, and landed silently and got away without so much as a dog's bark. How had the thief gotten in? And out? And the flashlight? The fact: he, or it, was invisible. No, visible, then invisible, then visible, then invisible.

Jed woke. The dawn had come and gone with the fog on little cat's feet. There was a tiny bit of spliff in the ashtray. Jed got his lighter. He lit and sucked the mystic berries down into his lungs. And exhaled for what seemed to be minutes. The smoke came out of everywhere. His ears, his feet, his fingertips. *I smell like a blueberry pancake.*

A croaker lizard clacked once from some obscure tree. A flock of tiny green pocket parrots chittered overhead. *What if I should live here? I mean, permanently.*

He stood up, head-rush, wobbled to the four-poster. Fell like a castaway walking land for the first time. Slept. Gently sea-tugged, forward, backward, side to side, in the surf of unknown dreams.

*

He was awake.

"Hello?"

"Did I wake you?"

"No, I had to get the phone."

"Funny. And how are *you?*"

"A bit groggy."

"All grog maketh Jed a dull bog."

"Clever."

"Stephen Wright. Any news on the *finding front?*"

"No. But someone's stalking me," Jed said.

"An herb stalk, perhaps? You sound stoned."

"What if I am?"

Marcia chuckled. "Well, how's it going? Really. . ."

"I think someone's trying to kill me or at least rob me."

She didn't say anything. Then, "We're not paranoid, are we?"

"You were going to tell me which half of the sculpture I'm supposed to look for."

"Lay off the ganja, will you? It makes you crazy. You're jumpy and I'm sleepy. I was up all night working on someone's script. Why don't you writers learn how to write? I have news. My client owns the top half of the sculpture; he wants you to find the bottom half."

"How large is the sculpture?"

Marcia sighed. "He said it could sit comfortably on a book shelf. I have a photograph of it for you. Now listen. This man's really rich. And very much preoccupied with obtaining the bottom half of this sculpture.

There's a bit of a story here. My client knew Noel Coward. Knew him well enough to spend months at a time down there at Blue Bayou—"

"Blue Harbor."

"Uhuh. So—to make a long story longer, my client not only knew Mr. Coward back in the day, but he also knew the subject of the sculpture. It's a portrait, you see. A life study, or whatever, of a young, very cute island boy."

"—And I'm to find his bottom?"

"In a manner of speaking. OK. Gotta go."

A few minutes later, Jed got a picture on his cell. The youth in clay—naked, handsome. And there were a half dozen locals around Blue Harbor who could've been him. . . once upon a time.

Dream away, ganja brain. . .

I'm actually getting a little buzz off the idea that I might be able to solve it. What if I should find the bottom half of the upper half, bringing the two together and making one exactly as the client desires? How much would that be worth? And, if I don't like the price—considering I'm here and he's there—maybe I'll disappear for a while and sort of ransom the thing. All I need is a little help from Mr. Bond. Find it first. Then ransom it. Then spend the next forty years down here inhaling blueberry pancakes.

*

Slept then, sitting up in the familiar wicker, thinking: this has to be Noel Coward's favorite chair. The indent in the seat, the curve at the back. Curiously, Jed's ass configured perfectly to the indents.

The long sprawl of dragon coast and the first glimmer of fireflies—blinkies, they call them in Jamaica. Or peenywallies, the ones that stream and gleam as they go jazzing through the darkness.

Jed was smoking the second blueberry spliff Mackie gave him. Veils of delectable smoke. Hint of rain. Patter of drops. Scent of salt. And humus. Then the downpour turning day into night and the raindrops ricocheting off the metal roof and the feeling of nausea fading and the stability of iron rain turning everything to gloss, the almond leaves shining, nodding, dancing in the mad wind off the rugged rocky coast. Snowy breakers thudding on the reef.

*

For the first time it doesn't feel like a dream. Probably because it isn't. It's something else.

Noel Coward with a bath towel wrapped and tied with a string of pandana vine around his waist. Someone beside him, someone else beside *him*. Somehow I am aware the dark-haired one is Cole Leslie, and the boyish one next to him is Graham Payne, Mr. Coward's friends and lovers.

They are each similarly toweled.

Mr. Coward looks up when he sees me. His cat's eyes are piercingly serene. The other two look surprised to see me here, there, here, wherever it is I am. They're planting something. A small body. I stare at it. A stillborn creature in fetal crouch.

I am trying to see through the rain, but the rain is blinding.

*

I wake—or think I do.

I'm no longer in the night gardens of Blue Harbor; I am back in the trusty four-poster. How did I get here? I turn and face the open doorway through which I can just barely make out the dawning sea. The croakers have stopped shrieking. A flock of West Indian grackles is jabbering in a Jamaica tall.

I feel small fingers combing my hair. Turn and see, a little girl, naked, rain soaked, wavy wet hair down to her ankles. Playfully, she throws her hair over her face and body. Now she is a curtain of tresses. She comes close. She parts her hair, so that just her nose sticks out, nothing else.

She shimmers, goes ivory, goes gray, goes away into the ozone-filled air of mist and pearl. In her place I see the figure of a model, a very lovely model, blonde, naked, golden skin peppered with tiny beads of silver rain.

On second glance, she's not completely nude. She wears a man's heavy leather belt upon which a sheath hides part of one shapely hip. A bone-

137

handled knife graces the top of the sheath and makes the woman's hip that much more noticeable.

"Cut! That's a wrap!"

The woman is Honeychile Rider from the film *Doctor No*.

It's a movie set and I am set in it, and no one can see me; nor can I see myself.

Honey's personal assistant courteously covers her with a terrycloth robe.

Where's Bond?

I look at my arm. It's covered with hair. I've not said a word but I know I have a Scottish accent.

*

At breakfast, Julie listened to Jed's weird tale of the night before. She had the guileless ease of all Jamaican listeners, who hear someone else's story as if it were their own.

"You're not crazy, you just see a duppy is all."

Jed watched her put before him a white plate of green calaloo, a boiled banana and hot fried johnnycake. Jed folded into the food.

"What color she is?" Julie asked as he began to eat.

"The little girl? Blue, I think. Yeah, blurry and bluish."

"Oh," Julie said with a shake of the head, "That remind me—your coffee! Soon be back."

The calaloo tasted like fresh spinach, without the bitterness of spinach. The boiled bananas weren't the sweet kind from the States, but rather the hard green kind that are boiled to the softness of a potato. It was all savory beyond belief, and Jed left not a single crumb.

"Is blue, you say?" Julie folded her arms, shifted her heavy frame to one leg that she placed at a right angle to her left foot, as if she were about to dance.

"You touch dis duppy?"

"No."

"What is that there on your arm?"

Jed shrugged. "Bumped into something the other night."

"Duppy do that?"

A gravelly voice answered her—Mackie leaning quietly against the doorjamb. He was wearing an expensive freshly ironed, lime-colored fisherman's shirt.

"Him get likkle bonks, Julie."

"Duppy dat?"

"Tief mon duppy!"

"What de rass!" Julie said, then she and Mackie burst out laughing. Then Julie covered her mouth, shook her head. "Reverend give me grief when I say sintin like dat."

Mackie's laughter followed her as she left the dining room and disappeared into the kitchen.

"Is *rass* so bad a word?" Jed asked.

Mackie nodded. "Nuh suppose to use a word like that. It mean ass. *Rass clot, bumba clot*, dem is all bad word."

Mackie gave him a short glass with a milky substance in it.

"What's this?"

"Aloe. Good for evry likkle ting, ya know. Dem call it sinkle bible. I mix it with fresh, warm cow's milk, likkle honey and one egg."

Jed took it down in one swallow. "You mean a lot of honey."

"Sinkle Bible mean Single Bible cause dem use it for every single ting. Good medicine."

"Chase wey de duppy dem?" Jed asked.

Mackie laughed. "When you learn patois?"

"Listening to you and Julie and Pansy."

"Not bad," he said with a grin. "Good fe right 'ere, inna de belly. OK. Soon come."

He returned a moment later with a finger-length of aloe. It was dripping green.

"Put dis on your elbow."

"I won't say that aloe-milk tasted good, Mackie."

"No, mon. Me seh, good fe *you*. Me no seh good fe you *taste*. But I like it."

Jed daubed the oozing aloe on his elbow. The scrape darkened, purplish.

"Good fe hair, too," Mackie said. "Is why dem call it "one Bible, ya know. Good for all that ail you."

"What's ailing me right now is the duppies. Last night I saw a strange little blue girl, Mr. Coward and two of his friends. . . and the actress who played Honeychile Rider in the movie *Doctor No.* Not one of these phantoms was real, right, Mackie?"

"No, mon. Dem was real."

"I dreamed them, Mackie, after smoking ganja."

"No, mon. *Them dream you.*"

Jed shook his head, shrugged.

"Look," Mackie said. "Inna dreamtime, there's no past, no future. Just what is, is."

"I get that. But you just said they dreamed *me*. How?"

"Dem pull you into their world."

"So. . .what you're saying is, their world is going on all the time, just like this one."

"Yah, mon. Just the same."

Jed thought about this for a moment. "My agent wants me to stop smoking ganja and find a buried treasure. Something hidden here on the property. Maybe I'm not supposed to be messing around in such stuff. Maybe that's why I'm being haunted like this."

"Duppy no dead," Mackie said. "Dem live just like we. Maybe you s'posed to find the treasure an ting."

"Others have looked?"

"Everybody look. Since the time of Henry Morgan. Him place him cannon on the point, y'know." Mackie aimed his finger at the rocky cliff towards the double bend in the road towards Port Maria. "And him bury nuff gold on Cabarita Island and on Firefly Hill."

"Mackie, do I look like a man who is looking for something?"

Julie came into the dining room and set down a small plate of sliced naseberry.

Mackie smiled. "Me love dat fruit, ya know."

Julie said, "Me know, Mackie. Blue Mountain?"

Jed nodded. "Best coffee in the world."

Mackie smiled again. "Blue Mountain have no acid. No other coffee like that. That why Japan buy up the whole of our mountainside."

"And charge twenty dollars a cup," Jed said as he took a sip.

"Maybe your treasure is just some bag of bean from Blue Mountain."

"At least I won't go home empty-handed."

An hour later, he was still thinking of Honeychile Rider as he sucked down his ninth cup of coffee.

*

But that day Jed worked.

Spent the morning and afternoon going systematically through each of the villas. The piano studio, which was now a suite of bedrooms. The guest cottage by the sea. The main house. Villa Rose, Villa Chica, Villa Grande, as they were called by the present owners of Blue Harbor.

It was all sweat, bother, and foolishness. The Coward sculpture, the blithe-spirited, bottom-end, nowhere to be seen. And there were attics and trunks and sea chests and wicker hampers from ancient days. He and Mackie wetted themselves up good, came out smutted with cobwebs and cricket skeletons—but no truncated sculptures.

A friend of Mackie's named Raggy turned up with the original blue print for the main house, Villa Grande, but that yielded little more than crawl spaces not made for humans. The slumbering dust of the Forties slumbered on.

Raggy, as it turned out, was a charming ragamuffin of indeterminate age who had a typical Jamaican passion for lost treasure. He spoke about the plastic bags that washed up on the beach one day. "Enough cocaine me did see in them bag!" Another drug deal gone sour on the sea. A man's hand turned up the following day. There was just enough wrist on it for a Rolex. The barracudas had hit the hand and the watch, but the watch was the better for it.

"What about the coke—what happened to that?" Jed asked Raggy.

141

He flashed a gold tooth and said, "That man, Pirate, y'know, him live down yonder? Him get to the coke last, but the first man there, him think that white dust is house plaster, and him paint the inside of his shack with it. Me see a whole heap of thing at 'old Blue Harbor, mon."

"Ghosts?"

"Y'mean duppy dem? Yah, mon. Many a dem. You?"

Jed lit a Rothman. "A few."

"Y'see de likkle girl?"

"Just the other night."

Raggy accepted a Rothman from Jed. He sucked on it hard. Smoke plumed from his nose. He chuckled. "Her a dead, that likkle one. Her seem like a living. But she dead."

"You ever see Mr. Coward?"

"Mr. Coward, now," Raggy said, cackling. "That mon an old pirate from dem time."

"He was a great playwright."

Raggy nodded, blew smoke, said, "Yes, him do dem ting. Him was talent. Him was a batty mon."

"A batty man?"

"A batty man. A gay," Mackie explained. "Dem do ting dem should not do."

"That should nah go happen," Raggy added, shaking his head.

"But it 'oppen," Mackie said. He cleared his throat, spat in the grass.

For a while the three listened to the sea pound the coral heads. The dark shadow of a John Crow rode a thermal and rippled over the lawn, disappearing over by Reef Point.

Mackie said, "There are four brother that work this property long ago."

"One a dem was Mr. Coward special helper," Raggy said.

"Special? How?"

"Him was handsome—"

"—handsome to pieces," Raggy added.

"An that one bwai was the model for Mr. Coward and his artist friends."

"Nothing wrong with that," Jed offered.

"But them mek that bwai undress. Him model wid no clothes."

"Did Mr. Coward do a sculpture of this boy you're talking about?"

Raggy's eyes flickered. "You haff only fe see David on the street today fe know how many time he did model fe dem."

"Why do you say that? Is he still so good looking?"

"No, mon. Him always dead drunk. Stoned on hundred proof white rum. David haff him living wage til death do him part, but him all ready dead. A walking dead."

"Did you ever see a sculpture of David?" Jed asked looking first at Raggy, then at Mackie. But Mackie looked away and Raggy just laughed. Tossed his head back and laughed. Then he grew serious and his eyes glittered again. "Ya want-y?"

"That sculpture? Yes, very much."

"Me a go show ya, mon. But me seh right now dat ting bruck."

"Bruck?"

Raggy smiled. "Yuh noh speak patois?" He laughed. "Me seh bruck."

"That mean broken," Mackie said, still looking into the far distance of the reef, and beyond to the hills of Port Antonio.

"You mean, like half of it. . . you know where half of it is?"

Searching my eyes, Raggy frowned. "No treasure dat, mon." Then: "Get your swimsuit."

Jed went up to his room on the second floor of Villa Grande. He undressed and slipped on his bathing suit. His hands, he noticed, were shaking a little. *Whatever this is, it could be it. So calm down and let it happen. Could be nothing. Could be something. Could be a whole lot of something.*

*

The day dragged. Raggy did not show.

Finally Mackie came " up top" as he called the second story veranda. Jed was reading *Blithe Spirit* again, the pages rattling in the sea wind. Mackie had a friend with him and it wasn't Raggy; it was a small Chinese guy.

143

"This is Chinkweed," Mackie said. "I told him you like his herb."

"You make the blueberry?"

The little man laughed. "I am the one," he said. "You like it?"

"I love it. There's nothing like it in the world."

"You should have more then."

"I could never afford it," Jed told him.

The three of them sat down in the wicker chairs overlooking the long, wave-crested coastline. Chinkweed handed a paperbag to Jed, who accepted it with surprise. He looked inside, and the aroma of a summer morning in Maine hit him in the face. It was redolent beyond belief. It surrounded the three men and enveloped them in succulence and the sea could not take it away; the sea could not even put a dent in the overwhelming essence of that tingling blueberry herb.

"I don't know what to say," Jed said. "No one's ever given me anything like this."

Chinkweed smiled beatifically. He put his palms together. "It is the healing of the nations," he said. "I was with Bob, you know, during his last big tour. I was there in New York when he collapsed. I was with him when he bravely stepped on stage in Pittsburgh. His last concert. I make this holy herb as a sacrament, a gesture of goodwill to the world. Mackie says you are a good person. That is all. Some pay. Some don't have to pay. It is that simple."

The treasure was in Jed's hands, in the paper bag, and he knew that no matter what else happened this day, this was quite enough. This *was* the healing of nations, the blessing on high. There was nothing more to say, so the three of them, smoked some, talked some, listened some, and after a while no one said anything.

Jed closed his eyes. . . .

*

Robin Hood stepped quickly and cut a good staff of ground oak, straight, without flaw, and six feet in length, and came away trimming the tender stems from it. Jed trimmed his own staff of light bamboo. Robin saw him, furtively. He was a broad fellow, Robin was, many palms across the chest. "I will baste thy hide right merrily, my good fellow," he said, and his voice was lusty and loud and rang in the wood and a singing bird answered with a clarion call.

They circled the healing spring, once, twice, thrice.

And then Robin made a feint to one side, and then whirled his body so that he came round-about the other side, and with a soft thump, a testing blow, caught Jed in the ribs.

The move was right deft, Jed thought. But now he countered with one of his own. Lowering his staff, he quickly hopped over it, raised it up from behind so that he held it backwards behind his head, then he let go his left hand and with his right propelled the bamboo in a wide quarter-staff move that struck Robin square on the top of the head.

"Nicely done," the other said, "Well-turned. I deserved that crease."

It was then Jed knew the white-toothed smile, the narrow mustache, the broad shouldered heft of the man before him. It was Erroll Flynn.

But it didn't matter who he was any more than who Jed was in this instance. They were now in the business of warding blows. A crack on the crown here, a bump and a bash there, a tumble and roll and spin. Once Jed tripped into the spring and saw the mother of that water, a mermaid. She was lovelier than life though with the teeth of a fish as well as the breasts of a woman, and she wished to do her business upon him. He popped out of the spring and sought his staff. Flynn had it and tossed it to him in a friendly way.

Their heads hummed as the cudgels stroked the hours, and hours. They tired, breathed heavily. Yet they kept on, and on. Until, in the end, Flynn said—"Breathes there a man twixt here and Canterbury Town who could do the like to me that thou hast done!"

They were both on all fours when he said it. And so Erroll Flynn stood up, hands on hips and grinned at the sun.

And a voice broke the silence—"Cut!"

*

Jed woke with a shudder. Raggy was there.

145

"Bring your wetsuit and follow me now," he said as he turned to go down the stairs.

Jed peeked into his bedroom and saw the solitary, priceless bag on the bureau.

Down on the rocky beach, the wind was from the west. Jed wormed his way into his one-ply neoprene wetsuit. Raggy had only a ragged pair of cutoffs equal to his name. They swam in the heavy surf out toward the reef, battered by swells and pasted with seaweed torn loose from the sandy bottom.

Nearing the reef, Raggy pointed to the rock cliff just below the Blue Harbor garage. The building was in such bad repair, the back end of it, from this angle, seemed ready to slide off the cliff.

"We haffa get to the cliff," Raggy shouted over the boom of the waves. Then, jerking his snorkel away from his mouth and off to the side of his head, he added, "That's the easy part."

"What's the hard part?" Jed asked.

"The cliff."

They treaded water for a little more, then Raggy headed for the limestone drop-off.

Raggy led the way between the greenish coral heads. He was quick as a fish. But when they reached the base of the cliff, Jed saw that it was a sheer fifty feet of vertical rock. Seagrape sprang from every crack and made the climb look impossible.

"We climb up," Raggy said matter-of-factly. "Use the withe dem fe hold on. Pull yuhself up. No problem."

The withes were vines, a tapestry of them, woven in and around the seagrapes.

He told Jed to go first. "You fall, me a go catch." Raggy laughed at his own joke.

Jed hooked his mask and snorkel to the light weight belt he wore. The belt equalized the buoyancy of the suit, but now it was extra weight he didn't need.

Hand over hand, Jed crept up, a little at a time. There were ledges for footholds and the roots of the seagrape and the withes for grasping. A small amount of slippage slowed them down. Small rocks tumbled off the cliff-face as they ascended. A white bird shot away from a fissure that widened into a big crack as they neared the top of the cliff. *It's this very crack that's sucking the garage into oblivion.*

When they almost were up to the crumbled foundation of the building, Raggy said—"Dere, look dere, mon!"

Jed had the sun in his eyes. Even shading them with one hand, he couldn't see very well. "What am I looking for?"

Raggy, right beside him, elbow to elbow, held a withe and used his chin to indicate a place to the left of Jed's shoulder.

Jed squinted. The crack in the rock where Raggy nodded was a small cave.

Jed saw it then. It was coated in milk-white guano. Maybe that was what had preserved it. Anyway, it was chalky; and unmistakable. Caught in a cleft, covered in leaf trash and sea grape sticks.

In the cave shadow, it stood out. The halved torso, slim-hipped and angular. The calves muscular, feet very large, splay-toed.

The eye-catcher was of course the erect member. The half torso of a man-boy—sitting absurdly in a helter-skelter of seabird scatter, the whole thing as bright and well-preserved as could be. In fact, better than the day it was done forty years before. Nature had a hand in this. Nature had completed it.

"Want-y?" Raggy asked.

Jed nodded with a crooked smile.

Then, "Get-y," Raggy said.

For a moment, Jed felt himself suspended between his imagination and the cliff. Lightly hovering in the air, he breathed. But did little else. For, in his elation at seeing the sculpture, he'd glanced downward. The sharp rocks below beckoned. One look and all sense of gravity was gone. He gripped the vine. Held on for dear life.

I know as surely as I am not attached to anything, that I am also stoned on blueberry. That my brain is not where I am. That my mind is somewhere else, holding me up, but I don't know how. . . I am on the verge, hanging. Caught between life and death.

He pressed his cheek to the rock and imagined himself hidden from death. At the same time he saw the barracuda coming at him like a torpedo. Its upper jaw was at right angles to the lower which gave the animal a certain cruelty. No doubt, any second, it was going to strike. The sun glaring in the water-glimmer blinded him. But still, somehow, he knew he was Bond. And for that reason, he couldn't, wouldn't allow himself to die. The barracuda struck. There was a wild tearing of neoprene, and flesh. A cloud of blood obscured his sight. But now he reacted to the searing pain in his shoulder. Raising his spear gun he triggered it. The rubber thongs whammed home; so did the spear. It struck the crazed fish full in the face, dislocating its upper and lower jaws. Unable to do anything else, the barracuda tore off madly in an erratic retreat which instantly brought other silvery meat eaters, more cudas, down upon it. The blood spectacle continued. Bond would live and let die another day. He released the vine when the command, "Cut!" thundered in his water-logged ear.

Raggy was laughing—"Wanty wanty, no gety. Gety gety, no wanty."
You want it until you get it, then you don't want it.

Jed blinked in the scorching sunlight. He'd let go of the withe and was holding on to bare rock. How he was holding on was another thing.

His head rocked. His pulse throbbed.

Marcia said tonelessly, "Get the goddamn thing, you idiot!"

Then he sort of slid sideways.

Raggy had mercifully tied a withe around his waist. His body was supported by it. And he was half-in, half-out of the cave. He was so near the sculpture, he could smell it.

I can smell it. It smells like bird shit. My mind is back. I'm clear again. The blueberry taste is still in my mouth, but the rest of me is sound.

"How'd it get here, Raggy?" he heard himself say.

Raggy, always laughing, laughed again. "Miss May—her trow dat ugly sintin down de cliff."

"Who's Miss May?"

"Mr. Leonard wife."

"Who's Mr. Leonard?"

It was an odd conversation to have on cliffside after blacking, or whatever, out.

"Dem people dem was housekeeper and cook and driver fe Mr. Coward back in de old time dem. She—Miss May—still live up inna Grant's Town. Her didn't approve of David nekkid. Nor him big hood made a clay."

"Hood?"

"Yuh call dat a cock, me tink."

I worked my hand into the sticks. Much of the nest collapsed into the fissure, but Jed grabbed the best handhold there was. Then, knowing he had it securely, he began the final climb. Shoulder and elbow, foot and toe. Vine in his right hand. David's cock in the other.

The fissure had what amounted to a stairway of stone—little ledges all the way to the top. Soon they were safely there.

For a long time, Raggy and Jed just sat on the promontory, staring at the glittering sea. David's better half sat next to them.

How much history does the world need? It devours all. Eats and shits it out into the void. What's left after years and years? Some irrelevant detail, some little ledge-caught pecker of a promise from the past. Some bit of gooey memory someone can't get rid of.

Jed looked at it, disgusted with himself. Filled with loathing for his quest, his passion to find what did not want to be found. Without another thought, he kicked it over the edge of the cliff. This time it went all the way down. When it hit a coral head at the bottom, it turned into red and white smoke. One puff on the wind, and gone.

"Yah, mon," Raggy said. That was all he said. But he patted Jed on the shoulder.

*

Jed was in his favorite position—prone in the four-poster—when Marcia called that evening.

"You want the good news or the bad news?"

"There's *both?*"

"Okay, the bad: Mr. Handsel doesn't want the bottom half of the sculpture after all. I hope you haven't gone to too much trouble trying to find it—"

"Naah. And the good. . ."

"—news is. . . Karin at Doubleday wants the book."

"The book?"

"The one you're going to write about searching all over hell and gone for that priceless piece of art. She read me parts of your outline over the phone. The parts that sold her."

"But I didn't send her an outline!"

"The next thing you're going to tell me is you didn't write one. Well, there's a six-figure advance in the offing."

"Six? Are you sure?"

"As sure as I am that I wrote the outline for you."

"You—*what?*"

"I did."

Jed couldn't tell what he liked best—that she *had* or that he *hadn't*. It didn't really matter one way or another. He hated outlines, and couldn't write them. Marcia had written some of his best. . . but that was years ago.

Marcia continued to talk while Jed, still musing over the way things had turned out, gazed down the beach towards Castle Garden. Six figures would buy a lot of chinkweed.

A lone figure was walking between the rocks.

A tall shapely woman.

It was Clover, the new housekeeper.

"See you tomorrow then. I'll call you with the flight number," Marcia said. "Jed—are you still there?"

"What?—you're coming down here—*now?*"

"Tomorrow. We have to work out the terms for this thing, you know. By the way, get some sleep, will you? You sound like you've been up for 40 nights."

"Well, you only live twice."

Marcia laughed, once, said goodbye.

Jed thought, *What a good girl Marcia is. How infinitely loyal and intricately clever.*

He thought about this as Clover came up the garden path.

The Night Heirs

by Warren Lapine

The full moon rose up over the city, gloriously shining through and reflecting on the mists rising from the pavement, the only remnants of a late afternoon storm. The moon seemed enormous in that illusionary way that it can just upon rising. I would have liked to be able to enjoy the beauty of that magnificent orb, but I knew the portents. My life was about to change and I didn't want it to.

Business was good, entirely too good. I moved away from the cash register to help a slim, young woman who was fingering a wooden stake.

"Can I help you?

She looked up, a thoughtful, far away look in her eyes. "I'm not sure. I really don't know much about this, but I think I need one of these."

"Well, if you need one of those I'd also recommend that you purchase a mallet and some garlic."

"Yes," she said, her mind seemingly a million miles away, "I think I heard or read something about garlic."

"Do they sparkle?" I asked her.

"Excuse me?"

"The person you plan to use this stake on, does he or she sparkle?"

"Now that you mention it, yes I suppose he does sparkle a little bit if you look at him in just the right light."

"Then you'll also want a copy of *The Book of Mormon*."

"*The Book of Mormon?*"

I nodded, "I'm not sure why, but it seems to work better than the Bible does on the ones that sparkle."

I got her supplies together and she handed me her credit card. A moment later she walked off into the night, reflected moonlight glinting silver in her long, straight hair.

Since the store was now empty I returned to my office to watch a rerun of Neil DeGrasse Tyson's *Cosmos*. But I'd only just settled into my chair when I heard the bell on the front door chime. I walked back out into the storefront to find three very stout, very short men walking down one of the store's many aisles muttering angrily to one another.

"Can I help you, gentlemen?" All three started as if no one in a store had ever asked them if they could help them before.

"Who are you?" the largest of the three demanded.

"Vic," I said helpfully, "I own the store."

They grumbled a bit more, I thought I might have heard the words "too tall" and "pretty boy" among others. Then the biggest and clearly the leader pointed up at the wall behind me. "How much for that?"

I glanced over my shoulder. High up on the wall in a glass case was a sword gleaming much brighter than it had any right to considering how little light was actually falling upon it. I turned back to my grumpy customers. "I'm afraid that's for display only."

"Name your price," Grumpy growled.

"It's not for sale. Is there something else I could help you gentlemen with?"

A bit more grumbling and then the leader said, "We need provisions for a. . . um. . . we need to outfit for a. . ."

I decided to cut to chase and save us both some time. "Are there thirteen of you or are there seven of you?"

"That's none of your damn business," Grumpy spat at me.

"Fine, suit yourself, you'll excuse me if I don't show you the way out."

Grumpy flew into a rage. "How dare you speak to me like that. Do you know who I am? I am Thor—"

"Look, Thor," I said interrupting what I am certain would have been a marvelous monologue. "It's up to you, I don't care if you want my help or not. If there are seven of you then I'd recommend the Whistle While You Work package of mining tools. If there are thirteen of you then I'd recommend the Misty Mountain package that includes weapons and some dragon repellant."

His anger evaporated. "You have dragon repellant?"

"Guaranteed to repel dragons for up to sixteen hours per application."

"Does it work?" one of Grumpy's friends asked?

"No one has ever come back looking for a refund," I answered, smiling.

Twenty minutes later I was helping the three of them load their gear into a rather anachronistic cart pulled by two ponies and steered by an old man in a funny hat.

As I made my way back into the store the phone began to ring. I reached it on the 4th ring. "This is Vic, can I help you?"

The voice on the other end belonged to a very young girl and she sounded not quite scared, but close. "I hope so. An owl banged into my window tonight. I think it's still breathing, but I'm not really sure. But anyway, it had a message tied onto its right leg. And well, um, there's no way I can get to London in time to buy. . ." The caller's voice trailed off.

"I'm assuming you need some robes, a spell book, a wand, and other assorted things?"

"Yes," she said, brightening. "Do you have them in stock?"

"I do. Just bring your letter here tomorrow and we'll get you all fixed up."

"Wonderful, this is all so I exciting, I can hardly wait."

"Then we'll see you tomorrow, goodnight." I hung up the phone before she could say anything else.

I was happy for the kid, really I was, she was about to start a grand adventure. But right now all I could think about was how my life was about to change; and, that really, no matter how tonight turned out I couldn't imagine that my life was going to be the better for it. When I signed on for this I could never have imagined it playing out this way. But then I guess that's the secret of life: nothing ever goes as planned.

I locked the door and flipped the phone over to voice mail. I needed to think, to clear my mind for what I knew was coming. Really it had all started three years ago when Sabrina had reached out to me.

*

155

She'd called my cell, I almost never gave that number out so I was very surprised when it rang and I didn't recognize the number calling. "This is Vic, can I help you?"

"Vic, this is Sabrina."

"Sabrina?"

"Yes, you remember, Sabrina from All Saints Cemetery."

"Oh, yes, certainly." It had been twenty-five years since that night in the cemetery, but you don't forget watching the Powers duel, nor do you forget a face as beautiful as Sabrina's.

"This is awkward, I'm calling about your master."

"My master? Oh. . . you mean my boss."

"Right, when was the last time you saw him?"

"I'm not really sure I should be having this conversation with you."

"The last time I saw your boss was when he visited with my master. The two drank three bottles of Chianti and then they just staggered off arm in arm into the night. That was almost four weeks ago and my master hasn't returned since. My sources tell me you've been working the store alone of late."

I paused trying to gather my thoughts. Could this be some kind of a trick? "That sounds about right. Yeah, four weeks."

"Did he say anything to you about where he and my master might be heading?"

"Hell, he didn't even say anything about going to visit your master."

"I'm worried," she said, sounding worried.

"I am too," I confessed.

"Perhaps we should pool our resources and try to find them."

I thought about that for a moment. I was worried about my boss, sure, but could I trust Sabrina? Even if I could, should I? "You could come to the store and we could discuss this if you'd like."

"Your store is awfully public. We have no idea who might be behind these disappearances. I'd rather meet someplace more private. You could come to our place. It's on the edge of the city and it's rather secluded."

I had not realized that the two lived anywhere near the city. "Okay, what's the address?" She gave it to me and I hung up the phone after agreeing to be there in an hour.

I looked up at the sword on the wall and wondered if I should take it with me. This could be a trap. I'd trained long and hard on the uses of the sword. But my boss Sam—not his real name, real names have too much power—had instructed me not to use it unless I was certain that it was needed. He also told me that when the time came I'd be certain. And I wasn't certain what I needed to do, so that ruled out the sword. And really nothing says I trust you like showing up wielding a sword. Still, one likes to take precautions.

I opted for my trusty Colt 45 in a shoulder holster. That necessitated my wearing a light jacket that the weather didn't really call for. Honestly, I wasn't worried about Sabrina or her master trying to set me up. The rules don't work that way. You can't just kill one of the Powers, or their apprentices, in a drive by or with a weapon other than one of the swords. And even if you have one of the swords at your disposal you can only use it when the conditions are correct. Remembering how every fiber of my being vibrated with power during the last duel, I knew the conditions weren't correct. But what if some other player had entered the game? What if someone was hunting both sides? Did they have to play by the same rules we did?

At the appointed hour I found myself driving up a long, winding driveway. The house, really a mansion, was tucked away from the road by a series of rolling hills. Finally the driveway opened out into a wide parking area in front of the well manicured lawn. Just down the hill from the house was a large gazebo overlooking a sprawling ornamental pond. The overall effect was one of enormous wealth. I knew my boss also controlled vast amounts of wealth, but he chose not to display it quite so openly. In fact, he'd been rather put out when I'd purchased the convertible Aston Martin I was now driving.

I parked the car, looked up at the clear sky, and decided not to bother putting the top up. I pushed my sunglasses back onto the bridge of my nose and got out of the car. Gravel crunched under my shoes as I walked to the front door. Sabrina opened it before I got close enough to ring the bell. I hadn't seen her is nearly 25 years. If she'd aged even a day it didn't show. She had a very pretty face framed by long blond hair that seemed to be moving about in a breeze, except that there wasn't one. Her eyes had a hard edge to them, but they were green and beautiful, and I knew that if she smiled her teeth would be very white and quite perfect.

"Thank you for coming," she said, showing me those perfect teeth.

I nodded.

"Please come in," she said moving aside.

I did that thing.

"Can I take your coat?"

I smiled, "Thank you, no it's really quite comfortable."

She smiled back at me and I noticed she was also wearing a light jacket.

She lead me to a bay window with two comfortable chairs and a small coffee table. The window looked out over the ornamental pond I'd seen coming in. There was a pot of tea and two cups on the table. "Can I offer you some jasmine tea?" she asked sitting down.

I took the other chair. "Yes, please," I said, taking off my sun glasses and placing them into the inside pocket of my jacket.

She poured tea into both cups and handed one to me. As I was thanking her she took a sip of hers. Well, that made it clear it wasn't poisoned, so I took a sip of mine. It was very pleasant with just a hint of honeysuckle under the subtle jasmine.

"This is very nice," I offered.

She smiled, but the smile didn't reach her eyes. "So you don't have any idea where our masters are?" she asked, getting right to the point of our visit.

"None. Honestly, I don't think my boss was planning to leave. I've gone through all of our accounts and I can't find any transactions that suggest he planned anything at all."

She seemed to shrink a little into herself. "I've gone though all of ours and came to the same conclusion. My master never went anywhere without plans. If you knew where to look you'd always know when he was planning something. I'd tried to explain to him over and over again that computers leave traces, but he just couldn't understand it."

I chuckled.

She stood up and approached the window, her back to me. I realized right away why she'd done that. A tear had slipped out of the corner of her eye and she hadn't wanted to show me that moment of vulnerability. I'm not sure why I did it, but I stood up and placed my hand on her shoulder, she turned slowly towards me and then I hugged her.

She let me hold her for a long moment and then broke away. She wiped at her tears, which were streaming freely now. "Why did you do that?" she demanded.

"You looked like you needed a hug."

She studied me long and hard. For a moment it almost seemed as though she was reading my mind. "You mean that don't you? You didn't have any ulterior motives at all."

Sabrina might very well be the most beautiful woman I had ever met, and she was certainly my type, but in that moment my only concern had been for her pain. "I didn't," I said barley above a whisper.

And suddenly she was in my arms again. But this time her lips sought out mine and she kissed me with a passion fiercer than any I'd ever experienced before in my long life. There was an awkward moment when we each ran into the other's holstered gun. But her laugh broke the awkwardness and the passion returned.

I spent the night and in the morning we decided to search out our missing mentors together. We went through all the records that they had left behind. In the end we spent three months traveling the world, moving from one place of power to the next. We met with hundreds of people who had had dealings or connections with our missing mentors, but no one had seen or heard from either of them. Looking back on it, those were some of the most glorious days of my life. As much as we were genuinely seeking out our lost mentors we were also getting to know one another. The time was very much like a three month long honeymoon.

Honestly, it was my first real relationship. Sam had always warned me about getting close to anyone. If we loved, the enemy would use that against us. So we could never let ourselves care too much about anyone lest they be used as leverage against us. Of course, falling in love with Sabrina meant not having to worry about the enemy using her against me; she *was* the enemy.

We spent hours amiably debating our positions. I'd tried to get her to switch to my side, but she insisted that she owed it to her master to continue on in his footsteps. She'd tried to get me to defect, pointing out that virtually all of the ills of the day were created by science. Global warming and pollution were the new dark ages, she'd argued, and only magic could put right what science was destroying. In the end neither of us could sway the other, but still our relationship grew stronger and I was almost glad we didn't find either of our missing mentors.

On the night we arrived home I decided it was time to tell Sabrina something I'd come to realize. "Sabrina, I love you."

She had been looking down at something and she looked quickly up at me. "You know that eventually one of us will have to kill the other."

I nodded, "But that doesn't change how I feel for you, and I've never been any good at lying to myself."

She smiled, but the smile didn't make it to her eyes. "You are a wonderful man, and I'm glad that fate has tossed us together as it has, but. . ."

'But?"

"But if I let myself love you, then it might slow my hand when it is time for me to kill you, or once I've killed you it might torment me for eternity that I killed the only person I'd ever loved. I'm not signing on for that."

I resisted the urge to tell her I didn't think she had any chance of killing me in a duel. My father had been a gold medalist in fencing in one of the early Olympics, and I was considerably better with a blade than he had ever thought of being. It was that ability that had attracted Sam's attention to me. And in the more than one hundred years that I'd been in Sam's employ I had studied with scores of sword masters in every style imaginable. Frankly, other than Sam, and perhaps Sabrina's master, I wasn't certain that there had ever been a better swordsman than myself. Still, her master wouldn't have chosen her if he'd thought she had no chance of defending herself. There's a saying that no swordsman should ever forget: A good big swordsman always beats a good small swordsman. Instead of giving voice to any of these thoughts I said, "Does that mean we're over?" I think a tear might have slipped from my eye.

She laughed, "No, it just means I don't plan to let myself love you. I can't imagine having a relationship with anyone else. How would I explain who I am and what I do to them? No, being with you is as uncomplicated in that department as it could possibly be."

*

That had been three years ago. My love for her had grown deeper than I would have thought possible. She still would not admit to loving me, but I could live with that; she was there and that was all that mattered. But I could feel the power growing around me. It was going to happen tonight. Tonight I would heft the magic blade to defend the powers of science and light and Sabrina would brandish her darker blade for the powers of magic and darkness. There were three ways it could end. One of us could die and that would fix the course of the world for all of eternity. One of us could bind the other and then the course of the world would be set for hundreds of years. Bindings had caused the dark ages and the industrial revolution. Or we could fight to a draw, and that would give us, if the records our mentors left behind were correct, another twenty-five to two hundred and fifty years before the power rose again. There was no way of knowing how long between times.

But really, I'd be lying if I said I had any other concern than how I was going to live without Sabrina. I couldn't sacrifice my own life for her no matter how much I loved her. Not and have mankind fall into an eternal dark age. It was also too risky to try to fight for a draw. If one of us bound the other it would be hundreds of years before we'd have any kind of interaction again. And even if we were fortunate enough to fight to a draw, how could our relationship possibly survive such a life and death conflict. Tonight my life changed forever and damn it, I didn't want it to. I liked my life exactly as it was.

Some indeterminate time later I looked up and there was a wall of fog pressed up against the glass of the shop's door. I hadn't seen it roll in; one moment it hadn't been there and the next it was. I recognized the fog, I'd seen it before. Morosely, I walked over to the case that the sword hung in. I fished a key out of my pocket and unlocked the case. My boss has always kept it in a case that could only be opened by smashing the glass, but as the one who had had to sweep up the glass afterwards, I'd insisted on a cabinet with a very good lock instead.

I reached into the case and took the sword down by the hilt. I'd held the sword in my hands before and each time I had I'd been able to feel its immense power like a strong current just below the surface. This time, however, the power came roaring through the blade and flooded my being. This was strength like nothing I'd ever experienced before. How could anyone or anything hope to stand before it?

Resolutely I walked to the door and opened it. The fog seemed to open up a tunnel for me to follow. I locked the shop's door and walked into the tunnel of fog. As I strode towards what I knew would be my first, if not my last, battlefield it felt as if I were walking on one of those electric walk ways that they have at the larger airports. Each step covered far more ground than a single pace.

When I came to the end of the tunnel I was not surprised to find myself at All Saints Cemetery. There was no fog here. The full moon shown like some cold, Greek goddess that had no care as to which Power might triumph. It was a beautiful symmetry that our first duel should take place where our mentors' final battle had taken place. Tears welled up in my eyes as I looked at Sabrina. The landscape about us was in darkness and shadows, but my blade reflected and multiplied the moonlight, giving me enough light to see all that I needed to see. She was beautiful, with her pale blond hair moving about in a nonexistent breeze. She was dressed all in black, but the blade in her hand was blacker than the darkest void. It seemed to be drawing light into itself.

Aligned behind her were dozens of creatures of darkness scurrying about. They were misshapen and twisted like something out of a very bad horror movie. "We don't have to do this." I said, "You don't owe your master anything now that he's gone."

She smiled that smile, the one that never makes it to her eyes. "No, I cannot betray his memory. But as I recall he offered your master a joint reign. I will offer that to you now, as well."

I'd be lying if I said I hadn't been mightily tempted. Why not try? Why not see if the two of us could entwine science and magic for the good of all mankind? But Sam's words came echoing back through the years to my ears. "The enemy is seductive. But their power corrupts, we cannot allow it to abide."

I shook my head. "No, I can't accept that offer. Tonight we end this." She nodded and then I said the words I'd promised myself I wouldn't. "Sabrina, no matter how this ends, I love you."

She didn't respond to my words as she moved toward me blade swinging faster than I would have thought possible. "Abaddon, Balberith, Lerajie, Sorath," she intoned."

"Tyson, Sagan, Hawking, Einstein, Curie." I responded.

"Lucifer, Vassago, Rahab, Kunopegos, Ronobe."

"Kant, Kierkegaard, Nietzsche, Aedesia."

The world seemed to bend and fold in upon itself and I knew that we were now locked in a battle outside of space and time.

I had expected to take the battle to Sabrina, but her dark blade seemed to be flashing at me from every direction. My blade parried blow after blow, but she was so fast that I could not even consider trying to riposte for fear that I would miss her next blow.

I have faced fencers that were faster than me before. And in those instances I would wage a defensive fight and wait for them to tire. But Sabrina was so fast that I wondered if I could last that long.

I drew power from my blade as Sam had taught me and decided to try a bat parry. Sabrina's blade came towards me and I knocked it away with every ounce of strength I had while directing my blade to move from the parry directly to her torso. But when my blade reached where she had been standing she wasn't there and I felt a burning along my right bicep.

"Damn," I swore as I realized that she'd scored a hit.

"You can't win," she said. Her words did not bother me nearly as much as the fact that she seemed not to be the least bit winded when she spoke.

"The night is yet young," I replied with a false bravado that I hoped she could not detect. In more than a century as a fencer I had only faced one opponent who was better than me and that had been Sam. But I knew with absolute certainty that Sabrina was better than me. I had no hope of defeating her. And yet I had to try. If I somehow escaped this night with my life I would have to redouble my time with a blade in anticipation of our next encounter.

"Where did you learn to fence like that?" I asked trying to distract her.

"In Hell," she said, her blade lunging directly for my heart.

I beat the sword aside and tried to step into her as her momentum pulled her forward. Perhaps I could land a blow to her head with my fist and even my odds. Unchivalrous I know, but this wasn't the Olympics. Again I missed and again I felt a burn as she passed. This time it was my left shoulder. How the Hell could anyone be this good? Neither wound was deep; she didn't dare commit the time it would have taken her to push the blade deeper for fear that my strength might be able to come into play. I could see that her plan was to kill me with a thousand cuts if necessary.

You learn interesting things about yourself when you think you're going to die. I realized I didn't really fear death, but that it still made me angry—angry that I could dedicate more than a hundred years of my life getting ready for a single moment and find myself not good enough when that moment finally arrived.

I fought with everything I had, but Sabrina never once broke tempo. She was never in danger of my going on the offensive. Unless she made some major blunder she was going to carry the night. While she showed no signs of tiring, I realized that I was not tiring either. Our swords were feeding us the energy we needed to keep moving and we were, by the standards of this game, young. Perhaps I could fight to a draw—keep myself alive until dawn. The thought had no more then escaped my mind when I felt a burn across my right side. I hadn't even seen the blow. Had she not been worried about my strength she could have killed me with that one.

A cold sweat broke out along my brow and I realized then that an even colder wind was blowing through the cemetery. The creatures that watched, Sabrina's all, erupted into cheers and shouts. I staggered back and parried wildly at the barrage of blows that followed. She knew she had me and she was moving in for the kill.

I pretended to drop back even father and then as she came on I threw myself at her with abandon. In that moment I could see, from the widening of her eyes, that I had surprised her. Even so my blade missed her by the slimmest of margins. Still, it had been worth it, as she had had to forego a death blow and settle for stabbing me in the thigh. It was deep and I felt my leg buckle and I crashed to the ground. The fall saved me a second time as her blade flashed through the spot I would have been standing in if my leg had not failed me.

And then the cock crowed. It did not seem to me as if we could have been fighting all night, but then this place was outside of time. Sabrina knew the rules as well as I; this fight was, if not a draw, over. I had somehow survived the night.

She lowered her blade and the murderous expression on her face softened. And then as she and her master had all those years ago she started to fade. "Will you still be coming over on Friday?" she asked quickly.

I laughed, relief flooding my very soul. "Of course."

Before she completely faded away I saw her smile, and this time it made it all the way to her eyes.

There Shall Be No Moon!

by Roger Zelazny

"Percy."

"Yes George?"

"I believe you have finally overextended yourself."

The younger man threw back his head and laughed. Anyone but his companion might have thought him demented. The larger man knew better, however. He shifted his gaze to the placid surface of Lucerne, gesturing with his walking-stick.

"That pink cloud reminds me of Southey."

"Oh?" chuckled the other. "In what way?"

"It makes a great show of being huge and colorful, and inside it's as miasmic and weightless as a London fog—and about as valuable."

"Well-turned, but I daresay you are changing the subject."

". . .and those peaks in the distance, my! How they must echo with the turning of the spheres—as my poor ears with the sounds of your Project."

"Now, that's unfair!" protested the other. "I haven't seen you for two weeks, and I've made great progress."

"Doubtless you are producing something of great merit and exquisiteness. . .but, if I doubt its efficacy along the lines you have professed, pray forgive me my doubts and grant me leave to remain a Thomas until I have thrust my hands into the wounds."

He smiled. "Ah! Whenever you are being irreligious, George, I'll concede almost everything. But this time you are mistaken."

"Then advise me."

"I conjured a fog last night, and an image."

"This is foggy country."

"A fog that tries to speak?"

"How much sleep have you had this week—not to mention wine, and perhaps a touch of brain fever?"

"No more than usual. But the rhythms are almost perfect now."

"Then why the delay? Bring him forth! There are some things I have always wanted to ask!"

"The moon will not be full for another week—and the land, I am afraid the land must be dispensed with."

"Oh? You have purchased a balloon from the Montgolfiers? —I fancy brother Bill might be a trifle distressed to awaken several hundreds of feet above the ground."

"No, no! The land is too stable and element—too firm, too venerable a *métier*—the invocation must be spoken upon untrammeled waters, there—where the wilder powers hold sway!"

His eyes dimmed as he spoke, and he swayed slightly, himself.

The other lit a cheroot, partly to end the flight of his friend's imagination in its stinging blue cloud.

"You have rented a barge?"

"A small boat. I have been purifying it all week. I'll anchor off-shore when the moon shows full. —I wish you could be there."

His friend tossed his dark locks, and a sinister gleam danced deep in his eyes.

"The son of the Devil at his father's Mass? No, I'm sure you are qualified to manage it without me."

"It's not the Black Mass!" he protested. "It is a personal ritual, designed to summon up the shade of William Shakespeare!"

"I'll try to be there, Percy, but I can't promise. I have a delightful engagement which I trust shall last well into the next day."

He smiled his lopsided smile, managing to condemn his thoughts and enjoy them at the same instant of reverie.

"Noblesse oblige," smirked the other. Then, changing back to his original proposal, "But seriously, I think you, of all men, would be best qualified for the undertaking. When you only dabbled at it you had better results than anyone else. . . ."

"My dear Shelley, I will tell you the trouble with your invocation, without having heard it.

"You invite, you entreat, you appreciate—that is wrong. You must command!

"You approach whatever power you call upon as you do the English language," he finished, "a bit too humbly. You must order it to do your bidding like the lackey that it is!"

"But that is not in my nature." He shook his head. "I sometimes wish that I could, but I lack your seigniorial prowess."

The other hung his head.

"Noblesse oblige," he muttered more softly. "But come! you say you have some fresh Kirschwasser!"

"Ah, yes! Red as the lips of one's beloved, and far more lingering!"

"Ha!" The other turned to the road with surprising agility. "Let there be no more talk of spells and incantations—only spirits! Tonight we drink!

They started up the road.

"But this one, Byron! I know this one will do it! I've worked so hard on the metrics, have chosen words with all the right vibrations. . ."

Silently, the other limped along beside him.

*

"Mary! Another bottle, please! The peerage is a bottomless lake!"

"Hollow hoof," snorted Byron, and he closed his eyes as Mary entered with the ruddy liquors. She smiled, but small lines on her attractive face betrayed a mood which had not been present two weeks previously.

Byron's eyes blinked open and bored into hers.

"You are troubled," he announced.

"And you still sober. Goodness!"

She placed the drink before him.

"There is that within me which never sleeps, nor drunken grows, though seas of grapes surround."

"Is that from *Childe Harold?*"

"No, it is from the moment. What's the matter?

She bit her lower lip.

"Oh, nothing. Doctor Frankenstein and his problems," she offered. "I'm following your suggestion and writing it out, since you men are too busy—"

She started to say "with," but chewed the sentence off.

Byron climbed to his feet, glass in hand.

"A toast! To goblins, werewolves, demons, and gods," he pronounced.

Shelley raised his glass drunkenly. Mary hurried from the room.

"To William Shakespeare, Englishman and Greek," he said.

Byron quaffed his drink and seated himself once more.

"You have her worried," he began.

"Huh?"

"Mary is troubled. The climate of your pursuits has upset the poor girl."

"Nonsense," he slurred. "She's fascinated by the stuff."

"Nevertheless, entertain a friend's suggestion. A holiday in Italy might be in order."

"Go to, m'lord—I shan't say where. What's in Italy?"

"It's warm, sunny, healthy—just the opposite of this place. Life is focused upon itself in the latin climes, not the metaphysics of involution."

"Ha! The pa' calling the kethle brack! You go to Italy! You won't help me there!"

"It would not particularly amuse me to speak with Shakespeare. He'd probably be tongue-tied anyhow." He smiled his twisted smile.

"No one could speak like one of his characters—which is both their tragedy and ours."

"Don't be so subtle when you're drunk. Lemme read you some Wordsworth."

"I'm afraid I have to be leaving soon."

"What have you got against Wordsworth?"

"As I said, I must depart shortly. I can't afford the entire night."

"All right." He closed the edition of *Lyrical Ballads* which he had stealthily inched from a drawer.

". . .But next time," he observed, "I shall convince you."

Byron spun his cloak like a great wing, and it settled about his shoulders. He retrieved his stick from the chair.

"Say good-night to Mary, lay in more wine, and write me at the inn."

Shelley snored softly.

*

The innkeeper's son tapped gently but impatiently. Finally, his knocking produced a yawn on the other side of the door. After another five minutes, that great oaken panel creaked inward. Resplendent in scarlet silk, Byron regarded the youth.

"A letter for you, m'lord."

"Very good—here, lad. Spend it not on one wench."

"No sir, I shall buy chocolate."

"Mm. To each his vice. —Thank you."

He pushed shut the door and crossed to his writing table. Seated, he brushed aside a mountain of cantos and unfolded the letter.

"Hm."

Two bold sentences uncoiled in his hands and slipped into his drowsy mind: "Tonight the moon is full. Your presence is requested."

"Damme!" he announced, rising again.

"Shelly! Why do you do these things? —Do you know what you ask?"

He crossed to the window and slapped the casement.

The day was bleak. The boy ran across the yard and stood beneath a willow. He began tossing stones into the stream.

Of course!

Hastily, Byron reseated himself and sharpened a quill. Without pausing, he filled a page with bold strokes:

Dearest Ariel,

Though you dwell in the Empyrean, doubtless you have not looked about of late. Pray do! The gods frown down today, and the havens darken. There shall be no moon!

As above, so below,

Manfred

Smiling, he melted a piece of red wax and dripped it onto the overlap. He looked about for a bell-pull and remembered there was none. Hurrying to the casement, he flung it wide.

"Boy! Catch this letter. Take it to the man who gave you mine. —And buy some more chocolate!"

The boy had recovered the letter and the coin before the window was closed.

Byron returned to his table to write another dozen cantos as he awaited breakfast.

A murmur: "Schedules must be maintained. . ."

*

"He's right," she observed, reading over his shoulder. "You said yourself that the moon must be full and clear."

"It may yet clear," he muttered, rubbing his blond stubble. "Come, let's walk down by the lake."

She took his arm.

"I will enjoy it more if you talk to me, and stop staring at the sky."

"It will clear," he stated.

"Perhaps," she sighed. "Why do you want to summon Shakespeare, anyway? What do you wish to ask him?"

"I don't know. I will know when I see him."

"There may be a storm."

"And there may not."

"I have finished *Frankenstein*."

"Good."

"Will you read it?"

"Tomorrow."

"Percy, you are impossible!"

"I trust you are correct."

"Perhaps that is why my concern is almost maternal. You are a careless child with a new toy."

"Then, daedal before the gods, shall I spin it."

"Byron will not be here."

"Who needs him?"

"You. So let me take his place."

"Never. A woman would vitiate the incantation."

"If it clears, I shall worry all night."

"Your privilege."

They drew near the cove where the boat was moored.

"I am sorry, you may not come aboard."

He vaulted over the rail, commencing a soft chant and paced from bow to stern, counting his steps. Everything above and below the deck was painted white. Black pentacles decorated the floorboards. Shelley opened a locker and checked a brazier, a supply of incense, and herbs. From his pocket, he produced a roll of foolscap which he placed alongside them.

He closed the chest and looked up.

"All right. All is in readiness. I'm going to remain aboard until it is time. You might as well return now."

"It's starting to rain." She held forth a pale hand, palm upwards, for an instant reminding him of a child beggar he had seen at Charing.

"It will pass."

Silently, she turned and walked back, wiping rain from her eyes.

*

The moon was a blind eye, peering from a lightless room through broken panes. Sightless, through opaque shards of sky, it looked down, past and through the trees, walls, and people of the city.

Byron cursed.

"Why? Why have I a nonsense conscience? —A gift of the gods for my blasphemies? Giving up a warm fireside—and more?"

His drenched cloak plastered his muscular limbs. The thunder prowled tentatively, then belched a long rumble.

"Cochon!" he spat. "Ariel stands beneath your moon, mouthing iambs at you!—Nature, you lack breeding! You should smile, not slap his face in insults of wind!"

He vaulted into the saddle, clucking at the soaked animal.

"We ride, my poor mount, though a beast deserves better tonight."

*

The beast of ink raised its thousand hands, jerking the boat to starboard.

"Oh Winds of Time that was Elysium. . ."

An instant study in black and gray was followed by a crash. The boat dipped to the left.

"Tides of Time, receding forever. . ."

He choked upon the aromatic fumes from the brazier. The smoke lay flat upon the deck; the pop and hiss of the fire emerged between passing gusts.

"I do conjure thee. . . ."

A devil-throated howl crossed the waters, racing footless the sweeping clouds.

The moon did not blink, staring down, past and through the boat, the man, the waters Shelley's words were cipher within the demon-siren of the passer.

Then all lay still.

173

The smoke flumed upwards, the moon blazed beacon, the ship was an arrow, quivering in the dark, flat field where it had fallen.

"Appear before me here, I charge thee. . . . "

A sudden spark, and the smoke billowed in all directions. In the distance, a sound like Atlas dropping the sky; an island of cloud crossed the moon, like its wandering pupil seeking the center of the retina. . . .

"Speak!"

The dark land shrugged, raising its hands once more; it grasped the arrow out, with a twist of fury, threw it flat, then bled rivers upon it.

"I do hear thee!"

*

Byron drew upon the shore. The tiny blink of the brazier beckoned his gaze. The rain hesitated, then held back a moment.

"Good Lord, why so far out?" he groaned. "The next one will catch you!"

Dismounting, he drew off his boots and unclasped his cloak.

The waters grew still.

He finished undressing and plunged in, swimming with the powerful strokes of a man who knew he could cross the Hellespont. The waves did not beat about him; the lake was as placid as a mountain rill on a sunny afternoon.

He bore toward the bobbing flicker—and the mountain fired its heavy artilleries. Like a boxer fighting an omnipresent opponent, Byron lashed out with double fury.

"Shelley! I'm coming!"

The waves fell upon him like a collapsing wall. He went under. Seconds later he bobbed to the surface and began to wrestle his adversary, timing his movements to give way before each buffet.

Then the light tipped and went out.

With quick strokes, he tried painting a mental picture of its last location. He fought forward until the dim hulk loomed before him.

"Shelley!"

He heard something that sounded like a sobbing coke. He beat his way about the fallen vessel.

"Shelley?"

This time the choke-sound was louder. He reached out through the darkness. . . .

Flesh! Shelley was clinging to the side of the boat.

He pried loose his weakening grip, then seized him cross-chest.

Then he began the long return toward what he hoped was shore.

"Jester of the gods!" he panted. "What moves a man to such extremes?"

Shelley coughed and did not anser him. Byron pulled on his boots.

"You should have tried the balloon," he snarled. "They don't sink!"

Shelley coughed again.

"Couldn't you have put it off for a month?"

"He came," said Shelley.

"Who?"

"Shakespeare answered my summons."

Byron shook out his cloak and threw it over his friend's shoulders.

"I suppose you had time for a lengthy colloquy?"

"No, only a few words."

The horse nuzzled him, suggesting that people with good sense did not stand out in the rain.

"What did he say?"

"I'm not certain."

He assisted Shelley to mount, then climbed up behind him.

"What did you ask him?"

"I asked him the meaning of a man's life."

"Is that all? —Well, what do you think he said?"

"It sounded like, 'Though his bark cannot be lost, yet it shall be tempest-tossed.'"

"Hm. Appropriate enough. —That's from *Macbeth*, by the way—the Third Witch. —You heard me calling and filled in your own words."

"No, it sounded like Shakespeare—the way I expected him to sound."

They plunged around the bend.

"Mary will probably have dry clothes waiting. Some rum too, I hope."

Shelley coughed again. They approached the welcoming windows of the cottage.

"George— There are no words—but no other man could have beaten the waters. . . . Thank you."

The other laughed. "Foul Weather Jack Byron would have sailed onto the Styx, and Mad Jack bearded Jove and a bolt or two, I've heard. Is the son to be less than his fathers?"

"In your case, never."

They dismounted, and Byron led the horse into the shed. Shelley paused on the step.

"I keep a messy journal, George—and I know you are writing your memoirs. Include this please, that I may acknowledge a perpetual debt—and future generations may be inclined to remember me when they read it."

"They will remember you without it, Percy. But, as you wish—some future Mad Jack may be amused."

"Your memoirs will blaze through all generations."

"I daresay. Now, get inside, it's chilly out here." He pushed him.

Mary opened the door, a twisted handkerchief at her waist. She peered out, blinking heavily.

"I'm sorry, Mary," said Shelley.

Her eyes blazed as she stepped aside.

"Tempest-tossed, indeed!" noted Byron.

Halflife

by Theodore Krulik

He was screaming when they brought him into the burn unit. I had been dozing next to an empty bed and sat up wide awake, shocked by the pandemonium erupting before me. He was a large man belted onto a gurney and the two paramedics wheeling him in fought to keep him from ripping out the restraints. I watched with a mixture of horror and commiseration.

His face looked like it was cracked down the middle, only half of which resembled something human. It was a face I'd seen on the news often enough to recognize immediately. Still shouting in agony, the big man was held by the paramedics and several interns as they transferred him to the bed next to mine. Gathered around him, the interns attached an intravenous feed and one of the doctors studied him carefully. While they were examining him, his groaning began to subside. After awhile, the IV drugs put him to sleep and the doctors left. Men (four? six? I couldn't tell) dressed in some unfamiliar military uniform stood at the nurses' station and at the entrance to the ward. They had holstered weapons on their belts.

I knew who the big man was, of course. Everybody did. Like the whole population of the planet, I'd seen him on the vid-screens and read the news stories over the years. The media gave him the sobriquet HalfJack for obvious reasons. He was a biomechanical astro-pilot—half-man, half-machine. His given name was Jack Shandon. For the past thirty minutes, the vid-screen at my bed announced the crash of his spacecraft. He was airlifted to the nearest hospital. This hospital.

I was engaged in my own little piece of hell. Car accident. Three days ago. Unconscious for hours. Didn't remember much about the crash when I came to. I was told my car went up in flames and a couple of good

Samaritans pulled me out. But not before I had suffered severe burns to the back of my head and upper body. My head, scalp, and back itched like I'd been lying on a bed of sawdust and blazing ash. I was bandaged around my head, neck, shoulders and ribs. I might've had a concussion also, and the doctors were keeping me for observation while my burns healed.

I had my intravenous feed removed earlier that day and could walk the hospital halls, a semi-free man. At noon, sometime after they brought Jack Shandon in, I took pleasure in finally getting some solid food handed to me on a tray. Hospital food. I tasted it. If it tasted like anything, I couldn't determine what. I ate it anyway.

I got out of bed and took my first real look at Jack Shandon. The uniformed men at the nurses' station watched but didn't move.

Jack's chest rose and fell regularly under the hospital blanket as he slept. I saw a good portion of his face and shoulders. The left side of his face was charred and raw. The IV was plugged into his left forearm. Apparently that side was flesh—darkened and blistered—but it was human skin nevertheless. The right side however, that was something else again. Metal surfaces that once gleamed with a black sheen—I'd seen many photos of him in the magazines—were now warped and stripped to a dull gray. The rotation hydraulics of his right arm-shoulder unit were melted and fused solid. Unusable.

Jack's eyes opened. Startled, I took a step back.

"I *am* quite a sight," he said. His voice was sand and crushed rock.

I stepped closer. "You're awake."

"Observant." His legs rustled under the cover as he moved to sit up. He let out a sharp cry and fell back.

"Here," I said, and adjusted the upper part of the bed to raise him up. "That better, Mr. Shandon?"

He looked at the IV feed on the pole beside his bed and then back at me. "That's not doing much good. The pain's still there." His gaze upon me softened. "Call me Jack," he said. "You?"

"Name's Roger." I sat on the side of my bed.

"What's your game, Roger?"

"Game?"

"What do you do? When you're not inhabiting burn units."

"I'm a writer."

"Oh." He looked away, seeming to ready himself to turn onto his side and show his back to me. Instead, he pushed himself up, something rasping under the blanket, and let out a groan. He considered me with lucid dark eyes. "Not a reporter?"

"No. I write fiction. Mostly."

Jack sighed. "What you've been reading in the news. Or seeing on the vid-screen about me—I *am* fiction. Mostly."

I opened my mouth to say something smart, stopped, opened it again. "That IV must be working now. You were screaming in pain when you came in."

"Yes. I was." He looked at the ceiling, reading something there I couldn't see. "I lost something important to me. Something vital." After awhile, he looked back at me. "Know what I'm talking about?"

I nodded slowly. "*The Morgana*," I answered. His spaceship.

He gave me a wry half-smile. Pulling down his bedcovers, he revealed his legs. My eyes widened in surprise. They looked like flesh, *both of them*, right up to where the hospital gown covered them. *One* of them, the right one, was supposed to be prosthetic. It wasn't. It was skin, clearly the genuine article. The other one was scarred and blistery from the accident but it, too, was clearly flesh-and-blood.

He rose into a sitting position and the snapping sound of heat-hardened flexion inserts thwacked inside him. He started to cry out but stopped himself by sheer will. He let his legs dangle over the side of the bed and faced me. His fused right armature hung at his side. Loose tubing within the prosthetic forearm pinged.

.He gave me a half-smile. "Not entirely human yet." With his good hand, he rubbed his knees. "Had that new leg implanted before that last—" A long hesitancy—"flight."

Just then, a uniformed man marched over to us.

"Need anything, Mr. Shandon?" he asked. He was eyeing me suspiciously, his hand covering his holster.

Jack watched my reaction and then looked back at the man, something like amusement in his half-face. "No need to concern yourself. Roger and I are just talking like two old buddies. That okay?"

"Whatever you say, sir."

He left us alone again.

"Are you a good writer?" asked Jack.

Recovering from the interruption, I looked at Jack, searching for an intelligent response. "People seem to think so."

"How much have you written?"

"Oh, about two dozen novels, a bunch of short stories, a handful of poems, a smattering of essays."

"Prolific, then. Think you might write about me?"

I couldn't read the expression on his half-face. I spoke with deliberate care, uncertain what he wanted to hear. "Maybe. Someday. I'd probably want to turn it into fiction, though."

"Good. Do me a favor."

"What?"

"Don't write it right away. Wait until I'm long gone. Do that for me?"

"Okay. But as I say, it will probably be fiction. A short story most likely."

"That's fine, Roger. I don't mind if you make up the whole thing. Because I need to tell someone the truth. I want to say it one time only. And be done with it."

I drew in my breath and exhaled slowly. "I'm listening."

"This leg—" He smoothed his right knee with his good hand. "I had it grown from my own DNA and grafted on weeks before this last trip out. It was wrapped in cushioned layers, cocoon-like, when I went inside *The Morgana*."

"That's why that leg wasn't injured in the crash," I observed.

"Yes. That was the first thing *Morgana* noticed when I positioned myself into the control web. *Morgana* asked why I had replaced a significant part of my ship systems contact points with something so inessential. What could possibly be the reason for deliberately hindering my efficiency as her pilot?

"I told her that I was considering retirement. I was older and wanted to spend the rest of my days earthbound. I said I couldn't take the gravity changes and acceleration stresses anymore."

"Sounds like a reasonable decision," I said.

Jack frowned at me. "I was lying to her."

"What part?"

"All of it. I had none of that in mind when I decided to reverse my implants."

"Why, then?"

"Kathi. I met her some time ago. Left her abruptly after I revealed what I was. She said she liked me that way. I didn't really believe her—or I knew such a difference between us would come to matter at some point. Anyway, I left, never intending to return."

"What happened?"

"I thought about her. I never stopped thinking about her." He paused, looking at something beyond the wall behind me. "I wanted to go back, to see her again. But so much time had passed. I didn't know if she would want me back. I called her a few months ago. I was a continent away and scheduled for another run outbound. But we talked on the phone for more than half an hour. We spoke of things as if no time had passed. No, she said, she wasn't involved with another man. Yes, she would enjoy getting together the next time I was in town. That changed everything. There was a time when I believed I was only alive traveling among the stars. But now Kathi means more to me than being out there. When I leave here, I'm going to her."

We sat silent a long time.

"So," I began, "Kathi doesn't know about your leg graft."

"No. I didn't tell her anything about my intentions. I want to see her. See if she really wants to spend a lifetime with me." Jack winced. Not in pain, or so it seemed, but because of a thought. "There's something more."

"What?"

"About the crash. I—."

Suddenly, unbelievably, the storm troopers double-marched in like a herd of buffalo. Within their phalanx, a bearded man dressed impeccably in a three-piece suit wheeled a well-cushioned mobile chair.

"Mr. Shandon," said the bearded man. "Come with us, sir. We've just learned that the Wexler Laboratory in Fort Lauderdale has specialized facilities we require. We're flying you there immediately."

The burn unit's chief physician came over to protest the move but the bearded man dismissed him with a word or two I couldn't hear. The bearded man removed Jack's IV and gave him an injection with a syringe, probably to ease the pain. Several of the uniformed men lifted Jack into the mobile chair and whisked him out of the ward. He was gone and I never knew what he was going to tell me about the crash.

.After I was released from the hospital, I got back to work writing a new novel. Two months went by while I tried not thinking about Jack. I was sure he'd forgotten about me. Then I received an Instant Message on my computer and opened it. It read:

Roger—I'm planning to go back outward. About Kathi and me, things didn't work out. My new ship's almost ready. So am I. You should hear from someone about the launch date. Abide.—Jack

I didn't know how he found me or why he had bothered. Perhaps he saw a kindred spirit in me, someone who was as alone as he was. Thinking back, I realized I hadn't told him a thing about my personal life. He must've checked my background. That still didn't answer all of my questions.

I sent a reply on my computer but he didn't respond. I returned to my novel.

Months later someone rang my doorbell. A man in military uniform stood there, envelope in hand. I was too old to be drafted, so. . .

It was a letter requesting my presence at the maiden launch of a new Intergalactic ship of the line to be piloted by Jack Shandon. With the letter was a single pass, authorized by the President of the United States.

On a hot August morning, I sat in the bleachers with a hundred other people. The spaceship on the launch pad gleamed under the rising sun. The name of the ship was *The Cassandra*.

Huge outdoor screens went from images in the central control room to men outside *The Cassandra* completing systems checks. We hadn't seen Jack yet. Then all screens cut to the ship's interior. A camera mounted on the ship's console showed a shadowed figure sitting in the pilot's chair. Something crossed the screen and a light came on, illuminating the area.

Immense on the outdoor screens was a silver-colored manikin—its head and shoulders looking much like a bust of Buddha, rotund and hairless. Inanimate, eyes closed, it sat on what appeared to be an elongated narrow chair matching the figure's silvery sheen. It took a moment for me to realize that the Buddha wasn't sitting *on* the chair. It was integrated into the chair.

The camera shifted downward momentarily and I heard a united gasp from the people around me. There were no separate compartments in the ship. We saw into the vast expanse of the ship's interior. I learned later when I saw the schematics that there were compartments near the ship's base for cargo and fuel and redundant equipment. But there were no living quarters and no compartmentalized work stations on board.

The 'chair' was a kind of metallic stalk that ran vertically through the interior of the ship. And like the bud at the end of a long-stemmed flower, the humanoid Buddha's head-and-shoulders were at its top.

Its eyes opened. The hairs on the nape of my neck bristled as icy slivers crackled along my spine. I recognized the eyes and the sudden smile of Jack Shandon. His face seemed natural but I couldn't tell if it was flesh. That silvered hue gave me doubt that it was his own skin. He gazed at the camera and lifted a tubular armature with pincer-like fingers in a brief wave.

"*Cassandra*, this is mission control," a voice came over the massive speakers on either side of the bleachers. "How do you read? Over."

I recognized Jack's characteristic grin as he spoke: "A-OK. Reading you loud and clear." His voice was of a higher register than I remembered it being. "Checking hydraulic systems. Stand by."

Jack stared off-camera and adjusted something on the panel. Suddenly the camera lost him, picking him up seconds later as the Buddha-figure dropped down the interior shaft to a console much lower down. On the large screens, we saw Jack swivel one hundred-eighty degrees. Another camera picked him up at a different panel of dials and monitors.

Jack's artificial face gave us a very natural smile. "Hydraulic systems a go. Over."

"*Cassandra*," said the voice in the control room, "secure entranceway. Final systems check. Over."

Jack dropped several more meters and swiveled forty-five degrees, different cameras in sync with his movements so that the big screens picked him up with each position change. Jack's armatures moved rapidly as he responded, "Entranceway secure, Control. Over."

"*Cassandra*, check computer upload for flight plan sequencing. Over."

"Checking upload for flight plan sequencing." Jack altered position, dropping to another work station. "Flight plan sequencing at the ready. Over."

That voice, I wondered. *The inflections are Jack's. But there's something else. A sort of lilt that doesn't quite fit.*

One of the big screens showed the workmen descending the platform to the ground. We heard the Klaxon sirens signaling everybody to evacuate the launch area.

The large screens showed a split-screen image of Jack in the ship's cabin and a bespectacled man in shirtsleeves and loosened tie in the control room. "*Cassandra*," said the man, "Ground crew is secure. Ready to proceed with launch. Over."

From Jack: "Control, this is *Cassandra*. Event timer started. Over."

"This is Control. Launch sequence T minus twenty minutes and counting."

The back-and-forth between *The Cassandra* and Mission Control continued. Paced speech, calculated notifications. Inexorable, one measured tick at a time.

He's not coming back, I realized. *Not in my lifetime, anyway.*

The ship rippled at ignition. White flame and billowing smoke exploded from *Cassandra* as it lifted. The immense ship tore into the blue sky, heading sunward. We watched as it diminished from a massive human construct impossibly defying gravity into a shimmering needle in the sky. Even as it disappeared from view, we continued to watch the image on the viewing screens grow smaller and more distant. People around me stood in the bleachers shouting and cheering while it slowly faded into nothingness. I stood too, my eyes red and watery.

What did it matter? I thought. *Even if he returned while I was still here—he would never walk among people again.*

He was Jack Shandon. And she was *Cassandra*. And there was no way of knowing where HE began and SHE ended.

The Lady of Shadow Guard

by Lawrence Watt-Evans

The inn called the Sign of the Burning Pestle stood beside the coach road overlooking the ocean, as it had stood for more years than anyone bothered to count, forever in Twilight. Its nightwood beams were black with smoke and age, and Rosalie had once looked up at them with wonder, wonder that they had lain faithfully in their places for so very long.

Now she viewed them with sympathy, for surely they were, in their inanimate way, as weary of the place as she was herself. She had been weary of it for a very long time now.

Her Jack, tall and gray-clad, had promised to take her away from this place, to take her to his castle, Shadow Guard, that no man save himself had ever seen. Instead his words had kept her here, waiting for his return, and now that she had finally realized that all his words were lies, that he was never going to come back for her, she had nowhere else to go. She was no longer the young beauty who could ask whatever she wanted of the handsome men who came through the inn's door, who could reasonably hope to make her way in the world with a smile and willingness to learn. She was just another tavern wench, fetching drinks for travelers.

The inn door creaked open, and she turned to see who had arrived, to judge whether she should call to the kitchen to heat up the stove. The weather was clammy and unpleasant, and the inn almost empty, not a single person was seated at the tables just then, and any new arrival was a welcome diversion, however slight.

Whoever had opened that door did not hurry in, and given the wet chill of the outside air that was something of a surprise. Rosalie got to her feet and straightened her apron.

Then the customer pulled herself through the door and stood panting in the opening, her face red in the firelight, her long black hair damp and tangled—more so, perhaps, than the weather could explain. She clutched the doorframe and her eyes focused on Rosalie, but she did not step across the threshold.

The woman was ill, Rosalie decided, and she ran to help. She lifted one hand from its death-grip on the frame and wrapped it around her own shoulders, then took the woman's weight—more than her own, even in their current respective conditions—and helped her down the steps into the central dining area. She settled her onto one of the sturdy wooden chairs, steadying her.

The woman still had not said a word; now she sat gasping, one hand on the table, one on Rosalie's shoulder, and stared into Rosalie's eyes.

"Are you all right?" Rosalie asked. "Is there anything I can get you?"

That gaping mouth closed wetly, then fell open again. The dark eyes blinked.

It was very obvious that she was *not* all right, but Rosalie had not known what else to say. Now she studied the old woman's face, trying to judge what might be most helpful.

She was indeed old, perhaps twenty years older than Rosalie, and her skin sagged on her face and neck, pulling tight over her cheekbones and hanging in folds below—she had once been plump, but was no longer.

She had not had enough to eat in some time; that much was obvious. The way she was gasping, as if trying to suck the moisture from the air, convinced Rosalie that she had not had anything to drink lately, either.

"Wait here," Rosalie said. She lifted the hand from her shoulder and set it on the table's edge beside its mate, then turned and hurried to the kitchen.

The inn's proprietor was not there; he had gone off to the market in Broken Wheel to restock the pantries. His surly nephew Aldreth, currently serving as the inn's cook, was sitting by the stove with a glass of wine in his hand, his head tilted back to study the black-on-black patterns left on the ceiling by centuries of smoke. "Al, we've a customer," Rosalie said. "I need a bowl of soup."

Al's head snapped forward. "What sort of soup?"

"Whatever's fastest. She isn't well."

He frowned. "Is it catching?"

"I don't think so," Rosalie said. "She's old; I think it's her heart."

"Can she pay?"

"*I'll* worry about that; you get me some soup."

Aldreth muttered something, then got up from his chair. There was always a pot of broth kept simmering, for those occasions when a customer wanted something hot quickly, and it was simple enough for Aldreth to throw a few slices of this and that into it, and open the stove vents beneath it to bring it to a boil. A moment later Rosalie had a bowl on a tray and headed back to where the old woman sat gasping, hands clutching the table's edge.

Rosalie spooned the first mouthful into the old woman herself, and was gratified when the sagging mouth closed around the spoon and the woman's breathing seemed to ease. She swallowed, and took the spoon from Rosie's hand.

A few minutes later the old woman still had to pause every so often to pant a little, and her hands trembled on the tabletop, but her eyes were clearer, her manner calmer.

"Thank you, my dear," she said.

"Is there anything else I can get you?" Rosalie asked.

"I have no money," the old woman replied.

"Oh, don't trouble about that," Rosalie told her. "Tell me what you need, and I shall see that you have it."

"A little more to eat, perhaps, and to drink. And if I could sleep here for a time—not a bed, I can't afford that, but this chair would serve me well."

"You'll stay until you're well enough to travel, and I'll see if there's a bed to be had, whether you can pay or not. What sort of people would we be, to cast you out in your condition?"

The crone's mouth twisted. "The sort I have met more often than not, my dear."

"Well, you won't find that sort *here*," Rosalie replied, with far more conviction than she actually felt. She was not at all sure what Aldreth and his uncle Bodge might do, given the chance, but *she* did not want to see this pitiable old thing sent out into the gloom to perish. "You just wait here, and I'll see what the kitchen can spare."

A moment later she was back with bread and cheese and beer, and she sat by and watched as the old woman nibbled away at the food.

Other customers arrived as the hours passed, but Rosalie kept them from disturbing the old woman, and later she took the woman to her own bed in the attic. Climbing the stairs was a challenge for the stranger, but there was no hurry.

Why Rosalie took it upon herself to tend the old woman she could not have said; perhaps she saw too much of her own future in her unexpected guest. Nonetheless, tend her she did.

Bodge, the proprietor, was not happy about this when he returned from Broken Wheel, but so long as Rosalie paid for her guest, he would not object.

Rosalie paid. She had saved up her meager wages for years, against a time when she could no longer work for her keep.

The old woman gave her name as Beatrice. Her history, as she described it, had been adventurous and far-ranging, very unlike Rosalie's own—but there were commonalities, as well. Both had put far too much faith in the words of the wrong men, and wound up with little to show for their trust.

Beatrice told Rosalie about her travels, and Rosalie sighed enviously. She asked why Rosie had stayed, if she had wanted to see other lands.

"There was a man," Rosalie explained. "His name was Jack—Shadowjack, he called himself, and he dressed always in black and gray. He swept me off my feet with sweet words and strong kisses, and stayed for a time. Then he told me that he had certain business to attend to, and that he had to go, but he promised me he would return, that he

190

would be back for me soon, and I, fool that I was, believed him. So I waited for him."

"But he never came," Beatrice said.

"He never came," Rosalie agreed.

"What sort of a man was he, that you would wait so long?"

"A darksider, actually. He even claimed to be a Power, the Lord of Shadow Guard." She laughed bitterly. "As if a Power would come here to Twilight!"

"There are stranger things."

Rosalie waved that away. "I was a fool, taken in by his pretty lies. He said he would make me the Lady of Shadow Guard, his mighty castle that no other man had ever seen, and I half believed even *that* nonsense! He spoke of it with such conviction. . ." She shook her head. "But he never came back. It was all lies."

"Perhaps he meant to return, but could not. Perhaps he died."

"He was a darksider. They do not stay dead."

The old woman could scarcely argue with that.

The two shared the attic room, and Beatrice recovered, not as quickly as she had hoped nor as slowly as she had feared. Somewhere along the way, in her years of traveling, Beatrice had picked up something of the Art, had learned a few of the secrets of magic, and she taught Rosalie what she could, in payment for her food and lodging.

Rosalie proved a surprisingly apt pupil.

Time passed, a year and more, until Beatrice was again on her feet, and able to help out around the inn. Eventually there came a day when Rosalie went to Bodge, in the privacy of his office, and suggested that perhaps it would be fair to pay Beatrice for her help.

Bodge shrugged. "I can't pay you both," he said.

"You barely pay either of us."

"There, you see? I am as generous as I can afford to be."

Rosalie had seen enough over the years to have an idea what Bodge could afford, should he choose to do so, and she felt a swelling in her heart. For a moment she stared at her employer, and then she nodded.

"Very well, then," she said. "Let her have the pittance you pay. I'll be going."

Bodge's mouth opened, then closed. He blinked, and then shrugged again. "As you please," he said.

When Rosalie told Beatrice what she had done, the old woman asked, "Where will you go? You have no other home."

"I don't know," Rosalie said, as she gathered her scant belongings. "Perhaps I'll go looking for my Jack."

"How will you live?"

"I have the skills you taught me. I'll make do."

For a moment Beatrice watched thoughtfully as Rosalie bundled her clothes on the narrow bed. Then she said, "If your darksider died, then he may be in Drekkheim."

Rosalie paused. "What?"

"Drekkheim, in the far west. When the darksiders die they are reborn in the Dung Pits of Glyve, at the west pole of the world, in the center of the dark side. That lies within the demesne of the Baron of Drekkheim. Any who are caught on the Baron's lands must pay a few years of service as a penalty for trespassing. The rebirth itself can take years, and the Baron's lands are broad and barren, not an easy crossing. It's true that darksiders do not die as we do, but one who is slain may take several years before he can return to his old life. If your Jack *has* died since you last saw him, then he may be working out a term in the Baron's service—or he may still be regenerating in the Dung Pits."

"Dung pits do not sound like an appealing destination."

"From all I've heard, they aren't one—but the Baron of Drekkheim does not care to live in filth any more than does anyone else, and his castle is far to the east of Glyve, almost at the further end of his lands. You could ask him whether your Shadowjack has passed through of late."

Rosalie stared at the older woman for a moment, then demanded, "Why have you never suggested this before?"

"It's a slim hope, Rosie," Beatrice replied. "It's far more likely that your Jack is indeed the liar and scoundrel you have long believed him to be. I did not want to send you off in pursuit of anything so improbable. But if you're leaving anyway, I can suggest it. You may find nothing—but if there is even a slight chance that your lover is toiling in the Baron's castle, what can it hurt to take a look?"

Rosalie had no answer for that.

It took almost three years to reach the castle of the Baron of Drekkheim; she had to find her way thousands of miles across the darkside. It took the better part of another year before her petition for an audience was granted. At last, though, she knelt before his throne.

"You have come all the way from Twilight to see me," he said. "We do not see many mortals this far west—at least, not by choice. Why have you come?"

"I am seeking a man," she said. "A darksider. Jack, he's called—Jack of Shadows."

The Baron started, and looked around at the torches that lit his hall. "Do not say that name again," he said. "And move out into the light, away from the shadows."

Puzzled, Rosalie rose and obeyed. She felt a surge of hope, though, for the Baron clearly recognized the name, and seemed to respect it. Could it be that her Jackie really *was* a Lord and a Power?

"What do you want him for?" the Baron demanded. "Why do you come *here* seeking him?"

"He made me promises, long ago," Rosalie answered. "I want to know why he has not kept them. I thought perhaps he had died, and was now in your service."

The Baron shook his head. "I have not seen him in many, many years. If he has died, I am not yet aware of it. As for his promises—do you not know he is also called Jack of Liars? He is a thief and a rogue. Even among the soulless, he is considered untrustworthy."

Rosalie's heart sank in her breast as she heard these words. Her new skill with the Art let her see that the Baron was speaking the truth—or at the very least, what he believed to be the truth.

"Thank you, Lord," she said.

The Baron considered her for a moment as she stood before his throne. "What will you do now?" he asked.

"I don't know, Lord."

"I thought I sensed a spell. You know something of magic?"

"A little, Lord."

"Enough that you can sense intruders?"

"Under the correct circumstances."

"I know you have come from Twilight, and are not accustomed to living in full darkness, but would you consider employment here, perhaps?"

Rosalie blinked in surprise. "Employment, Lord?"

"You have come here because you know all those who are resurrected must pass through my lands, and it is my custom to charge them a few years' service for that passage. There are those, however, who avoid that just toll—my realm is a broad one, and great as my powers are, they do not inform me of every skulking revenant who seeks to evade me. I therefore employ certain entities to guard the outlying portions of my domain, and I have found that human Wise Women—that is the correct term, is it not?"

Rosalie nodded.

"Yes," the Baron continued. "Wise Women can serve well as guardians of my borders, to see that my rightful prey does not escape. I have a vacancy in one district at this time; do you think your skills are sufficient to essay this task?"

"I. . . I do not know, Lord. They may be."

"The position has its perks. You will understand, of course, that I do not need additional wardens in inhabited areas; if you accept my offer you will be watching over a broad stretch of otherwise uninhabited wilderness. If you are prone to loneliness this may prove unpleasant, but you will have regular visits from my staff, who will bring you food, and whatever else you might desire, within reason, and who will obey you, within reason, and perform services you ask of them. Your authority within your district will be second only to my own. In exchange, you will report to me, by messenger or by spell, every stranger you observe to cross my lands, and you will hinder them as best you can, so that I have time to intercept them. That is all. I do not expect you to engage in duels of either spells or wits with anyone, nor do I think a single human woman can reasonably be expected to employ force against a determined darksider. If you simply tell me of each trespasser, you will have done all I demand, and anything more shall be at your discretion."

"I don't. . ." She stopped without completing the sentence, unsure what she had wanted to say.

"And should that man you seek, your Jack, happen to die and return," the Baron said with an unpleasant smile, "perhaps it will be *you* who finds him and alerts me to his presence. That might provide a modicum of vengeance for his lies and mistreatment, yes?"

Rosalie's eyes lit up at that. "Yes," she said. "*Yes.*"

And so it was that Rosalie, long of the Sign of the Burning Pestle, became the Wise Woman of the Eastern Marches, in the service of the Baron of Drekkheim, dwelling alone in the wilderness near one of the borders of his realm.

She found the job suited her. After a lifetime of living among travelers and innkeepers who barely noticed her, the solitude of the waste, and the solicitous attention of the Baron's men when they visited her with her regular supplies, were a welcome change. Simply sitting on a rock watching the stars, with no thought that she might be ordered to fetch someone an ale or clean up a drunkard's vomit, could keep her happy for hours.

She was also able to practice her Art undisturbed, and her prowess grew steadily. Within a few years of her arrival she felt herself truly worthy of the title "Wise Woman," and could effortlessly sense everything of consequence that occurred within the territory the Baron had assigned her.

On those occasions when the pleasures of isolation paled, she reminded herself that ending up alone was her own fault for listening to the pretty lies Jack of Shadows had told her. Someday perhaps he would pass here, and she would be able to make him pay for those lies. She would have a chance to tell him what he had done to her. Lady of Shadow Guard, indeed! Instead she was the Wise Woman off the Eastern Marches—which was to say, mistress of a hundred square miles of desolate stone, inhabited only by a few scattered lizards and an occasional passing monster.

And once, when the Baron's men brought her the regular portion of good cheese and hard bread and salt pork, and jugs of red wine and strong ale, she took the opportunity to engage one of them in conversation, asking for news of the world beyond Drekkheim's borders. They spoke for some time—he giving her the latest gossip about the upcoming Hellgames and rumors of doings on the distant dayside, she telling him about those long-ago promises her deceitful suitor had made.

The man considered her silently during a break in the discussion, then asked, "Are you waiting for him? Is that why you're here—your magic tells you he'll come this way someday?"

"Oh, it's nothing so certain as that," she said. "He *may* come this way eventually, but I have no assurance of it, and if he does, it may not happen until long after I'm dead. But I hadn't anything better to do."

"So you're here because you *might* see him?"

Rosie thought about this for a moment, looked at her own motives as honestly as she could, then nodded. "That's right."

The man said, "He means a great deal to you, then, even though you haven't seen him in so many years."

"Yes."

"I'm not sure I understand, though," the man said. "Do you *hate* him so very much, to devote your life to punishing him, or is it that you still *love* him, and want to see him again?"

Rosalie stared out at the wasteland for a moment, then turned and stared at the man's face instead. At last she shook her head. There were questions even a Wise Woman could not answer.

"I don't know," she admitted.

Rock and Road

by Michael H. Hanson

The grizzled hitcher shuffled out of the cab of the red Chevy pickup and waved a thanks and goodbye to Randy and Leila, the handsome, sort-of couple who had picked him up hours ago. They and their poetry book AI had been good company over the long ride. A gregarious duo, they had a fun time teaching old folk songs to Billy as the miles flew by.

"Thanks again," Billy said, grabbing his rucksack.

"A single act of kindness throws out roots in all directions," Leila yelled out just before she pulled away, "and the roots spring up and make new trees!"

Billy chuckled. Their generous lift had saved him about a week's worth of walking, subjective road time.

About another half-day on Shank's mare and he should be able to find an off ramp for The Eagles first show in L.A. He fingered the few wrinkled one-dollar bills in his right jeans pocket knowing he'd make it in without having to spend a cent.

Decades of crawling, begging, conning, threatening, and lying had made him a Prince among concert gatecrashers.

Vehicles whipped by and he had to stay far to the right of the shoulder to keep from being messed up by tailgate-winds. That and the occasional surprise rainstorm kept him on his toes.

"Tach it up, tach it up, buddy gonna shut you down," Billy sang.

William "Billy" Petersen, AKA "Freshness," "The Ladies Man," "Dude," "Smooth Groove," "The Riding Dutchman," and occasionally "Bill" had been hitching the highways of America for two-thirds of his life. And at a prematurely grizzled and sun baked forty-nine years of age that was a good chunk of thumbing it.

197

Even now, with grey replacing his once red beard and smile lines becoming more and more visible around his eyes and mouth, he could still remember first stepping onto this endless stretch of asphalt and concrete.

*

It was 1968 and sixteen year old Billy wanted to have some fun. Most of his friends had already split their homes to check out the scene down in New York City, the old man was hassling him to get a haircut and a job, and Debbie had just ditched him for some college prick. He'd read articles about how brilliant things were in Haight-Ashbury, San Francisco, a place where pot grew out in the open, everyone was groovy, and hot chicks were practically giving it away.

The roads called out to him.

With a pocket full of cash ripped off from his mom's cookie jar, a pair of his older sister's ill-fitting Birkenstocks, his favorite pair of worn levis, and a garish tie-dyed t-shirt he'd made in art class, it took Billy a week of hitching, begging, and running away from older guys trying to feel him up to make it down to Interstate 80 in Massachusetts. Last Christmas he'd read a really cool Time Magazine article about a bunch of hippies who had a psychedelic drive from Boston to L.A. all of it on Interstate 80. That's what Billy wanted. Four days of sex and LSD and sleep deprivation with people who could dig him.

Illegal or not Billy made his way up a long onramp to the highway just beating the morning sunrise. A couple of squares drove by ignoring him or giving him the eye. And then came the white van.

It was something out of a Greenwich Village pipe head's dream. A 1968 Volkswagon Minibus covered in hastily painted rainbows and peace symbols. They came to a screeching halt and opened the side door. Billy barely had time to open his mouth to say hi before he was pulled inside by a mass of friendly hands.

Simultaneously, the back door was popped open and what looked like a large grey garbage bag was dumped out the back. They shut the doors just as quickly and sped off. The adventure had begun.

Billy should have known something was up the second he'd sat down in the floor of the crowded van.

"Uh." Billy muttered. "You guys going to a Halloween party or something?"

He was answered with a chorus of laughs, giggles, and chuckles. His question, however, was not far off the mark. The four men and four women whose company he'd just joined sported a bizarre and colorful variety of clothing, headgear, footwear, body-paints, tattoos, jewelry, and what appeared to be some form of cosmetic fish scales over the very long and delectable legs of two gorgeous green-maned women.

Billy also noticed that the driver, a rather hirsute blonde who appeared to have two, three-inch-long antennae jutting out of his head, was swerving quite a bit between the lines. In short, he was higher than a kite.

"Yo dude." Billy's voice wavered. "Lets keep it on the straight and narrow eh?"

"Oh Flazzbo's cool!" One sexy fish-girl cooed. "We just scored come C-20 Hallucinogenic Fungus. Helps him focus on the temporal exit-shift! You fetch me, flipper?"

Billy smiled, shrugged, and decided to play it cool. These were grade-A hippies and until now he'd been strictly small-town in his anti-establishment antics. He still had a lot to learn. So what if they were talking total nonsense?

And then it happened. Flazzbo suddenly jerked the steering wheel to the right. The passengers all lurched to the side and Billy felt his intestines contract as he cringed in anticipation of the inevitable head-on collision with the twenty-foot tall highway concrete barrier.

Billy suddenly felt himself immobilized as if the air in the van had just transformed into transparent jello. In a panic he realized he could barely breathe.

A few seconds, or possibly a lifetime, later Billy came back to his senses.

"Screeeelaaaaaa!!!!" Flazzbo ululated in a haunting alien voice.

The rest of the van cheered in response and Billy lamely joined in.

What the hell just happened? He thought wildly.

A few moments later the sunlight started flickering weirdly through all the windows, as if a million butterflies had appeared overhead.

For a split second Billy grew dizzy and wondered if he'd inhaled some spent hash without realizing it.

One minute later it had suddenly turned pitch dark and Billy could see thousands of stars in the night sky.

A short while after this things evened out a bit and the sky appeared a uniform dull grey.

Flazzbo maintained his steady 60 mph and the folks started chattering away in what Billy realized were at least three different foreign languages, none of them sounding the least bit familiar.

Flazzbo waved a free hand over the unusual glass cover on his van's strange dash and suddenly an incredible live recording of The Doors *Light My Fire* started blasting forth from every direction, though try as he might Billy could not see any speakers anywhere. Overhead, some strange device pressed up against the ceiling started sending out multiple colored beams of light, reminding Billy of the laser blasts he'd seen in *Destroy All Monsters* at the local theater a few weeks ago. These proved harmless enough but were definitely adding to Billy's realization that he had most definitely stepped through the looking glass.

A few minutes later all four of the women (the two buxom ladies with the green hair and odd skin modeling, and the two petite, gorgeous redheads that Billy suddenly realized were identical twins) simultaneously stripped off their skimpy clothing and pulled a shocked Billy into a pornographic fantasy beyond his wildest hopes and dreams. The other passengers smirked at Billy's surprise before re-engaging in their previous conversations, as if this sort of thing happened all the time.

Jefferson Airplane's *White Rabbit* next filled the interior of the van with pulsating power.

Billy's amazing journey had begun.

*

The sun was shining down pretty heavy so Billy pulled a soiled bandana out of his right hip pocket and wrapped it around his head in a tight dew-rag.

He wondered if he'd bump into himself at all this trip. Thing was, lately he'd been doing that more and more. He was never one for keeping records or journals, and even though his memory had always been good, all the gigs, and concerts, and play dates had started blurring together in his mind of late.

Sometimes when he'd come face to face with a twenty or thirty year younger Billy, he'd panic and have second thoughts and try to convince the boy to sober up and find his way home. This always scared the kid off, and ever since the Angels messed up his hip and knee at Altamont he was never in good enough shape to run after himself.

Poor little Billy must think he's some kind of escaped lunatic.

Funny how time plays tricks on the mind, middle-aged Billy couldn't blame teenage Billy for taking off from him every time they ever met. Heck, he remembered when he first found out about the Temporal-Exits (or Tempxits in roadspeak) how some old weirdo seemed to be tracking him every now and then, some filthy old bum with a dirty red beard. Oh well. Life and the road go on.

Billy spotted an old man dressed in a ratty, threadbare, brown U.S. Army uniform, circa C-20, maybe the forties, on the other side of the highway. The man, balding and wearing spectacles, carried a small duffle bag over one shoulder and a rusty looking trumpet in his other hand.

"Hey Glenn," Billy shouted to be heard over the roar of traffic, "you may have a gal in Kalamazoo, but you ain't got a snowball's chance in hell of hitching a ride back to dubya dubya two!"

Glenn scowled at Billy and flipped him the middle finger before continuing his slow hike in the opposite direction.

A sleek metallic vehicle (probably something from C-24) shot by at about 600 miles per hour. It traveled roughly three feet above the road surface and it's tail wind nearly knocked Glenn off his feet.

Billy laughed and shouted aloud, "Duck Dodgers in the twenty-fourth and one half Century!"

*

Young Billy's eyes opened wide when they stopped at a nightclub just a couple of hours after his ride had started. For some bizarre reason it was evening already and the sky was full of stars. It had been morning when he'd been picked up.

The next shock came when Billy found out they were in Detroit, MI. *How the hell did we get here so quick*, he thought, *we weren't driving that fast*.

As the party van troupe walked through the front entrance of the nightclub Billy did a double take just before entering when he saw a sign above a side door that read, *Negro Entrance*.

Sitting at a small table near the front stage, Billy couldn't help but feel conspicuous as he suddenly realized that most of the small crowd consisted of squares in suit or dress. There wasn't a dude in the bar with hair that touched his ears and Billy felt more than a little conspicuous with his shoulder length locks. Flazzbo kept the heat off, though, with non-stop drink orders and eyebrow-lifting tips.

The final slap to Billy's rational mind occurred when he found himself sitting a mere ten feet from a very young Nat King Cole singing *Smile*.

*

A maroon 1975 Mercury Marquis Brougham pulled over to the side of the highway. The passenger door opened and Billy stepped out. Before shutting the door he smiled and yelled "thanks for the lift, Jimmy. You saved me a whole day."

The grizzled driver, looking to be in his sixties, smiled back, "any friend of labor can step into my cab any time. Rock on, Billy."

The car sped away in a spray of gravel and dirt, and the hitchhiker resumed his long walk.

Billy felt a few kinks kick in so he sat down on some brush grass and put his lanky frame through a series of yoga movements he'd mastered the Summer of '67 at an Ashram in Arizona.

After awhile his muscles started to loosen up and the day's stress slowly bled away. It would be a good night. Must be five years since he'd seen and heard Glen, Don, Bernie, Randy, and Tim performing and singing that sweet four-part harmony. Billy hoped they'd open with *Desperado* and *Take It To The Limit*. Those were his faves.

Sure, *Hole in The World* carried a ton of existential angst Henley never showed in the majority of his popular work, but Billy was an admittedly shallow, non-intellectual music fan when it came to his lyrical tastes.

Songs gotta be felt in the gut, he thought, *not ripped apart to find its hidden meanings.*

After a few more calve-extensions and some deep breathing exercises Billy stood back up and moved forward. He figured half a day would do it.

*

Young Billy was tripping on time travel, and the temporal exits were his dealer.

Every day was a new adventure as Flazzbo took them on and off some road into different decades, sometime even centuries. For the most part though, the party van liked to hit events and gigs in the 50's, 60's, 70's, and 80's, 20th Century or C-20 in roadspeak.

Flazzbo was apparently from the not so distant future, and financed this incredible road trip by making bootleg 3-D holographic recordings of live music venues, and selling them on the global-net gray market in his own time track.

Billy once tried to get Flazzbo to explain to him the history of the road. Had it been built by aliens or super humans from the distant future? Flazzbo and the others just laughed and said The Road was The Road. It had always been here and always will be here. It existed throughout the width and breadth of time from the birth of the planet to its eventual demise, millions of years in both directions. Driving one direction on The Road lead you to the past, and the other direction to the future. It was as simple as that.

The suddenly appearing and disappearing exits, off ramps, side-roads, trails, and footpaths were each a doorway into a different time period.

Apparently, some folks had a natural affinity for knowing when and how to find the Exits to and from The Road, because it was something that could only be done in certain moments, as they only flared into and out of existence for no more than a single second, when the temporal exit shift occurs. Folks like Flazzbo didn't really need this natural connection to the road, as they loaded up on mind-altering drugs to expand their consciousness and all of their senses. People from the far future didn't need this sixth-sense either, as they had expensive technology that would tell them when and where to drive onto or off of these strange exits.

As far as Flazzbo and the gang was concerned, though, The Road was nothing more than an advantageous ticket to party hardy.

The immediate future spread before Billy as an endless party of grooving to great music, non-stop sex with wild erotic women, and multiple drug-induced highs and trips.

Billy felt like the luckiest kid on the face of the planet.

*

Billy knew he was making lousy time and pushed himself harder. Lately he was getting short of breath after only a few miles of walking at a shot.

To take his mind off his heavy-feeling chest, Billy pondered his regrets like a stack of cards. The first ten years of hitching between exits had been one long drug-induced vacation. Concert after concert, venue after venue, it was quite a run. Then one five-month stretch behind bars in Macon County Prison for possession, he sobered up.

And he realized he was no longer a teen runaway but a man well into his 20's. He suddenly felt a strong desire to return home and see his parents and little sister, and so Billy got back to hitchhiking as soon as he was paroled. Unfortunately, matters were not quite that simple.

Try as he might Billy could not find the exit or path back to his own time. He traveled the highways for years and learned from other temporal-Hitchers that the exits, onramps, roads, paths, and trails they'd all used were mutable. That is, if each and every temporal exit were not used on any kind of regular basis, they dwindled, faded, and even eventually disappeared. The few times he was lucky he found himself near his home, but several decades before he was actually born, or in a decade where he would have already been dead of old age.

And then, after fifteen more years of searching for the way home, he realized how pointless it all was. Entering middle age the gulf between him and his lost loved ones was just too big. Even if he did find his way back to his proper place in time he could never explain his absence. The Road was now his home.

It was in the middle of this sobering realization that Billy found the answer to one of the world's greatest mysteries. Why do thousands of people disappear, annually, reportedly near the major highways of the world, never to be seen again by family or friends? The United States alone was home to tens of thousands of unsolved cases of road travelers never reaching their destinations, forever lost.

The Road's time exits, the lure of fantastic adventure, the difficulty and near-impossibility of finding one's way back to their proper time-track, and then not sounding like a lunatic needing to be institutionalized when trying to connect with or confront old friends and loved ones, appearing as much older or much younger than you should have been at that time.

Billy could easily imagine the number of psychiatric establishments flooded with irrational individuals insisting they were victims of supernatural forces beyond their comprehension, subjected en mass to butcher/neurosurgeon Walter Jackson Freeman's transorbital lobotomies. Years later when such medical atrocities fell out of favor, such patients were merely doped to utter indifference with large quantities of Thorazine.

Billy rested for about twenty minutes then got back on his feet. He saw what looked like a turn-off just a few hundred yards in the distance. The tingling began in his belly. A portal was going to form just up ahead. He smiled.

*

Time was a rollercoaster and in a few months Billy struck out on his own.

It had been a wild ride with the party van. He'd lost his virginity, popped all manner of drugs and stimulants, and seen and heard great music performed by people old before his birth.

But he felt the urge to choose his own destiny and so bid the wild travelers goodbye. Flazzbo tried to warn Billy that going off on his own meant that he would lose the semi-safe predictability of the few dozen well-traveled pathways through time that the van driver had limited van troupe to over the past three months.

Billy, taking a long hard pull on his joint just smiled.

"I'm a big boy now Flazz," Billy laughed, "I can take care of myself."

Billy never saw Flazzbo or the others again.

And, it didn't take Billy long to find out that he was a Road-Man himself, blessed with the psychic gene to sense when a temporal exit was going to appear on one of life's grand highways, an ability greatly enhanced by pot and acid.

Thirty years passed like a dream.

* Dancing in the audience to the thrill and power of Janis Joplin singing *Ball and Chain* at the Monterey Pop Festival. . .

* Popping ludes with Brian Wilson between recording sessions on the album *Good Vibrations*. . .

* The surreal experience of watching The Doors opening for Simon and Garfunkel in NYC and singing *The End* before a stunned uptight audience of thirteen thousand folk music lovers. . .

* Buying Bruce Springsteen a beer after one of his first gigs at a bar in Newark, NJ. . .

* Nearly going deaf due to teen girl shouting while watching The Beatles perform *A Hard Day's Night* at Shea Stadium/Candlestick Park, August 15, 1965. . .

* Getting chased out of Lawrinson Hall student dormitory at Syracuse University, September 1982, during The Greatful Dead's U.S. Festival. . .

* Grooving to The Rolling Stones performing *Sympathy For The Devil* and getting the shit kicked out of him by the Hell's Angels at Altamont Speedway, Livermore, CA, December 6, 1969. . .

* Woodstock, Summer of 1969, Yasgur's Farm, a speed-induced orgy in Max Yasgur's calving barn. . .

* Conning a 22-year-old Madonna Louise Ciccone into thinking he is an exec with Sire Records and getting the midnight ride of his life Summer of 1980. . .

Damn it life was good.

In fact, the past year had proven the most interesting of all in Billy's bizarre time-traveling life. It seemed his presence at multiple music venues all over the planet, several at the exact same time, was being noticed and picked up on by a few curious filmmakers, videographers, photographers, and chrono-historians. The myth of the *Eternal Roadie* or *Rock Fan Phantom* was a semi-popular fable among concertgoers and music reporters. Nobody had put the theories and observations to print yet, but Billy figured it was only a matter of time.

And what would be the effect on causality and temporal stability if he and his kind got outed? Back during one of his lucid stretches of weeks one summer he'd bumped into a science fiction writer outside of a small sci-fi conference in Santa Fe, New Mexico. Loosening up and sharing a portion of his life story with the man, Billy found himself the audience to a wealth of well thought out contemplations on time travel theory and the dangers and contradictions of temporal paradoxes. The lanky author, balding and smoking a meerschaum pipe, was a warehouse of endless speculations on time dilation, warping space, and general relativity. When it came to Billy's suggestion of the concept of *a physical road through time*, though, the writer just laughed. A few hours later Billy bid Roger goodbye and left the combination coffee and head shop with the firm decision that his life was better off just staying buzzed and hitting rock venues. If the time/space continuum was heading toward a cataclysmic explosion or implosion, then fuck it.

Time to have some fun while it was still to be had, Billy thought as he popped a tab of acid. If he timed it right he should be able to hitch The Road and in two days catch Dillon performing *Masters of War* at The Gaslight Café.

*

Billy reached the exit and groaned. He'd screwed up again. Must have missed it by a good two years he figured. Suddenly a van pulled off onto the shoulder of the road and its side door popped open.

"Need a ride man?" A strange lisping woman said.

"Sure" Billy answered and ambled his way over and into the flower-child mobile.

The vehicle drove right onto the off ramp and away from the highway just as a temporal-exit-shift blurred the air in front of Billy's weary bloodshot eyes.

"Smooth move, Exlax." He said.

The big blonde guy driving just nodded his head in reply. Something funny about the freaks Billy was now riding with though.

Oh they weren't all that unusual at first glance. The driver was a gene-splice from the Funshuku-Satellite Colony, still sporting his cranial downlink prods. The green chicks obviously a couple of pleasure-shemps from one of the Atlantic underwater globe resorts, and the two redheads a pair of XZ gratification clones. The rest were your usual mix of C-15 through C-22 hitchers and road whores, not all that different from Billy himself.

"Yah!" The Driver shouted out. "Boston. Massachusetts. C-20 alright. Maybe late 60's. . ."

No. Billy thought desperately. *No.*

"Hey. I see some fresh meat looking to lift," One of the shemps trilled. "And he's young and cute. Lets stop!"

Billy squinted his eyes and saw his life come full circle. There he was, a sixteen-year-old boy about to embrace eternity.

"Don't stop," Billy shouted and started standing up.

A split second later a sharp staggering pain flooded his right arm and chest. Billy dropped back down struggling unsuccessfully to breathe. His heart, abused with drugs and booze and concert-vendor fat-fried food for over thirty years, just gave out.

"Ewwwwwwww," One of the Shemps squealed. "Gramps took a dirt-nap!"

Two men, a couple of passengers looking like village-rejects from an old Frankenstein movie, quickly stuffed Billy's fresh corpse into a large grey disposal bag as the van came to a stop. They dumped his body out the back door just after the young Hitcher was pulled inside.

They sped away.

"Uh." Young Billy muttered. "You guys going to a Halloween party or something?"

The Aspect of Dawn

by Shariann Lewitt

They had all come to Keenset to stand against Heaven. Why Keenset? Innovation among the humans seemed to have visited this city as if it were the Aspect of a Deity, though of course to even think that would be heresy. Yet humans here were inventing, rediscovering technologies or perhaps creating them anew, who could say? It was all very strange that so many new ideas emerged in this one city in the South, but there it was.

Naturally, Brahma blamed Sam. This time Sam wasn't going to back away.

Sam, of course, also known as Siddhartha and the Buddha, was ready to fight the forces of Trimurti for Acceleration. Ratri, goddess of the night was with him, as were Kubera and the Rakasha and many of the lesser gods. Kubera drilled the thousands of men who mustered to defend the city where piece by painful piece men had rediscovered the printing press and plumbing, and perhaps more to come. Sam held his councils of war and awaited Nirriti with his troops of the dead.

Along with them was one inconspicuous ape. Among all the others who stole fruit from laden tables and swung between branches and the deep eaves of temples, no one noticed one ape in particular. They all looked the same. In any case, who cared to notice when gods gathered and demons ran free across the plain and everyone knew that something great, something mighty, was about to unfold. Most reasonable folks were afraid. Many of those younger, who had grown up on tales of adventure without any concept of what real battle entailed, enlisted.

Ratri did not stay at the Palace where Sam and Kubera had made their headquarters. She had withdrawn to her Temple in the center of town. Not one of her larger establishments, it was still elegant and quiet, built of black marble that had been richly carved with stories from her various

211

lives, lit by fires burning in tall brass stands that shed more shadows than light.

An armorer attended her in her private chamber, having been called upon to make black armor for the battle to come. He had never made armor for a lady before, let alone a goddess, let alone a goddess of such distinct beauty. The breastplate fit tolerably well but his hands trembled as he tried to buckle it in place and he averted his eyes from his creation.

"You will not be able to fit it correctly if you do not look at me," the goddess complained fretfully. "Now adjust it as if I were any soldier, or at least any general, who you were fitting."

"Yes, Lady," he said, and bowed, but he could not bring himself to actually judge how the metal lay against her skin (luscious skin that sparkled like the depths of the night, almost the color of the midnight sheen he had worked so hard to burnish into the metal now on her body.) He dared not touch her as he adjusted the straps and so he could not tell if they needed to be tighter or let out.

"Oh here, let me," a voice interrupted his confusion. And since he could not look, he could not tell at first that it was not a man who had spoken. It was, in fact, an ape, with clever hands and no fear of the goddess at all.

Ratri smiled. "Thank you, Tak. Have you heard anything of Ushas? She should have been here before now. I know she is in the city."

The ape shook his head. "Not a thing, Lady. I've gone out to listen. People talk in front of me, but Dawn came as usual this morning across the sky and disappeared into the sunlight. She didn't stop here. And I haven't heard anything about any demigods leaving the main pack and heading this way, either."

Ratri paced. "I know my sister. Ushas would have joined our main body by now if she hadn't been delayed. By them."

Tak, the ape, knew exactly what she meant and tried to diffuse her clear concern. "She was going to try to bring a group with her. She needs to convince them, and many of the demigods can be. . ."

Ratri smiled. "Lazy. Selfish. Completely mercenary, which is how they achieved their rank in the first place. Ushas is such an idealist. I tried to talk her out of it, make her see reason. I tried to get her to leave earlier but she was so sure she could turn a few of them with her Aspect. What do you think of the armor?"

"Looks magnificent. They'll have to carve a whole new chamber in the Temple to commemorate this. But how does it feel? Can you move easily? Is it too heavy on your shoulders? Does it dig in anywhere?"

"Chafes a bit under my arm, now that I think about it," Ratri said to the armorer. "Can you do anything about that?"

Not having to actually touch her, and called on in his realm of expertise, he recovered his composure. "Swing your arms around as if you were swinging a sword. Now up and down as if you were mounting a horse. Now walk a bit. Anything other than the chafing? Show me exactly where it is uncomfortable."

The armorer marked it with a yellow wax crayon. Ritra sighed. "That color makes me think of Ushas. Can you fix the armor?"

"Yes, of course Lady. Now move again and make sure where I marked is the only place it is uncomfortable. I'll have this for you tomorrow."

Ritra swung her arms a few more times and climbed up on the seat of a chair to make sure she could get onto a horse, then shook her head. "I think that's got it." The armorer unbuckled the goddess and left with pieces that he hadn't contoured quite right wrapped in midnight quilting.

"Can you find out what is keeping her, Tak?" the goddess asked when the armorer was well away. "I'm afraid something's gone wrong and she's in danger."

The ape blinked. "I do not think I can get to Heaven without a ride, or it will take me a very long time."

Ritra laughed. "Oh, no, dear Tak. Ushas is here in Keenset. She has a lovely pleasure palace outside the city walls near the river with the most charming glade and grotto and courtyards. She's been here for nearly a year. Why do you think this revolution in thought started here? That is her Aspect, after all. Didn't you know? No, what I mean is why has she not joined us here for our councils? I know she had asked some of the demigods who she thought might be sympathetic to be her guests in the hope of winning them to our side, but I have heard nothing from her for days, not a call, not a note, nothing. It is not like her. I don't know why she thought they would be any use to us, though perhaps keeping them from fighting for the other side would be useful. I don't know. But I haven't heard from her for days and a few of her guests are not the better sort at all and oh, Tak, you are my friend. You understand?"

"Of course, my goddess." He lowered his eyes and remembered, and wondered if she remembered too, when he had been a man and the Archivist of Heaven. When she had once danced with him on rose petals. When she had favored him.

What she asked was a little thing, something very easy for an ape to do. And in any case, there was little else he could do. It was not like he could contribute much to the war effort in his present form and often he felt that he was only in the way.

*

"It bugs me, that ape hanging on that tree outside the window. He keeps sneaking in here, too," said Bhairav.

"No one else is eating the bananas," Maya observed. "So why do you care if he steals a few?" She shrugged her lovely shoulders and picked delicately at the repast that sat in front of the large window where the ape was not the only animal that hung outside waiting to forage.

Small songbirds fought with doves and even peacocks for the bits of cashew and grains of saffron rice that littered the table. A sloth had picked at an ornamental leaf and two ravens boldly wandered about the detritus of the meal tearing any stray meat they could find clinging to bones. The smaller raven stuck his beak into two of the cups and slurped noisily, clearly satisfied with the wine.

Why, then, notice one more creature picking at their leftovers?

Bhairav made a face. "It just bugs me, you know? Maybe because he takes whole ones instead of picking up the pieces."

"There are no pieces. No one's been eating the bananas. You're just nervous," Maya said. "Do you really think that anyone is going to notice that little bitch is gone, or look for her? And really, we can just tell them the truth if it comes up."

Bhairav glanced at the gloriously beautiful demigoddess tied up in the far corner of the room. Her golden veil had been bound through her mouth as a gag and pale rose scarves secured her firmly to the armchair brought for this one purpose. She tried to scream out but the veil effectively cut off her voice and so nothing but the faintest sound emanated from her contorted face.

Maya stood in front of the prisoner and grinned. "You thought you had it all over me, didn't you. You and me, it always comes down to that, doesn't it, Ushas? Well, I win this time. You and your friends, you're not going to get away with it. And your friends will all agree with me anyway. They only came here because you invited them and you have such a pretty place. That's all you do, start the sunlight, so sweet." Maya made a face at the bound demigoddess. "If you promise to shut up I'll untie the gag."

The bound demigoddess nodded.

"On second thought, I'm not sure I can trust you. So we'll just leave you here while I go meet with your little cabal. Not that they will have any idea, of course. I can do you oh so well. And who shall I make Bhairav look like? Kamdev? That would be hilarious. I could just see you as the sweet little love god with the honey bees." She giggled. "Or how about one of the Ashwini twins? What a pair of goody two-shoes. Could be fun, though, to see Bhairav trying to impersonate one of them. What do you think, Mr. Warrior? Can you pull it off?"

The demigod of War appeared most miserable at the thought. "What about the real Ashwini? Won't they be there?"

Lady Maya, demigoddess of illusion, tittered. "No. They're such scrupulous good boys that they refuse to take sides. Healing is for all, as they keep saying. Any who are sick or injured have claim to their skills."

"But won't it be suspicious if one is there and not the other? Have you ever seen them apart?"

215

Maya thought a moment and then shrugged. "It's one of them or Kamdev, take your pick."

"Great, a wuss with a sugar cane bow, or a horse-head doctor. How about someone a little more exciting?"

Maya shook her head. "That's it, I'm afraid. For demis who are on the other side, or at least wavering, and I am dead certain will be absent."

Bhairav considered his options as the ape bounced on the windowsill and grabbed another banana.

"I'll go with the horse heads then. At least they're not idiots, and they're warriors when they're not healing people."

Maya nodded, and then waved her hand and a ripple of force flowed through the air like a wave deep in water. When it had passed, to the eye Bhairav and Maya stood there no longer. Instead of a four armed war god and lovely red haired goddess of illusion stood a horse-headed god of healing and speed and the breathtakingly beautiful goddess of dawn. Who sat bound to the armchair in the corner, the golden veil still gagging her mouth.

Ushas of illusion smiled at Ushas bound. For all her great beauty, it was not a pretty smile. "I believe your friends are meeting in the Courtyard of the Sunlight Lotus before sunset. We can't deprive them of your presence, and guidance in the matter of best to break with their betters. Ta, later."

And with that, Ushas and one of the Ashwini twins swept out of the room. Followed by fury in bound Ushas's eyes.

The ape on the table finished his banana, tossed the peel out the window as he had done with the previous three, but this time did not retreat back to the huge banyan tree that shaded this side of the palace. No, this time he hopped off the table onto the tiled floor and made his way over to the bound demigoddess.

"Do not worry, Lady," he murmured as he untied her gag. "But please try to remain quiet so that your captors don't realize you've been released. At least not quite yet." With that, he untied the lovely rose scarves around her wrists and ankles, and then rubbed the skin where the silk had bit cruelly into her legs and now made it difficult for her to stand.

"Ow, ow, ow," said the Goddess of the Dawn as the circulation returned to her hands and feet. She grabbed the sturdy arms of the chair that had held her for balance as she hopped from one foot to the other. Only after she had reestablished her ability to stand did she notice the ape standing at her side.

"Would you like a mango? I'm sorry, but the bananas are all gone." He held out a very tempting yellow fruit with a deep red blush, just the colors of the dawn. Ushas smiled at him.

"Thank you, but I believe I have some work to do."

"That is true, Lady, but you'll need your voice. Maybe some of this limeade, at least? Because that gag didn't do you any good."

She blinked. Twice. "You're not just some human stuck in an ape body for a passing thought the Lords of Karma didn't like," she rasped as the ape handed her a tall glass of sweet limeade. The drink tasted better than any soma she remembered in Heaven, especially when the metallic flavor of the gold in her veil lingered on her tongue. It soothed her throat. The ape was right, too, she would need her voice when she got there. If Maya and Bhairav hadn't already led out her faction of demigods and lost everything.

"Do not despair, Lady." A hairy hand patted her own. Which would have been sacrilege and possibly blasphemy, not to mention grounds for six more incarnations as an ape, had not his eyes shown only the most pure compassion for her. "Better to have your voice."

"You are in this form because you were an Accelerationist?"

"And fought for the cause," he confirmed. "But that's not important now. Now we have to get you to that meeting before Maya usurps the whole thing. But I think we can maybe get some help."

He whistled. The window filled with Mayura, the most beautiful peacock in all the world. Created from the feather of the Garuda bird, Mayura was a much smaller and more temperamental creature. It could not carry any of the gods, or even any of the larger goddesses. But Ushas had her own chariot that she drove across the sky before the sun every morning, and Mayura could pull that through the corridors of the Palace. And, like Mayura, the chariot could fly.

Ushas smiled, and the ape's heart melted. He had adored her sister Ratri for much of his life, but her little sister Dawn won him with that single glorious moment of gratitude. "Worthy ape, you deserve all the bananas you desire. And anything else."

"Can I come along?" Okay, he knew he was pushing it with that, but he could hardly resist.

She nodded, and he leaped aboard her tiny chariot of Dawn. She took the reins as the Mayura bird took to the air and they were out the window and across the courtyard where the ape had stood vigil in the window for so many hours.

Ushas' Palace, where she had hosted most of the lesser demigods of Heaven for the past month or more in luxury, sprawled beautifully. Inner courtyards tiled in marble and lapis flew beneath them, delicate fountains that reminded the ape and the demigoddess of Heaven interrupted creations of towers and balconies, wide corridors and reception halls. The great peacock screeched as she flew, and Dawn guided her to land in a particular courtyard where a carpet covered platform had been erected beside a pool where yellow lotus bloomed.

Two demigods reclined by the pool, appearing to all eyes to be nothing more than taking their ease in the pleasant shade and perhaps indulging in the heady scent of the blooms. A bottle lay between them, but these, being younger demigods, had never experienced the great vintages of long lost Urth and so were content with the local best. The ape recognized Bhumi and Candra, two planetary deities newly promoted from the ranks of venerable (or at least very desirable) humans. Shukra lay a little apart with a vague smile on his face, but then Shukra had never been precisely serious about anything.

And approaching the dais, accompanied by at least two more demis the ape had thought allied to the Accelerationist cause, was the false Ushas and the horse headed healer. Tak hissed and spat and had the urge to throw something nasty, only nothing nasty had survived the careful grooming of the grounds.

False Ushas turned to true Ushas and pointed her finger. "Spy," she screamed, her face screwed up with fury. "She's taken on my appearance to fool you, but at least I'm here and I can tell you. She's one of them, she's working for Trimurti." Then she turned to the ape. "And you," she hissed, this time her voice pitched so that the ape heard her clearly but no one beside her compatriot could make out her words. "I recognize you, Tak. I threw your spear beyond World's End. You have no power now, you're not even human. And you never will be again. And just you watch. I'm going to dismantle this entire little conspiracy right now and there's not a thing you can do."

Tak hid behind true Ushas' gold embroidered rose colored skirts as if he were terrified. He knew Maya, and even in his ape brain he understood something of how she worked. Maybe he understood even better with his ape brain then when he thought as a man.

"Leave him out of it, Maya. It's between the two of us and it always has been."

Ushas-Maya laughed unpleasantly. "You're an idiot. He was always part of it. Not with you, you never knew him. He was an ape by the time you got promoted. But me. You should have seen the way he looked at me when he was still a man and I came into the Archives looking for information. He was disgusting. Besides admitting his disloyalty to the gods. On top of everything."

"I hate to tell you whichever one you are, but we're all what someone might call disloyal to the gods. At least to Trimurti," Shukra said from his bed in the foliage. "I'm all over humans."

Bhumi twittered. "Yes, you are. As long as they're young and pretty. No discrimination. You make all kinds of promises, too, and you forget."

"What's the point of our positions anyway? We're planetary gods of planets half the sky away. Honorary positions entirely, just so they have some excuse to promote us and keep us around," Shukra said. "We don't really have Aspects, not the way they do." He didn't sound upset about this, not in the least. Everyone knew Shukra was simply lazy. So long as life was pleasant and easy for him, and he was adored and beautiful and had a selection of lovers, he was content. He certainly didn't want to fight.

"We could have Aspects if we develop them," Ushas pointed out. She did not go so far as to say that she herself had done so. Riding her Dawn chariot across the sky before the Sun rose was the least of her duties, though she had carefully shielded the true Power of Dawn.

She had come to Keenset to test whether she had, in fact, developed a true Aspect and not simply an Attribute, but she had seen her power slowly work its way through the human population. Minds opened and began to examine, and inventions followed. A printing press emerged, and a toilet. But it all went so slowly, that was the problem. She brought the dawning of realization, not the full blaze of understanding. They had to put in a lot of the work themselves.

"Yes, well, not everyone is as diligent as you," Bhumi said, and pouted. "No one can argue that you've not worked hard, but then you have a well defined role. Me, really, I never much mattered. Only that I was old Brahma's favorite concubine for a number of incarnations."

"Exactly," one of the Ushas said. "Which is why we are on the side of Trimurti. What has humanity to offer us? We were human, and not that long ago, let me remind you. And it wasn't all that much fun as I recall. Being a concubine was a lot of sit around and wait to be called to have sex with some god who could not care less about whether you were even there. No, you just existed for him to get off and he forgot you the minute he did."

"Well, not entirely," Bhumi said. "Or we wouldn't be here. We'd still just be humans."

Both Ushas sighed in unison. No one had ever said Bhumi was one of the more intelligent of the newly appointed demigoddesses. Nor would anyone. Ever.

"We have a war to wage," Ashwini jumped onto the dais and started to speak as other dreamy-eyed demigods and goddesses drifted in to the courtyard. The fountain bubbled softly behind his harsh voice. The scent of yellow lotuses permeated the soft breeze. Bhumi passed around a tray of candied rose petals and little squares of nougat.

Tak, who had seen a number of wars and not a few war councils, could not help but roll his eyes at this ridiculous collection. These demigods knew nothing of what they were about to do, or not do, or what war meant. Most of them had no idea of what they meant, when it came down to it. Tak was grateful that his ape form hid his tears of laughter, his grimace, his roar of hilarity at these poseurs.

"We have a war," Ashwini repeated himself. "The age old war of our kind, those who uphold the values of the Deists against the rash and radical plans of the Accelerationists. They've been trying since before most of us were conceived to tear down the fabric of our society, to teach humans to use science and technology they're not ready for so that those same humans will rip this world apart. The Gods, that is to say, us, we are the ones who keep order and peace. We give humans clear goals and a way to live, and we reward them for good behavior. We ourselves know that those promises are kept, for haven't we all become gods ourselves? Isn't this the fate of all humanity, to eventually partake of all the good of Heaven?

"The Accelerationists lie. They say that we want to keep all that is good here for ourselves. That clearly isn't true. We simply don't want humanity to destroy itself as it did on Urth. If the Gods didn't plan to share with humans, why did they elevate us to their ranks?"

"Because we were good lays," Shukra called out. A number of others joined his silver toned laughter.

Ushas sat and listened, folded in on herself. Tak could feel a glimmering from her, power that radiated softly like an additional layer of gold in the light of the sunset. It made him feel good, and thoughtful. He found himself examining Ashwini's words, but then he had always been of an examining frame of mind.

Ashwini snorted through his long horse nose, which brought yet more laughter. The two Ushas, who had been still, listening, turned to face each other.

"Traitor."

"Spy."

"We were all human," one of the Ushas announced in a voice that rang like the herald of the light. "We came from humans and we remember our lives as humans and mostly, those lives were not pleasant. Every time someone had an original idea, or created anything that looked promising, it was destroyed. I remember my mother teaching me to weave back when I was human. She had an idea for threading a loom so that she could create more interesting patterns in the fabric, using different colors without re-stringing the threads. It wasn't even very complicated once you saw the idea of it. And we were all so excited. She made beautiful saris with colors and patterns woven in, not printed. Or she did until the Temple found her. The next day all the looms in the village were smashed and my mother incarnated into a dog and me, I was taken away and placed in one of Ratri's establishments to sell my body and my nights. Fortunately, the goddess noticed me and made me Ushas, saying that the Goddess of the Night always had a little sister, Dawn. But how many of us have seen the same in our villages and neighborhoods? How many of us know about ideas for better living that disappeared, and people along with it?"

"But why do we care about them?" Bhumi asked. "I mean, I know everyone doesn't get the same, but then I'm not Brahma, either, after all. Why should I fight for humans? They didn't fight for me."

"Exactly. Everyone for themselves! We are gods, so we fight for the gods, easy as that!"

"If you have the intelligence of a mango," Tak muttered.

"Don't insult mangoes," Shukra said. Tak started. He had not noticed that Shukra had moved, nor that anyone had been close enough to overhear him. Shukra studied him then smiled. "Tak of the Bright Spear, if I am not mistaken. One of the most dangerous Accelerationists after

Siddhartha himself. And yet you do not speak at this meeting. I wonder why. Would you like some nougat?"

Tak took the sticky treat from the plate the Venus god proffered. Why a Venus god? What did Venus matter here? What, indeed, was Venus and did it even still exist out near lost Urth? But the gods had needed positions for their favorites in the Pantheon and dredged up old astrological gods who had no function here that anyone could tell. Except for Candra, who always complained that had his hands full with three moons (though what he did with them was anyone's guess.)

"I'm just an ape these days. What about you? Why is Shukra here at this clandestine meeting?"

Shukra shook his head and his perfumed ringlets swept his shoulders. "Clandestine? Do you think there is anything here the high gods do not know? No, they let us amuse ourselves and see who presents on which side. Me? I'm just in it for the show."

"For Trimurti," yelled Ushas, raising her fist.

"For humanity," intoned Ushas, her arms and eyes raised to the sky.

Then the two slowly turned toward each other and hissed. "You little. . ." But the words got confused as the two identical Dawn goddesses launched themselves at each other on the dais in front of the bubbling fountain. One tore at the other's hair, and one kicked at the other's knees. Ashwini rushed to aid one but then seemed confused. The rest of the demigods crowded closer. This was more entertaining than all the talk of war. Ushas slapped Ushas' face. Ushas bit Ushas' pinky. Ushas broke a nail. Ushas stomped on Ushas foot. Everyone could see that Ushas, both Ushas, fought like schoolgirls.

"I'll put my beach house on the one on the left," Shukra said.

"I'll take it. Against twenty rubies." A deep rumble accompanied to offer.

"Back off. No rakasha. That offer was for Tak only."

"It was an offered bet. I took it. You have no right to rescind, spawn of a slizzard and a drunken one-eyed bound thing."

"She's winning. Which one is she?"

Ushas screamed. Ushas kicked. Ushas tried to throw a punch but, alas, she had never tried this before and didn't have the knack. Her long nails prevented her from forming a tight fist, so she grabbed Ushas' choti instead and went to rip it open.

Ushas, being a modest virgin (and celebrated for such), squealed at the threat of exposure and pulled Ushas' left earring down. Hard. Blood spurted out of Ushas' ear as she screamed and collapsed inward, protecting her delicate lobe. Ushas held a bloody earring in her hand, took one look at it and threw the offending piece of jewelry into the pond among the lotuses.

Maya could not hold the illusion with blood pouring out of her ear. Suddenly she was visibly Maya again, crouched on the platform, cradling her ear in her hand.

Ushas winced and then turned resolutely from her adversary. "Tomorrow we will join Sam and his forces and oppose Trimurti on the battlefield."

But Shukra came up behind her. "How about tomorrow we just stay out of it? We're not much for battle. You can't even pull an earring without flinching. I don't think we're going to be any use as warriors. We can oppose Trimurti by depriving them of our presence, and that will be good enough."

Now Tak saw Ushas' problem. She had wanted them to join the battle actively rather than sit aside. Though, to be fair, Shukra was correct. Most of them were more likely to run than fight. He could not imaging any of them standing against the forces of Heaven. Honestly, he could not imagine them standing against a stiff wind.

Maya had not moved from where she nursed her injured ear and wept.

"It is not good enough to sit out. We can be a force if we want," Ushas called after the departing astronomical gods, but they were no longer listening. Bhumi was serving Maya nougat and bandaging her ear, calling her "poor baby" and promising that they would get a real Ashwini to take care of her immediately.

Hopeless, all hopeless—except Ushas, Tak thought. She had the determination, if not the skills. But unlike Ratri, she did not have an Aspect that could be of use in battle. Still, he could not leave her with the useless demis.

"Come, Goddess, come with us, to your sister. Ratri is one of our great allies. Come in your chariot. At least you prevented them from fighting for Trimurti. That's something."

She shook her head. "Not enough. I thought we had a chance to do something more than sit around and eat and smell flowers. Be like real gods, or at least real humans. Not like a bunch of brothel goods."

He patted her arm. He would have preferred to caress her luscious shimmering hair, to stroke her rose blush cheek, but he'd settle for what he could get. "Come with me back to our lines. At least you've got the means to get there. And we'll find a role for you, even if the rest of the demis are a lost cause."

She sniffled and wiped her face with the beautifully embroidered pallu of her sari, just the color of clouds touched with the first hint of light. Together they mounted the delicate chariot of Dawn. The Mayura bird, being a peahen (always ready to eat and not too bright,) had wandered behind a large tree and was rooting for grubs. Tak had a hard time convincing the great bird to come and be harnessed to the chariot yet again. She found no grubs, and Tak was able to lure her with a few pieces of nougat he had found on the ground where Shukra had apparently left them. Then the Mayura bird discovered she had a great taste for nougat and came along eagerly.

They arrived at the fortress near sunset, so Dawn's colors merged with the end of the day and did not give away their position. Tak left the young demigoddess in the care of her sister Ratri and went to report to the generals. "The demigods are divided," he told them. "Most will sit out the battle. Bhairav will fight for Trimurti, and perhaps Maya if she recovers from today. The rest will likely withhold. I can give you the names of those who I am certain will not join anyone tomorrow."

"Did we gain any allies among them?"

Tak shook his ape head. "Only Ushas. And as Ratri's sister, she was our ally in any case I think. But what use is Dawn in such a fight?"

Sam smiled gently. "There may be a role for her. She is well loved, and that is always a power. You've done very well, Tak. Thank you."

Joy spread like warm drink through Tak's body. Sam had noticed him, acknowledged him—even thanked him. This moment was all he had ever hoped, to be able to truly aid Sam. He bobbed his head and then scurried out the window.

*

The next morning Ushas woke as always before the world stirred. She dressed in her rose and gold sari and went to her little chariot with a heavy heart. Today she brought the dawn of the battle, and while she had the heart for the fight she recognized that she had few skills.

If only she had been able to rouse thought, knowledge, or curiosity in the demigods who had been her guests. She had tried so hard. True her Aspect was subtle, but she had practiced and flexed her power through Keenset for almost a year now and she knew she had gained strength. If only she had been greater.

She could wait the day, she thought for a moment. She could hold off the hours of battle, but to what end? Everyone was ready, eager even, to rush into blood fray. Even her own sister had preened in magnificent black armor before they had retired, and Ratri was often the gentlest of souls.

Her role, her duty, lay in the small chariot and the sky, and so she recognized that she could put it off no longer. She leaped into the chariot and took up the reigns, no longer with the Mayura bird but with her own Dawn horses, to travel their daily route.

Below her Keenset lay ready for battle. In the Accelerationist camp, warriors had already begun their day, polishing weapons, steadying mounts and eating a good meal before the fight. In the command Palace she saw sentries scanning the plain before them for any movement. One or two raised a spear to her and smiled grimly with the promise of victory. She only hoped they were true prophets, though she believed that Sam was the truest of the gods.

She moved onward, spreading her blue and rose rays ahead toward the camp of the gods. Below on the road she saw a band of travelers and she dipped lower for a look. Who would be on this road on this morning? Certainly everyone knew that this road would soon be drenched in death and dying.

They traveled as if in procession for a feast day, on horses and in palanquins, all brightly picked out with silk hangings and embroidered with planets, moons and suns, with flowers and fruits and small animals. One or two of the celebrants played the flute. Others sang, or danced, or clapped along to the music on the road of destruction.

Ushas recognized them, or at least thought she did. But she dared not stop. Instead she speeded up, driving her horses faster to encompass the sky so that she could return and discover the identity of the travelers. Because a hope fluttered briefly in her breast, along with a larger fear.

She finished her duties quickly and returned by chariot to the travelers on the road. They had made good time and were just at the gates of the city when she joined them. Yes, there was Shukra, and Candra, and even Bhumi. And at least thirty other demigods, many of whom she had not known all that well, despite their recent status as her houseguests. They moved very quickly although they appeared to be part of a festival procession.

"Ah, Ushas, you have joined us," Shukra said as she swung her chariot around and landed at their head.

"That depends. What are you doing?"

Shukra laughed, low and deep, and intelligence sparkled in his eyes. He had always been one of the smartest of the demis, Ushas acknowledged, and he could have done a great deal had he not been interminably lazy.

"Why, we are going to join Siddhartha of course."

Ushas cocked her head. "You mean you are going to actually do something? Or you just wanted someplace to watch?"

"Oh, no, we are ready to fight," Candra said. "We discussed it last night, and pulled out the weapons. Most of us were trained as warriors when we were human. And a few have other skills." He looked a Bhumi.

227

Shukra nodded solemnly. "I was a warrior for six incarnations. I know what I'm doing. Pretty much all of us do. And we can help. So if you'll speak for us to the command, they can let us know where we can do the most good."

"But why are you traveling like this, like you don't take anything seriously?"

"Because Trimurti doesn't take us seriously," Shukra replied. "If we left as if we meant to do something, that would give it away. If we acted as if we were just behaving the way they expect us to behave, they will ignore us. And they won't realize we've deserted until too late."

Ushas nodded and gestured to the guards at the top of the gate. "Let them in. Allies."

So she rode at the head of the troop of brightly dressed demigods to the chamber where Sam stood over a map and called him down. He inspected the motley collection and turned them over to Kubera to be assigned places in the battle line.

But before Kubera assigned them, Sam asked, "What made you come over? What changed your minds?"

Ushas watched as Shukra stood straighter. "We thought about it. At first the idea seemed ridiculous, to risk ourselves and our position, but gradually we could see the sense behind it. I don't know why it took us so long to understand that we have far more in common with humans and that Trimurti only uses us and relies on our indifference."

Sam nodded and the demigods marched off. Then Sam looked at Ushas, standing alone in the courtyard. "A powerful Aspect indeed," he congratulated her. "You are most worthy, Ushas. And a great help to our cause."

Dawn blushed. And an ape swung low from a tree as Siddhartha walked off and stroked her hand. "Very well done, Goddess," he said.

"Only a demigoddess," she corrected him softly.

"No, Lady. You have demonstrated a full Aspect and are a power on the field. You are, indeed, a Goddess."

And he bowed. Which was ungainly, in the way of an ape, but it mattered nonetheless.

"Come with me, Tak," Ushas offered. She leaped into her chariot and Tak followed, and she insisted her horses take them to the skies for a second time that day. Tak, and even Ushas, used spears from above on the battlefield below.

But Ushas' weapon was not the spear. It was the light that she brought, the early light of dawn that came not just to bring the day, but the light of Knowledge to the mind.

Afterword

Shannon Zelazny

Roger Zelazny. Known around the world as the science fiction and fantasy author of over fifty books and one hundred fifty short stories, a six-time Hugo Award-winner, three-time Nebula Award-winner, and an overall inspiration to readers and authors alike.

Known to me as Dad.

I was fifteen when my father unexpectedly passed away from colon cancer. In the physical sense, it should have come as no surprise, as it was quite evident that his health was slipping away over the course of his final year. However, the shock that reverberated throughout my being at the news of his passing stemmed from a doting daughter's belief in his consistent affirmation that he was going to beat it. He truly thought he would. After all, he did not view himself as an average human being. The theme of immortality so prevalent throughout his works was truly an extension of his own perception of himself. As such, I too believed him to be immortal; yet, This Immortal succumbed to the sands of time, as do all who walk the Earth.

Last year I was asked to speak at my father's 20-year anniversary memorial. After having difficulties trying to figure out what to say I decided to back out. However, the day before the event, I was going through an old storage box in the garage and found a notebook I had filled up with memories of my father a few days after he died, so that I wouldn't forget all the little details that grow fuzzy with time. The following day, I decided to share some of those memories I had unearthed, in order to give insight into the nature of the man who was my father and not the world renowned writer. It is my honor and pleasure to share some of these memories of the man who greatly shaped who I am today for reasons other than his writing.

Once a week my father would drop me off at Grandma's house, an opportunity she would seize to tell me stories about her beloved son. She lit up telling me a tale of how when he was a boy he wanted a dog so badly that he drew pictures of a little dog and himself smiling next to it, and left them all over the house for her to find. She said she would open cabinets, the refrigerator, drawers and more, only to discover endless pictures. She finally broke down and got him a terrier that he loved with all his heart. In our family home, he had a metal terrier dog statue holding open the door to his office.

Some of the most precious moments of my childhood were spent in our 1970's Chevy van which was beautifully adorned with orange shag carpet and rainbow interior. Often, when driving me to and from school, his latest work was swirling around in his head and he would randomly start reciting lines in his various character's voices. "Oh he's at it again," I would think, paying little heed to a master at work.

Driving also seemed to be a time when he felt most inspired to bust out his very particular "Aroo" language. He explained this was the language of the animals and would proceed to very casually, yet also very seriously, recite an entire what I can only refer to as a poem, in this Aroo language. "Aroo, aroo. . .aroo. . .aroo. AROO! Aroo, aroo. . .aroo."

He greatly amused himself a lot of the time. He was indeed a tremendously witty individual who took pride and amusement in the creative workings of his own mind. Off the beaten path on our drive home, there was a tiny bridge that I simply adored as a kid. I think because it was such a novelty to this Santa Fe girl. He would drive out of the way just so we could drive over that bridge. Just to make me happy, because he was a kind person. His kindness extended to kids other than myself. He would give talks at school about the writing process, inspiring the younger generations to do so.

In town, there was a train car that had been converted into a restaurant called The Super Chief Diner that we often frequented. Each day an obscure riddle or question was written up on a chalkboard, and if answered correctly would entitle one to a free milkshake. We *always* got free milkshakes, and boy a sweet tooth my father did have. A regular staple in our house was a case of Pepsi or RC cola and at least several 100 grand or 5th Avenue candy bars. To the left of his work chair in his office one could always find a pack of Juicy Fruit gum. He had a button he would sometimes wear that read, "Life is short. Eat Dessert First."Strawberry rhubarb pie or German chocolate cake were his favorites.

He embraced the casual style of New Mexican attire. He wore a sheepskin vest over his shirts most days, moccasins, and when it was time to dress up, would add a bolo tie to the ensemble. On occasion, he would wear the only hat he owned, a Cleveland Indians hat, having grown up in the suburb of Euclid, Ohio. He always carried a piece of string in his pocket tied at the ends, which he used to make hand figures out of. Also in his pocket was a handkerchief, a comb, and cash folded up sans wallet, until his dear friend Gerry Hausman gifted him a money clip. In his breast pocket he always had a pen and small notebook, just in case an idea popped up. He would carry a book with him everywhere he went in case he would have wait, even if only for a minute. Never was a minute wasted.

I remember sitting in his lap as he read *The Secret Garden* and *Peter Pan* to me. I would drift off and he would carry my dozing self to my room to put me to bed. Oftentimes, I would accompany him to a bookstore. After locating the latest *Nancy Drew* or *Sweet Valley Twins* book, I would timidly ask if I could get it, apologizing beforehand if it would be a waste of his money. I knew how hard he worked, day and night in his office creating his books that translated into our livelihood. I didn't want to willy-nilly waste his compensation on something trivial. His response was sternly always the same: "It's *never* a waste of money if it's spent on a book." And books did he have. There were rows and rows in his office, akin to a mini-bookstore. Among it all was a comic book stash of particular fancy, *Donald Duck*.

My father was certainly interested in eastern philosophies, alternative modalities of health, and martial arts. I would accompany him to the dojo where he had his aikido classes, and watch on as he and a partner threw each other around using various circular movements. Acquiring his black belt, he eventually began teaching the art. Daily, he would practice his tai chi routine. Together we took a tai chi class. Afterwards we would go get ice cream and talk about the class, Feng Shui and any other concepts relating to energy, the body and movement. He regularly received rolfing, acupuncture and took Chinese herbs for various ailments.

Growing up, living with a writer, was a unique experience. I didn't exactly know what he was doing, but I knew it was important. I knew *he* was important. Aside from doing a book report on *A Dark Traveling* and reading his children's books *Way Up High* and *Here There Be Dragons*, as they were dedicated to myself and my best friend in a beautiful limited edition, I paid little attention to his professional life while he was alive. However, I do remember at a science fiction convention my dad was signing autographs for some set period of time, one or two hours. I arrived at the table just before he was supposed to finish. Alas, the line of people waiting for an autograph was as far as the eye could see. He wasn't going to leave until he signed every last one. Though I sat with him, bored, I am grateful that I got to witness the looks on people's faces as they approached the table. People in awe, utterly ecstatic to meet this person who had created something so meaningful to them. I was proud of my dad.

It was a beautiful thing to watch the excitement that took him over as he was writing *A Night in the Lonesome October*, which he wrote in a month's time. I had never seen him so happy while writing a book before. He would unwind after a writing session by soaking in his hot tub, his prized possession. He got in it every day, even if only for five minutes.

After his passing, there were many times in my late teens and 20's that I questioned, "Why do I think the things I do? Why do I feel so different from my cohorts?"

At some point in my late 20's I started reading his books and a lightbulb went on. "Ahhh. . .I get it. I am literally my father's daughter!" I was so grateful to learn that various thoughts, ideas, and concepts that I was reading about in his books were of a similar nature to what I had privately entertained throughout the years. Well, I guess it makes sense.

His blood does flow through my veins. I do carry Roger Zelazny's genetic code inside of me. My grieving spirit found comfort in his work, discovering that I no longer felt alone. The deepest pain of my adult life is that he is not around to engage with in conversation as I traverse this dimension of Earth. I suspect we would have had colorful, dynamic discussions about a variety of topics, and I know I would have greatly appreciated his unique perspectives. Alas, he moved on, and I have to find his voice in both my heart and in his written words.

I share one final memory of my father to illustrate a place I think most of us strive for in our professional careers. One day, when I was about eight, I was in the kitchen and he came out of his office to get a cup of coffee. He had clearly just had a really good writing session that he was quite pleased with. He simply proclaimed out loud, "God *damn* I'm good at what I do." To which I replied in my childlike simplicity, "Dad! You're conceited!"

He matter-of-factly responded, "It's not conceited if it's true."

I was speechless.

Now that I am older, have read his works, and have seen the impact that he has had on the lives of so many through his timeless characters and the worlds he created, I realize that he was not being conceited. It was true. He was simply stating a fact. Why downplay it? So yes, God *damn* he was good at what he did, both as a father and as a writer.

About the Authors

George R. R. Martin is the international best selling author of the *Game of Thrones*. His first short story appeared in print in 1970; in 1973 his story "With Morning Comes Mistfall" was nominated for the both the Hugo and Nebula awards. In 1977 his first novel, *Dying of the Light*, was published by Simon & Schuster and was nominated for the both the Hugo Award and the British Fantasy Award. His 1983 novel *Fevre Dream* has been called one of the greatest vampire novels of all time and was nominated for a Stoker award. *A Game of Thrones* (first in his A Song of Ice and Fire series) was published in 1997 and reached #1 on the *New York Times* best seller list. The Daenerys Targaryen chapters won the Hugo Award for Best Novella. In 2011 *A Game of Thrones* was adapted into an HBO series, to worldwide acclaim. He currently lives in Sante Fe, New Mexico.

Steven Brust was born late in the Cenozoic Era at a place a mere 238,900 miles from the lonely, harsh desolation of the moon. From the moment of his birth, he launched a study of language, facial recognition, and tool using, while simultaneously beginning an intense regime of physical fitness. He fell into a life of crime under the influence of Tuli, the Evil Dog of Evilness, a life which continued for many years. At one point, aided by Captain Blondbeard the Space Pirate Kitty, he nearly succeeded in either taking over the world or destroying the universe, the record is unclear. The plot, which featured a machine (built by a mysterious parrot known only as "Doc") that could predict the future, failed when the machine turned out to be only able to predict the plot of action movies. This led Brust to abandon his criminal activities and begin writing science fiction and fantasy novels. Only time will tell how much lower he'll sink.

Kelly McCullough writes fantasy, science fiction, and books for younger readers. He lives in Wisconsin with his physics professor wife and a small herd of cats. He has more than a dozen novels in print or forthcoming either from PRH/ACE or Macmillan's Feiwel and Friends. His short fiction has appeared in numerous magazines and anthologies. His microfiction series DragonDiaries and Badnoir can be found on his webpage or by following him on Twitter or Facebook. He also dabbles in science fiction as science education, having written short fiction for the National Science Foundation and co-created a science comic for NASA and the Hubble Space Telescope.

Mark Rich writes, "When young as a writer I had a place in my heart for Zelazny stories — a place his writing has never surrendered. And now when my much-older hands reopen a book of his, that younger self appears as from nowhere, to re-enjoy it along with me." Rich's fiction has appeared in magazines and anthologies including *Analog, Amazing Stories, Science Fiction Age, Universe 3*, and Full *Spectrum 4*; his poetry, in many magazines. His most recent book is C.M. *Kornbluth: The Life and Works of a Science Fiction Visionary*. With partner-in-life Martha Borchardt and two Scotties-in-life, he lives in western Wisconsin.

Jane Lindskold: Before he died, Roger Zelazny chose Jane Lindskold to complete his unfinished novels–*Donnerjack* and *Lord Demon*. "The Headless Flute Player" is a prequel to *Lord Demon*. It is based, in part, on conversations they had when they were living together and talking about stories they planned to write. Jane is a *New York Times* best selling author of some twenty-five novels, seventy short stories, and various works of non-fiction. She lives in New Mexico with her husband, Jim Moore, assorted small animals, and the sculpture of the Eight Immortals, including the headless flute player, that inspired this story.

Gio Clairval is an Italy-born writer who used to live in Paris, France, and is now based in Edinburgh, Scotland. Her stories have appeared in *Weird Tales, Daily Science Fiction, Galaxy's Edge*, and many others. She translates literary works from French, Italian, Spanish and German.

Edward J. McFadden III juggles a full-time career as a university administrator and teacher, with his writing aspirations. His new horror thriller *Awake* is now available from Severed Press. His first published novel, a mysterious-dark-thriller *The Black Death of Babylon*, was published in 2012, followed by *Our Dying Land* and *Hoaxers*. He is the author/editor of: *Anywhere But Here, Lucky 13, Jigsaw Nation, Deconstructing Tolkien: A Fundamental Analysis of The Lord of the Rings, Time Capsule, Epitaphs* (W/ Tom Piccirilli), *The Second Coming, Thoughts of Christmas,* and *The Best of Pirate Writings*. He lives on Long Island with his wife Dawn, their daughter Samantha, and their mutt Oli.

Steve Perry has sold dozens of stories to magazines and anthologies, as well as a considerable number of novels, animated teleplays, non-fiction articles, reviews, and essays, along with a couple of unproduced movie scripts. He wrote for *Batman: The Animated Series* during its first emmy-award winning season, and during the second season, one of his scripts was nominated for an emmy for Outstanding Writing. His novelization of *Star Wars: Shadows of the Empire* spent ten weeks on the *New York Times* Bestseller List. He also did the best selling novelization for the summer blockbuster movie *Men in Black*, and seven of his collaborative novels for Tom Clancy's Net Force series have made the *New York Times* List. For the past several years he has concentrated on books, and is currently working on his 54th novel.

Gerald Hausman is the author of mythological animal books for both children and adults. Many have been translated into foreign languages. In 1994 he co-authored the novel, Wilderness with Roger Zelazny (Roger's only Western) and they became very close friends. Aside from writing, Gerald is also the editor of numerous books for Random House, Putnam, Viking, St. Martin's, Simon & Schuster and others. Gerald's latest novel is The Evil Chasing Way published by Speaking Volumes in Santa Fe New Mexico.

Roger Zelazny was a science fiction and fantasy writer best known for his ten book series the Chronicles of Amber. He was a six time Hugo Award winner and a three time Nebula Award Winner. He published more than 50 novels in his lifetime. His first novel *This Immortal*, won the Hugo for best novel, a shorter version of the book entitled "...And Call Me Conrad" had already won the Hugo Award for best novella. *Lord of Light*, his second novel, won the Hugo award and was nominated for the Nebula award. In 1970 *Nine Princes in Amber*, the first of his ten book Amber series, was published. This series would garner him an international following. He died in 1995 at the age of 58.

Theodore Krulik is the author of The Complete Amber Sourcebook. He is also the author of *Roger Zelazny*, a literary biography of Roger Zelazny. He is a distinguished scholar who completed his Master's thesis on a textual, critical, and biographic study of Mary Shelley's *Frankenstein, A Modern Day Prometheus*. His essays on genre and television may be found on Tor.com.

Lawrence Watt-Evans is the author of some fifty novels and well over a hundred short stories, mostly fantasy, science fiction, and horror, including the Hugo-winning "Why I Left Harry's All-Night Hamburgers" and the long-running Legends of Ethshar fantasy series. He has loved Roger Zelazny's work since he first read "A Rose for Ecclesiastes" in 1963, and is honored to be included here.

Michael H. Hanson is the creator of the ongoing Sha'daa shared-world anthology series. He has three collections of poetry *Autumn Blush, Jubilant Whispers*, and *Dark Parchments: Midnight Curses and Verses*. In 2017, Michael's short story "C.H.A.D." will be appearing in the Eric S. Brown edited anthology *C.H.U.D. Lives!* Michael also has stories in Janet Morris's Heroes in Hell anthology volumes: *Lawyers in Hell, Rogues in Hell, Dreamers in Hell, Poets in Hell, Doctors in Hell*, and *Pirates in Hell*. Michael is also the Founder of the international writers club, the Fictioneers.

Shariann Lewitt: Author of seventeen novels under five different names, Shariann Lewitt has written hard science fiction, high fantasy, young adult, military science fiction and urban fantasy. She has published over forty short stories; her story "Fieldwork" has been selected for Gardner Dozois' *34th Best Science Fiction Stories of the Year*. Roger Zelazny bears a fair bit of responsibility for this.

Trent Zelazny is the author of several novels, novellas and short stories in numerous genres including, but not limited to, horror, crime, thriller, science fiction, erotica, and humor. He is also a bestselling international playwright, editor of two anthologies, and has written for both television and film. Son of the late science fiction author Roger Zelazny, Trent was born in Santa Fe, New Mexico. He has lived in California, Oregon, and Florida, but currently lives with his fiancé, Laurel, and their dog, Banjo, back in Santa Fe.

Shannon Zelazny is a trained Massage Therapist and Naturopathic Physician, having earned her Doctorate at Bastyr University in Seattle, WA. After a 15 year hiatus, she has returned to her homeland of New Mexico where she is currently serving as a naturopathic consultant, studying Qigong and enjoying spending time with her partner and his two cats, Stella and Stanley.

Acknowledgments

The editors would like to thank the following people for donating to the Shadows and Reflections Indigogo. Without your help this book would not have happened.

Thomas Bull, Solomon Foster, Linda J. Weldon, Laurell Hamilton, Nathan Bardsley, Cliff Winnig, Joe Saul, Andrew Cherry, Elanor Finster, Cheryl Mankin, Kit Kindred, James Scott, Zach Shephard, Michael Stroup, George Terry, Christopher Petrilli, Madeline Ferwerda, Sheryl R. Hayes, Star Straf, Timothy Feely, Edmund Boys, Andy Modell, Cindie Hurley, Matthew Collier, Scott Drummond, Erik Ogan, Aaron Schutz, Kevin Winter, Jim Crider, Charles Lewis, Sandra Hohn, Elizabeth Ray-Trumitch, Matthew R. Sheahan, Zack Wood, Gio Clairval, Tina Swain, Lisa Adler-Golden, Paul Millhouser, Michael H. Hanson, James Manley-Buser, Sarah Williams, Elisabeth Flaum, Bruce Cohen, Garrett Boos, Elektra Hammond, Shelley Souza, David Shaw, Cecilia Tan, Jefferson Krogh, Kat Lemmer, Scott Bradley, Jean-Marie Bergman, James Lowder, Matthew Milne, Carl Rigney, Duffi McDermott, Rick Neal, Chris Martin, Rob Starobin, Chris Knight, Fred Kiesche, Christopher Kovacs, Peter Quinones, Gary M Dockter, Nathaniel Lee, Subrata Sircar, Joshua Wanisko, Richard Chilton, Bridget McKenna, Jason Durall, David W. Goldman, Steve Perry, Daniel Moran, James Zimmerman, Samanda Jeude, Dawn Vogel, Gordon Garb, Jeremy Zimmerman, Marti McKenna

CPSIA information can be obtained
at www.ICGtesting.com
Printed in the USA
LVHW091126120520
655425LV00002B/644